Earl

Book 5 in the

Anarchy Series

By

Griff Hosker

Published by Sword Books Ltd 2015

Copyright © Griff Hosker First Edition

A CIP catalogue record for this title is available from the British Library.

Cover by Design for Writers

Dedicated to

To Ron and Sue Ringrose; two lovely, generous people.

Part 1

The wars in the west

Prologue

Since my return from the east and my elevation to Earl I had not been as happy as I might have been. I bore a secret. The heir to the throne of England and the lands of Normandy and Anjou had left her husband and incurred the wrath of her husband. One of her knights, Rolf, had told me that she had left him and fled, possibly to London. The secret was that she might come to my home. I dared not tell anyone that she might arrive for fear of insinuations against both of our characters. I would have to appear as surprised as any if she did arrive. Such deception did not sit well with me. I was, I hoped, an honourable knight. I wanted a simple life. None could understand my moods. All thought I should be happy and joyful at the advances I had made. I had come from Constantinople with my father and in a very short time become first a Baron and then an Earl. I had done so without any sponsor. It had been because I fought well and was rewarded for being a good warrior. I had no confidante. The one to whom I could have entrusted my secret was Edward, also a knight of the Empress. However, since my return, I had not seen Edward. He had been with his conroi at Hexham enjoying the hospitality of the Baron there, Sir Hugh Manningham. I was desperate for his return. I needed to speak with someone. I hated secrets.

The other weight upon my shoulders resulted from the death of Osric, the last of my father's oathsworn. When I had been

4

in Miklagård I had retrieved two treasures from my former home. The servants there knew naught about them and I had hoped that Osric could have shed light upon them. One was the blue stone which had rested in Harold Godwinson's pommel until the battle of Stamford Bridge. The other was a golden wolf with two blue stones for the eyes. The blue stones were smaller versions of the pommel stone. It was a mystery and I knew not how to solve it. It was little wonder that I was so distracted.

And then there was the seal which King Henry had given to me. It was a wolf! I could not fathom how that came to be. The King could not have known what I had found and yet the ring seemed to complete the circle: a blue pommel stone from the sword of a king, a wolf sign with blue stones and a signet ring given by a king with a wolf upon it. Yet the circle appeared to trap me!

Surprisingly I had found some consolation, no matter how small, in the words of my new men at arms. When I had fought for the Emperor I had found some of the men who had fought alongside my father and they had left the service of the Emperor to follow my banner. Erre, their leader had told me of a tradition amongst the peoples of the North. They spoke of something called *wyrd*. It seemed to be Fate. My father and his oathsworn had also known this phenomenon. It had only come to light when we reached England. It was not an Eastern belief. I knew that the priests would frown on such pagan ideas but it actually brought me some peace. It seemed that there was another force directing my life. I liked to believe it was my father and my names sake, Aelfraed. I did not think it blasphemous to believe such things. When I died I believed I would go to heaven. Why should my father and his best friend not be in heaven too? Perhaps they were watching and guiding me. My father had always enjoyed setting me puzzles and tasks to stretch my mind. Mayhap this was another such.

Chapter 1

Edward did not arrive back until the late winter. The snows had been bad in the north and he had been trapped by roads made impassable by the snow fall. I was pleased to see him when he arrived at my castle.

When I saw him, I engaged in small talk. I was nervous of divulging my news. "How is Sir Hugh?"

"He has made the Roman Wall secure, Baron, and it prospers. It is now a fine demesne. We killed many wolves when we were there for the hunting is good."

My look must have startled him for he said, "What is it my lord? Have you seen a ghost?"

I led him to my eastern tower. I showed him my new ring, "I am now Earl of Cleveland."

"That is good news but what troubles you? The elevation is good news and yet your face was one of shock."

I told him of my discoveries and the wolf. He nodded. "I understand. This is almost witchcraft, my lord."

"I know." I then unburdened myself and told him of the letter from Rolf the Swabian.

"You can do nothing about this, my lord. I know of your feelings and those of the Empress but sometimes these things are not meant to be. You must obey our lord and master the King and we must defend this land. That is our duty. You are married and there is no honour in coveting the wife of another man no matter how young he is."

"And if the Empress comes to my home?"

"I pray that she will not. If she did then I fear that the world we know would end. The King would not countenance such an open act of disobedience." He paused. "Know that I will stand by you and the Empress no matter what happens."

"I know but this is my problem and I will deal with it."

As the winter drew closer to spring it seemed that the Empress would not visit with me as Rolf had intimated. During a visit from one of the priests from York upon his way to Durham I discovered a possible reason. Roger of Mandeville, one of King Henry's most trusted commanders, had been given the Tower and therefore London to guard. Matilda was under his protection; she stayed in the Tower. It was more likely that Sir Roger was her guard. He was a loyal and ancient friend of the King who would not gainsay him. She would not be travelling north. I actually felt relief for I did not know how I would have coped had the Empress visited me.

Our news came from such visitors. The ferry across the river was a safe route from York to Durham. It was why I had built the castle here in the first place. My father had been given Norton some four miles north of us. I recognised, as did my father, the value of this river crossing. Father Ralph, the priest, spent a night with us telling us news, gossip and the changes that were being wrought in the land. Our other news carrier would be Olaf and Dai the two sea captains who used my port to trade. Like visitors on foot they knew there would be a welcome and they knew that they would be safe. The land was still a dangerous place for travellers both on land and sea.

I threw myself into the management of my manor. I now had another six men at arms; they were recruited from the Varangian Guard. They reminded me in many ways of Athelstan and my father's oathsworn. All were still warriors at their peak but they were looking for a quieter life. I made them the guard for my castle. They did not ride but they were all doughty warriors who had served the most powerful man on earth. Erre was their leader and he would command. They could still take the field if needed but I knew that my family would be as safe as any with their swords to guard them.

Now that the King had given me my seal I incorporated that into my coat of arms. I paid the women of the town to sew them on the new surcoats I had had made. My retainers painted them on their shields and my wife sewed one on my banner which John, my squire, carried. I knew that I was lucky to have so much gold. My father had left me much and we had made more than enough on our journeys. It was why I had more men at arms than most knights.

With twenty-five experienced men at arms and eleven archers we could hold our own against most enemies. We would never have enough archers and Dick, my captain of archers, had spent the winter training young men to become archers. Although they would be able to use a bow in a couple of years they would need at least four to be an archer who could fight alongside Dick and the others. I had the satisfaction of knowing that my home would be well protected by these erstwhile archers and my Varangians.

I even went hunting with Aiden my falconer, as well as John and Leofric my squires. Adela was always telling me that I ought to spend more time hunting and enjoying my life. Other lords spent their whole lives doing that. I had been brought up differently and it did not sit well with me to indulge in leisurely pursuits.

When Father Ralph returned from Durham he brought a pair of letters for me from Sir Henry de Vexin, the knight who held Durham for the King, and the Dean, Brother Michael, whose life I had saved. They both said the same thing but in different tones. Sir Henry de Vexin felt he was my superior and his tone reflected that. Brother Michael wrote to me as a friend and as a priest who cared for his people. The message, however, was the same. The harsh winter further north had sent young warriors south to take animals, women, and slaves. They had chosen the Garth of the Bishop. It was close to the now derelict motte and bailey castle the Bishop of Durham had first lived in. Now that he had a stone castle it had been left empty. My manor was the closest and Sir Henry de Vexin wanted me to cleanse the land of the swarm of vermin, as he put it. Had Brother Michael not asked me to help the people there then I might have refused. Sir Henry had knights of his own.

I summoned Wulfric my Sergeant at Arms. "We ride tomorrow before dawn. I want half of the archers and five of those training to be archers. It will be good practice. We will need just six men at arms and my squires."

He nodded and then asked, calmly, "Where do we ride, my lord?"

I smiled. I expected him to read my mind. "There are thieves and brigands in the forests around the Bishop's Garth. We are to rid the forests of them."

Wulfric seemed quite pleased. "That is good my lord. The men were becoming a little fat and lazy. Why, three of them have even taken women! Can you believe it?"

"Have you not thought of taking a woman, Wulfric?"

He laughed, "I take them when I want them, my lord. I don't want to keep them and I certainly don't want a brood of whining, puling children around my feet!"

Wulfric was an old-fashioned warrior. War was all to him. He was good at it. When he went into battle with his war axe he was a frightening sight to behold and I would have feared to face him. I knew that I was lucky to have him as my sergeant at arms.

9

I laughed, "We will take Aiden. It will save time finding them."

"Should we bring the new warriors, my lord?"

"No for we shall be on horses. This is not their strength. We hunt and we need quick hands and eyes."

That evening, as we ate in my hall, Adela brought up my humour and my moods. "You have been distracted of late, my husband. Is there something on your mind? I would have thought that your elevation to Earl would have made you happy."

I hated lying to my wife but I did not like upsetting her either. I compromised. I told her what was worrying me about my new position. "The problem with being an Earl is that it not only gives you power it can make you a threat to others. Sir Henry de Vexin was affable and friendly when he first took over Durham. Now I am an earl I can read the resentment in his letters. The Barons here in the north support me but what of those to the west and the south? Will they see me as a threat? An upstart? A Greek who has insinuated himself into the favour of the King?"

"But you are not a Greek!"

"Half Greek through my mother but it is an insult I have heard from those who do not like me, like the brothers from Blois." I smiled, "Do not worry, once I am back in the saddle then I will become my old self again. Perhaps I am nervous of the task which lies ahead."

She shook her head, "No, my husband, you are the most assured and confident man I have ever met in my life. Perhaps you are right; you will grow into the role."

"And I shall be in the saddle tomorrow. That will help."

"Bandits and brigands?"

"They can cause as much trouble as raiding Scotsmen and they can be even harder to find. They will melt into the woods which surround the Garth."

Before I retired I summoned John and Leofric, my squires. "I want to be abroad before the sun rises. I am relying on you to have everything ready."

"Do you take Scout, my lord?"

"Aye, Leofric. He has a nose which can smell out trouble."

I had a restless night. I know that it was nothing to do with the bandits and all to do with my deception before my wife. I had a conscience. Many men did not. It could be a curse.

John shook my shoulder. I nodded to show I was awake. I crept from my chamber and went to my tiring room where Leofric waited with John. They both wore their armour and they soon dressed me. They handed me my sword. Each time that I took it I felt excited. I now had the pommel stone from the sword wielded by the last English King. I had not used it in anger since it had been fitted and I wondered if it would make a difference to the sword.

"It has been sharpened?"

"Aye, my lord and your dagger."

"Good."

We went to the hall where my steward, John son of Leofric the Moneyer, had the slaves Ada and Ruth waiting with warmed wine, porridge, ham, cheese and bread. "Good morning."

"Morning, my lord," they chorused.

"Have the men been fed too, John?"

"Yes, my lord, an hour since. Wulfric was keen for them to make an early start. Aiden left an hour ago too. He said he would meet you at the farm of Alan the Lame."

I nodded. Alan the Lame had fought for me when we had despatched the raiders from the west. He had been wounded in the leg and he limped. I had rewarded him with three cows we had captured and six sheep. I did not want my people suffering because they fought for me. He had a farm just three miles from the Bishop's Garth. It would be a good place to start. The ground would be hard from the overnight frost and Aiden would have his work cut out to find their tracks.

I wolfed down my food and washed it down with the sweetened, spiced, warmed wine. I looked at my squires to make sure they, too, had partaken. Their platters showed that they had eaten as only young men can.

"Bring spears. We will be back before nightfall, John."

"Aye, my lord."

Ada handed me my cloak as I stepped out of the door into the inner bailey. It was cold. We walked to the inner gate and entered the outer bailey and the stables. Scout stood stamping his fore foot. He was eager to be away too. The winter did not suit his temperament.

Dick, my captain of archers, had chosen five young archers. I could see the nervousness on their faces. Not only were they having to ride to war, they were under the scrutiny of Dick, Wulfric and the Earl of Cleveland. They all knew that success this day would bring forward the time when they would join my illustrious archers.

"Today we ride to rid this land of brigands but it is also the first time since Yule that we have drawn our swords in anger. Use your weapons well! I want you all to return safely! Ride!"

We headed north from the castle and skirted the walls of the town. Those elders who managed the borough for me had set a night watch over the gate and the figure of the sentry waved at us as we headed through the dark. I dare say they wondered what the lord of the manor was doing out at this ungodly hour. We rode by the farms and houses which dotted the road leading north towards the land of the Bishop. As we trotted along it the thought came to me that we needed to improve it. When next we captured slaves, I would have them make it a stone road. William, my mason, always had rubble left from his work. It would make a better surface than the one we rode upon.

Alan the Lame was waiting for us. I reined in. "Aiden asked me to wait for you my lord, when he rode through."

"Are there raiders on my land?"

He pointed to the forest to the north east of us. "I told Aiden, my lord, that I had found the carcass of a butchered deer. I did not think it was you for you always take the carcass back to the castle. I also found the prints of many men."

"Why did you not send me word?"

I saw fear flicker across his face as he thought he had incurred my wrath. "My wife and my children were ill with the winter sickness. I am sorry, my lord."

I was being harsh and I knew it. It was not my villein's job to watch my land. That was my role. "No, Alan the Lame, I am not chiding you. I would have you safe."

"There was one other thing. I normally see Thomas of Thorpe when I collect my firewood from the forest. I have not seen him these ten days since. Aiden was heading there."

"Thank you. Is your family well now? Should I send Father Matthew with medicine?"

"They are recovering, my lord. He smiled. You are a father and husband too, you will know how we worry."

"Aye, Alan. Take care."

I mulled over his words as I led my men towards the farm which stood on the ridge of Thorpe. It was on the way from the Durham Road to the Garth of the Bishop. I allowed the ones who lived close to the forest to use it to collect firewood. Many lords did not and punished those who did. Thomas and Alan the Lame would have used that to exchange news. If raiders had come then perhaps Thomas had seen them.

Thorpe was not in my manor. It was part of the Bishop's lands. I kept my eye on the land but it should have been Sir Henry de Vexin's responsibility in the absence of a Bishop. There were only a handful of houses and farms. They were spread out over a wide area. In fact, Thomas' nearest neighbour was old Thomas in Wulfestun. The land around Thorpe was difficult to farm. It lay on a ridge and the valleys thereabouts were steep. I knew that Thomas of Thorpe eked out a bare existence for him and his two daughters. With no son to help him and not enough coin for slaves I did not know how he survived.

Aiden was waiting outside the wattle and daub hut when I arrived. His face looked pained. He came over to me before I had even dismounted. "My lord, the raiders have been here. They came six days since."

His tone told me that this was bad news. "They have hurt these people?"

He nodded, "They raped the two girls and the wife. When Thomas tried to intervene, they cut off his hand."

"How is he?"

"He is not well. They have tried their best but..."

14

"Wulfric send a rider back to Stockton and fetch a wagon and Father Matthew. Tell him that Thomas of Thorpe has had his hand cut off."

Arkwright was soon galloping south. It was just four miles to my castle if one went by the Durham Road. He could be there and back within a short time. I dismounted and went inside. The two girls were huddled together by the back wall and were still sobbing. I saw blood on their shifts. The wife, I did not know her name, looked up from her husband who lay, pale and still, by the fire. I knelt down next to her.

She shook her head, "I have tried to stop the bleeding my lord. I fastened this to the arm." She pointed to a rag tourniquet. Blood still dripped from the stump.

Wulfric said quietly, behind me, "We must use fire, my lord."

"I know. Get a brand. Dick, see to the girls." I turned to Thomas' wife. "I have sent for a priest and he will tend to your husband but we must use fire to staunch the blood. Do you understand?" She nodded. "Go to the other side and we will do the rest."

I turned to Wulfric, "You had better hold him down."

"Aye my lord. I'll just give him some of this first. It is an old soldier's trick," He took out a leather flask. "Wine sweetened with honey." He held Thomas' head and poured some down his throat. He replaced the stopper and then pressed down on both shoulders. "Ready my lord."

"John, hold the stump for me and clear away any material." I had seen this done before. I suppose I could have asked one of my men to do it for me but I was the Lord of the Manor; I had responsibilities. He nodded when he was ready and I thrust the brand onto the flesh. There was an acrid smell of burning flesh

15

and I saw Thomas' legs as they jerked. He was a brave man and endured the pain well but his body reacted nonetheless. His wife bit her lip. I held the brand there for the count of three to make sure that the flesh was totally burned.

I handed the brand back to Leofric. "The priest will be here soon. Your husband should be kept warm. He will not die now. We must find these men." She nodded. "How many were there?"

Aiden said, "I should have told you, my lord, sorry. There were over twenty of them and they were Scots. She said that she found it hard to understand their words."

"Where did they go?"

Aiden pointed to the north west. "They were heading for the Bishop's lands."

"Then we will go and teach them a lesson."

The sun had risen but the ground was still frozen and the air was cold. The breath from our mounts rose like an equine fog as we galloped across the frozen ridge and through the trees which covered it. I knew that there were a handful of farms just a mile or so from the old fort. I dreaded what I would find. Once again Aiden waited for us. The first farm had been razed to the ground and Aiden pointed within. "I have seen the burned bodies. There are animal tracks."

The second farm, just a half mile further along the greenway had not been burned but the bodies of the farmer and his family lay as a grisly reminder of the raid. The animals of the night had come to feast upon them. Aiden pointed. "The old fort is just a mile ahead beyond those trees."

We rode into the trees and left the horses with my squires while Aiden hurried on. I saw that they were less than happy to be given that task but my men at arms and archers had more skills

16

than they did. John asked, as we turned to leave, "Will you want your helmet, my lord?"

I shook my head, "These are brigands. My coif will suffice."

As we moved through the woods we could hear them. It sounded as though they had only recently risen. Aiden returned, like a ghost and stood close to me. "They have animals and five slaves. They are abusing the women, lord. Some sleep yet. The animals are at the northern edge of the camp. They have one man guarding them and he looks to be half asleep."

"Are they in the fort, behind the ditch?"

He nodded, "But they are not at the top of the hill. They have set up a camp."

"Wulfric, Dick." My two leaders came. "Wulfric, we will take the men around the northern side of the camp. Dick, give us enough time to get into position and then use your archers to kill the leaders. They may flee but if not we will advance and engage them. You should be able to keep loosing without fear of hitting us."

Dick looked offended, "My lord! We hit only where we aim!"

I laughed, "Sorry, Dick I thought I had ordinary archers! Aiden come with us. You can rid us of the man guarding the animals."

I took my spear with me and fastened my shield around my back. These were no knights we were facing. They were bandits and brigands. As we moved north we could hear the squeals, shouts, and screams from the noisy camp. When we heard the sound of animals we knew that we could begin to head towards the camp. We left the woods and kept low as we went across the long

17

grass. No animals had grazed here for some time. I saw the bailey rising to our left. Aiden had missed the fact that there was a guard at the top. Fortunately, his gaze was to the south for I could see his back.

The animals were moving around the thick grass enjoying the feast of virgin grass. It helped to disguise our movement. Aiden suddenly darted off and disappeared. Wulfric shook his head in wonder. I held my spear above my right shoulder in case Aiden failed to silence the sentry. When we reached him, he was wiping his knife on the kyrtle of the dead Scot. Just then I heard a loud shout from the camp and saw five men fall clutching arrows which had hit their bodies.

"Keep in one line and I want no one to escape. Aiden follow us in case any manage to evade us."

We moved swiftly though silently. The brigands were caught in a dilemma. Did they try to find these archers or flee? I saw one man grab two of the captives and hold them before him as a human shield. He fell with an arrow between the eyes and that decided the others. They fled. There were twelve of them left as they ran towards the eight of us.

I flung the spear at the nearest man who was thirty feet from me. The heavy ash spear flung him back as it entered his chest. I saw that, although they were brigands, some of them had been warriors. One or two had leather hauberks and they held spears, swords and axes. One even had the small buckler favoured by the Scots. I drew my sword and I felt power surge through my body. Perhaps this was just my imagination; I know not. I had only set a blue stone in the pommel. I held my weapon in two hands and swung it sideways at the man who charged at me and thrust his spear towards my middle. I was already pivoting when the spear slid along my surcoat and mail. His movement and my armour took the head of the spear harmlessly away and my sword, used two handed, hacked through his leather hauberk and bit

18

deeply into his side. His scream was like that of a vixen and he fell dead at my feet.

Suddenly a wild giant hurled himself at my right side. I saw him raise his axe as he launched himself at me. I continued the turn I had made to kill the man with the spear. The axe sliced through fresh air. I lifted my sword and brought it down upon his unprotected back. The blow was so hard that I heard his spine as it broke. I quickly looked around for another attacker but they were all dead. Dick and the archers had come to our aid and all of the raiders lay in untidy heaps.

"Wulfric, see if they have anything of value. Dick and Aiden secure the animals." I looked up at the sky. We still had a couple of hours of daylight. We could go directly back to my castle and be there before night fell. Sheathing my bloodied sword, I turned to Arkwright and said, "Go and fetch my squires and the horses. It is time we were away from here."

I wandered over to the captives, all women, who were gathered in a huddle. I realised that they might not know who I was and I saw fear in their faces. They might think they had exchanged one cruel master for another. "I am the Earl of Cleveland. Sir Henry de Vexin asked me to come to your aid. I am sorry that I was too late to save your men. I will take you back to my castle where you will be cared for." I saw looks exchanged between the two older women; obviously they were the matriarchs. "Do not worry you can come back to your homes and your families but that will be when the weather is more clement." I looked at the young girls. "They will need comfort will they not?"

The leader of the two women nodded, "They will and we thank you, my lord. We are grateful."

We put the captives on the horses of five of my archers and made our way south to my castle. Leofric rode ahead of us to warn my wife that we had unexpected guests. For her it did not matter if the guest was the King, a priest or a poor farmer's wife. She would care for them all. She had been a captive once and knew what it did to a person.

It was almost dark when we saw the torches at my gates. The reassuring stone walls made the captives all burst into tears. Stockton was now a sanctuary.

Chapter 2

Some of the captives were still with us for much longer than I had expected. Some were afraid to return to their homes. For others it was different. I think that two of my men at arms had taken a liking to them and I suspected they would marry. It would be mutually beneficial. The women would have a man to protect them and the men would gain a farm without having to go to the trouble of courting one. They would still be my men at arms but there were times during the year when they were not in constant demand. I had been lord of the manor long enough to know that my men grew older and the lure of war was not as strong. It made my farms strong for some of the farmers were those who had been warriors.

I wrote letters to Sir Henry de Vexin, Brother Michael, and the Archbishop of York explaining what I had done. I was learning that others would take credit if I did not. As the weather had marginally improved I took the opportunity of taking my men at arms, including my Varangians, on a tour of my lands and fiefs. I did not expect trouble and so I left my archers at Stockton. They were more than capable of defending my home and it gave Dick a greater opportunity to train more archers and the fyrd. We had learned that the best use of the fyrd was as either spearmen or bowmen. Defence was their best strategy.

William pestered to accompany me. He was now big enough to ride a large pony and he wore a small surcoat my wife had made him from one of my damaged ones. Alf, my smith, had also made him a short mail hauberk and helmet. As it would be a peaceful progression I gave in. Leofric was charged by my wife to watch out for him rather than me. Leofric was the gentler of my squires. He showed the qualities one needed in a knight. John, in contrast, had more in common with Wulfric. He might never be a knight but he would make a good man at arms. My bigger squire had grown again during the winter and promised to be a giant even bigger than Wulfric.

We began our progress at Elton south to Thornaby; east to Normanby and then west to Yarm. Even though Yarm was just a couple of hours travel from our home it took us two days to reach it for we stayed over with my knights. Although I would enjoy the company of my knights I had taken my men at arms because they had to learn to mix with the other men at arms. When they fought together in one huge conroi then they needed to know each other. My Varangians were new. I knew, from Wulfric, that there was often conflict when new men at arms joined together in a large conroi. I wanted that to be away from the field of war.

When we left Yarm for Piercebridge and Gainford I saw that some of my new men at arms sported bruises and cuts. I asked Wulfric if there had been trouble. "Trouble? No, my lord; more a levelling of opinions. They will all be like brothers when we go to war."

We changed my plans when we reached Gainford. Hugh of Gainford had once been my squire. I had been looking forward to the visit. He was the only survivor of a raid from the west and he had had to build up his manor. He had succeeded beyond my wildest expectations. However, he was not at home when I arrived. His steward, Geoffrey of Bowes, apologised, "I am sorry, my lord but Sir Guy of Balliol has died. He was ill for some time. My master and his men are attending the funeral at the castle."

"Who is the new lord?"

"His son, Barnard de Balliol." He smiled. "His father thought so much of his son he named his castle in his honour on the day he was born."

I had often wondered why the castle was so named. "We will travel thence. It is but a couple of hours of hard riding."

22

As I headed north I wondered about this Barnard of Balliol. I had not seen him when I had visited his father and, as far as I knew, he had not participated in any of our battles against the Scots. Some young knights liked to use their youth to travel. Perhaps he had been one such. If his father had named the castle after him then it would seem he doted on him. I saw, as I approached the castle, that the wooden structure in which his father had lived was now being replaced with a stone one. It was in the early stages but, when finished, it would be a daunting castle. It had a superb aspect, overlooking the river as it did. Although I was an Earl, Sir Barnard owed his fealty not to me but to the Bishop of Durham. I wondered if this would cause a problem.

When we reached the castle, it was close to nightfall. Although we were admitted I suspected that my men might have to make do with the stables as there would be other guests for the funeral.

Sir Hugh introduced me to Sir Barnard, "My lord this is Alfraed, Earl of Cleveland and Knight of the Empress Matilda."

Sir Barnard gave a bow and said quickly, "I am honoured that you have graced us with your presence my lord. I hope you were not offended that I did not invite you to the funeral."

"Of course, not and you have my sympathy. Your father was a doughty knight who defended this end of the Tees valley well. I am sure the King will hope that you continue to do so."

There was the slightest of hesitation before he smiled and said, "Of course." He saw William at my side, "And is this your squire or your son?"

That pleased William who beamed, "I am the Earl's son, William, and I too will be a great warrior when I grow up!"

"Of course, you will." Sir Barnard turned to me. "I am afraid I only have a chamber for you and your son this night for we have many guests. Your men will have to sleep in the stables."

"They have endured worse and we came as unexpected guests. Think nothing of it."

He bowed, "Come we are still in the middle of the feast." He ruffled William's hair, "We will find a chair high enough for you, my little man!"

I turned to Leofric and John, "Tell Wulfric they are to sleep in the stable. I am sure he can arrange food." They nodded. I held up a warning finger, "Tell him, best behaviour! And especially Erre and his men! And tell him to keep eyes and ears open. He will understand." Wulfric was a great gatherer of intelligence. Men at arms gossiped.

I followed Sir Barnard who led William. Sir Hugh walked next to me and said, "I should warn you, my lord, there are visitors here. They are friends of Sir Barnard." There was a warning in his voice and so I was not as surprised as I might have been when I entered the hall.

As soon as I walked into the room I saw my Nemesis, Stephen of Blois. What was he doing here? I had learned to put on a face to meet my enemies. I smiled as I was led to the high table. I was, apart from Stephen of Blois, the most noble of the knights around the table. I would receive respect. I saw faces turn to me. My name was known as was my reputation. Some of those I saw I recognised. Not all were friends. I recognised some coats of arms and remembered them as being those who had fought alongside the Scots. I smiled, nonetheless.

Sir Barnard had a chair brought for William between him and me. Stephen of Blois was moved down and I had to endure his company. I wondered how long I could feign friendship. "Congratulations Earl! Your star is rising!"

"Thank you, my lord. I have been lucky."

"It is said that a man makes his own luck and you have certainly taken advantage of all of your opportunities."

I lifted the goblet of wine which had been poured. "I raise a goblet to a fine warrior who was true to his king and true to his friends." I chose the toast deliberately. I wanted to see Stephen's reaction.

Those within hearing distance raised their goblets too. I saw the briefest of frowns flash across Stephen's face. He knew that I was aware of his treachery. He had tried to have me killed before now. "Thank you, Earl. A kind sentiment."

I put the wine down and asked, "What brings you here, my lord? You are far from your lands in Blois. Did you know Sir Guy?"

"I know his son. He is a friend of mine." I lodged that information in my head. "I hear that the Empress is in London." We were like two knights sparring. He changed the direction of the conversation.

I was equally capable of feinting and using deception. I lied. "Is she? I had not heard. As you must realise, my lord, the north is far from the places of power like London, Caen, Rouen and Blois."

He shook his head and held his goblet out for more wine. "Blois is a backwater now. It is a land of old men who remember the days of glory and they are all long gone. England is the centre of the world now. Why even Louis the Fat has conceded that King Henry holds all of the power. Since the death of William Adelin he has stopped his attempts to usurp Maine, Anjou and Normandy. My brother stays in Blois and fights the bandits like Coucy and Puset who plague the borderlands."

"You do not need me to tell you, my lord that until Louis controls all of the lands of Charlemagne he will not be happy."

Food was brought and we both picked at it. "You are a clever man, Earl, we should be friends. We can do much to help each other."

I smiled back, "I am but a protector of the Tees and your lands are in Blois. Even if we were friends it is hard to see where the advantage would lie."

He leaned and spoke quietly. "You never know what the future might hold, Alfraed, Earl of Cleveland. Do not shut doors just yet. Who knows when you may need them opening?"

I nodded, "Thank you for the advice, my lord. I know that I am young and naïve and that I have much to learn. You are, I know, a consummate politician and know how the court works. I am just grateful for my little castle on the Tees where I am away from the intrigues of politics and power."

"I agree that politics are far removed from the glory of the battlefield but wars are won there too. Think on that. Those wars are bloodless."

"In war, my lord, there is always blood. You know that." We looked at each other in silence. He had tried to sway me to his side without revealing what his plans were. I could have gone along with him but my father and Athelstan had not brought me up that way. I would remain my own man who was true to himself.

Sir Barnard had arranged for a troubadour who came and sang songs about Sir Guy. They were not very good songs and the troubadour was not the best I had heard but William enjoyed him until he fell asleep and I had the opportunity to return to my chambers. I had much to think on.

Stephen's presence, here in the north, so soon after I had been made earl was not an accident. The fact that he was here made me suspicious of my host. What was their connection? Then I wondered about Stephen of Blois. I wondered how he had reached here. I decided that I would use my squires to ask pertinent questions which would not arouse suspicion. I had had little to drink and I would rise early. William always rose early and it would not seem strange for me to be abroad in the early hours when everyone else was recovering from a night's heavy drinking.

Although I had no need to doubt my hosts I slept with a chair behind the door and my sword close to hand. I had experienced a knife in the night before now. I would not risk it with my son so close.

As I expected my excited son had me up before dawn. I took him, when we had dressed, down to the stables. I woke John and Leofric. "I want you two to watch my son." They both nodded. "Without being obvious I want the both of you to discover where Stephen of Blois has been before he reached here. Can you do that?"

Leofric grinned, "Aye, my lord."

John was not as quick as Leofric and he just nodded and said, "Yes my lord."

William would help disguise their questions and the three of them left. I woke Wulfric and led him into the inner bailey. "I want to know the intentions of Stephen of Blois. Where is he going when he leaves here?"

"Is there trouble, my lord?"

"Let us say that I have an itch and I cannot scratch it."

"I got to know some of his men last night. I will do my best."

Sir Hugh and I left together just before noon. I would have left earlier but the night's carousing meant our host was still abed until late in the morning and it would have been rude to leave while he was in bed. It gave my spies the chance to gather as much information as possible. I would wait until I was back in Stockton before I asked for the details they had discovered.

I used the opportunity to catch up with Sir Hugh. The death of Sir Guy might have ramifications for the young knight. "What did you make of Sir Barnard?"

"I think, my lord, that he is good company. He has made me feel more than welcome." They were considered words. Hugh was telling me that he had been courted by Sir Barnard.

"Had you seen much of him before his father's death?"

He shook his head. "He returned towards the end of his father's life. I think his father's steward sent for him."

"Where had he been then?"

"He travelled my lord. Is there a problem? Should I be wary of Sir Barnard?"

It would not do to build barriers between Sir Hugh and his nearest neighbour. Perhaps I was making more of the presence of Stephen of Blois. Shaking my head, I changed the subject. "And how does your manor fare? Did you suffer much in the winter? It was mild in the east."

"No, my lord. We were not bothered by wolves and we only lost one or two of the old people to the winter sickness."

"You were lucky. Sir Richard lost a whole family to that vile contagion and many of my knights had similar problems."

"Perhaps I was due for a change in fortune." He had lost all of his family. His only relative now was Sir Edward's squire, Gille. "And will we be campaigning this year?"

"Eager for war, young Hugh?"

He laughed, "No, my lord but eager for the profits of war."

"At the moment there are no enemies for us to vanquish but I believe that will change. The whole valley prospers and that normally induces jealousy in others. The Scots are still our closest enemies."

We reached my castle at dusk after bidding farewell to Sir Hugh. As we dismounted I said, "Wulfric I wish you and my squires to dine with me this evening. I am keen to learn what news you gathered."

"Aye my lord." I smiled for Wulfric preferred the rough company of his men at arms to that of my wife. He was a rough and ready soldier but Adela would not mind his manners. John and Leofric often dined with me. Adela was keen to turn them both into gentlemen. Their backgrounds were lowly. I knew many such squires who never became knights. Adela was adamant that the two squires would, one day, both become lords of their own manors. She had an unwavering belief in my ability to improve my fortunes and therefore the fortunes of those who served me. I was lucky to have her.

After bathing and changing I sat at the head of the table while I waited for the others to arrive. Sir Hugh's question had been a good one. If neither the King nor the Bishop required me to go to war what should I do? I knew that I could not raid the lands of the King of Scotland. King Henry had forbidden that. What else could my men do? Idle hands oft turned to mischief.

My reverie was ended when William burst in dragging his mother. Adela shook her head, "He has been full of the journey my husband and is determined to tell me all!"

I laughed, "He was quite the centre of attention but he was a good boy my wife. You can be proud of him as I was."

William then gave his mother a blow by blow account of all the places we had visited. Wulfric and my squires entered whilst he was in the midst of it. They listened with amusement. It made it easier for Wulfric as he was able to relax as William was the centre of attention.

Adela was the cleverest woman I had met, outside of the Empress and, as the meal drew to its close she knew I wished to speak with my men. "Come William. It is time for your bed."

"But I want to stay with the other men!"

That made them all laugh. I affected a stern expression, "Then you should know, young William of Stockton, that my men all obey me without question! It is time for bed!"

He hung his head, "Yes, my lord."

I grabbed him and hugged him. "You did well, my son, and I am proud of you. In a few years you, too, might be part of these discussions but for now go with your mother."

He brightened, "Yes father!"

Once he had gone I stood and poured my men some of the red wine we had brought back from our last visit to Normandy. I sat and spread my arms, "Tell me all."

Wulfric began, "The Lord of Blois and his men were preparing to head west and visit Carlisle. There is a new castellan there, Geoffrey de Bois. He is a distant relative of Lord Stephen."

"And what did you make of his men?"

"They are well armed and armoured. They are paid well and I think they are good warriors. They have great respect for Stephen. They think highly of him and would follow him anywhere."

"What you are saying is that he would be hard to defeat."

"For others perhaps but we could take them. Erre and the others from Miklagård were not impressed by them."

I turned to the squires. As I had expected it was the more thoughtful Leofric who answered first. "They came from the north east, my lord. They came through the wall to the west of Hexham."

"Think you they landed in Scotland?"

"That was where they were evasive my lord. It was almost as though they had all been told not to say whence they had come."

I was intrigued. "How did you question them?"

"I said that they would have had a warm welcome had they stopped at Stockton when they travelled north. One of their squires blurted out that they had not come from the south but the north east and that the land there was cold and harsh. I could see from their reactions that he should not have said what he did. I said, as casually as I could, that Sir Hugh Manningham always kept a fine table. They did not recognise the name. I deduced that they had not crossed through his land. That only left the gaps in the wall to the west."

Wulfric nodded approvingly at Leofric's logic. "That would make sense my lord. When they have visited Carlisle, they can return from whence they came."

"You have all done well. Tomorrow, Wulfric, send two of your men north to Hexham with a message for Sir Hugh. I will write a letter this night. I would know where they go, these men of Blois."

He nodded. John ventured, "My lord his men are as loyal to him as yours are. They think he is a good man." There was a naïve innocence about John which was quite endearing. I hoped that others would not take advantage of such an innocent nature.

"He may well be, in his own way, John. However, he does not have the best interests of the Empress Matilda at heart and I do not trust him."

When they had left I summoned my steward and clerk, John son of Leofric. I dictated a letter to Sir Hugh. I asked him to keep watch for Sir Stephen and his conroi. I wanted to know what he was about. Despite John's words there was something about Stephen and his actions that I did not trust. Robert of Gloucester and the King had both chastised me for my suspicions. He was trusted by them. Perhaps it was the memory of Stephen trying to abduct the Empress all those years ago when I had escorted her back to the Emperor. Men can change and Stephen, like me, had been much younger then. Perhaps he was a different person now. I would watch yet.

Chapter 3

As the first hints of spring began to show I threw off the lethargy of winter and looked to my castle walls and my men. William the mason was already hard at work finishing off my gatehouse. I discussed with him the prospect of adding another large tower which would accommodate more men and add strength to the town end of the castle. He said he would draw up plans but that work would take a long time and much stone. I did not mind for I had seen greater castles than mine and knew just how strong they were compared to mine. He had drawn plans showing how we would make the town's gates stronger. That, too, would make my castle harder to take. With doughty men on my walls it was hard to see how an enemy could breach them. Then I set about organising my men and assimilating my new warriors.

Erre and my new men would not fight as mounted men at arms; it would take too long to train them but there would be times when they fought alongside my dismounted men at arms. Then their unique skills would come into their own. We fought on foot. We practised using the six of them and Wulfric as the heart of my line. I knew some of the others resented the place of honour being given to such new men but they had been brought up to fight and protect the Emperor. I knew that if we fought on foot then they would be able to stop anyone getting close to me.

I also set John to begin William's training as a squire. They used wooden swords, much as the Romans had done. John was firm with William. He was a good teacher. The aim was to harden my young son up. Each day they would spar for hour upon hour until William could barely raise his arm. Adela had questioned this at first but I dismissed her concerns. Women could never understand what was needed to train a warrior. It was hard and harsh; it was almost brutal but it was necessary to forge young squires into knights. William's tears soon stopped and he learned what it was to be a warrior. It would not be long before he would be able to ride to war with us. At first, he would not fight. But that would be another stage on his journey. Campaigning was yet a further skill to be added.

Some of my men at arms had now become married, as had some of my knights. It was a sign that they were getting older. When their wives became pregnant I was pleased for they would become warriors when they grew. Wulfric and Dick continued to train and seek replacements. It was too late if we waited until a warrior fell. There had to be someone ready to take their place. The new men were kept at the castle where they could be trained until they were good enough to fight with my warriors. I was acutely aware that we had been very lucky of late. Luck did not last.

Close to Easter Sir Hugh sent me a message that Stephen of Blois had left the north by sea from the River Wear. That meant he had passed through Durham on his way east. That disturbed me. He had been very close to my land and yet we had not seen him. Had he passed close by Durham? What connection did he have there? Sir Hugh's diligence had paid off. I was just happy that he was away from my heartland.

It was as I was just finishing my sessions and preparing for the visit of the King's collector of taxes when I had a message from Robert of Gloucester. It seemed that the Welsh, under the leadership of Owain ap Gruffudd, the son of the king of Gwynedd, had begun to push north and east from the stronghold of Snowdonia. They were ravaging the lands around Chester. The Earl of Chester was secure enough in his castle but the rich lands of Cheshire were suffering. I was ordered to march south with a force of my men to relieve the pressure on the Earl. It was a long letter and I took it as a sign of my recent elevation that Robert of Gloucester entrusted me with such knowledge. He would be bringing an army from the south. He commanded me to meet him on the plains of Cheshire. I was urged not leave the north undefended. The Earl of Gloucester only asked for a small force of knights.

Even as I sent riders to summon my knights I could see the Earl's strategy. I would be the anvil and Robert the hammer. When I approached the men of Gwynedd I had no doubt that they would outnumber me. Robert of Gloucester was clever. When the attention of the Welsh was on me then he would fall upon them. I only sent for four of my knights. I would take just those whose manors lay close to Stockton. My other knights would provide protection for our homes. The Earl had not said how many men he wished me to bring and I would not risk took many.

Sir Edward, from Thornaby, brought fourteen men; Sir Richard of Yarm sixteen, Sir Tristan of Elton ten and Sir Harold of Hartburn twelve. The bulk of the men in the conroi would come from my castle. I took Wulfric and twenty men at arms and Dick and nine archers. I left Aelric at the castle to work with my new archers. They would provide the defence.

As the knights were all so close they reached my castle within an hour of my summons. As was my wont I did not command, as was my right. Instead I asked if they were ready for a campaign in Wales. I was delighted when they all enthusiastically agreed.

Sir Edward rubbed his hands, "The last time we fought the Welsh we came home with more cattle than there are in the whole of Scotland!"

Sir Richard laughed. He too had profited from our raids against the Scots and knew this could be the opportunity to increase our wealth without risking revenge from those we defeated. "Do you have a plan, my lord? Or do we wait for the Earl of Gloucester?"

"I believe that the Earl is gathering a large army. He is relying on our proximity to enable us to get there before him."

35

Sir Edward snorted, "So that we can draw the sting from this Welsh wasp!" Edward had been critical of the Earl's strategy before. He had been a man at arms and saw every battle from that viewpoint. His men loved him.

"I do not mind. If the Earl is not there to give me instructions then I have a free hand."

Harold had been my squire and, I think, knew me as well if not better than any other. "How many men will you lead, my lord?"

"We will take forty-eight men at arms, thirty-six archers and half a dozen men to watch the horses and feed us. That will give us a force of almost a hundred men; fast enough to evade an army and yet big enough to be able to do some serious damage. Choose your own servants to look after your needs and your baggage. The bulk of the men at arms will be mine. You will each leave enough men to guard your homes but I have sent messages to the other knights in the valley to keep a close watch on our own homes. With a new Castellan at Durham and Carlisle as well as a vigilant Sir Hugh I think the normal Scottish raids may not materialise this year. I have a young priest from Norton, Father John, who will be our healer. I intend to leave Edgar here to command the men at arms."

Sir Tristan was the youngest of my knights. The son of Sir Richard he was Sir Harold's best friend. He was also the poorest of my knights. "Will we need our war horses, my lord?"

"We will take them. The Welsh are a small people and whilst the land of Wales does not suit destrier the land of Cheshire does. The sight of our fine horses charging them may help us win without even drawing a weapon."

"And when do we leave?"

"We will gather tomorrow at dawn by Sir Richard's Manor at Yarm. I intend to make the journey in less than five days."

"You will take Aiden?"

"Of course, Sir Edward. I will not run blindly into the Welsh defences. I want the element of surprise on our side. We have fought in that land before and Aiden is familiar with it." I rose. "If you have no further questions then I suggest you leave to say your farewells."

Adela already knew of my orders and she was resigned to being alone again. I knew that when I was away she would spend much time seeing to the poor of our town. She had a good heart and, having been a prisoner who was subjected to much hardship, she constantly sought to alleviate that in others. She improved the lot of the poor and the sick. My daughter, Hilda, had now grown enough to be left with Seara and Mary the slaves. They enjoyed looking after my children. The problem was William.

As I was packing the clothes and equipment I would need he came in to watch. "You are going away?"

"Yes, my son, I am. The King wishes me to go to fight the Welsh." I knew it was the Earl of Gloucester who had summoned me but I found it easier to use the word 'King' for now that I was now an Earl too it might confuse my son.

"You said I could come with you next time."

I turned and faced him. "Do not try to twist my words. It is not the behaviour I expect from my son. I told you that when you were old enough I would take you. You are not old enough as this request proves." I saw his lip begin to quiver. "See, this proves I am right. When you can take my commands without crying then, perhaps I will consider taking you."

He nodded and wiped the tears from his eyes. "I can do that."

"However, you have to be big enough to ride a horse alone, wearing armour and your helmet and you must satisfy John and Leofric that you can fight with a sword." I looked at him. "Will they say you are ready yet?" He looked at me and I could see that he was desperate to say yes but he knew it would not be true and he shook his head. I smiled, "See, already you are showing that you are growing and learning."

"I promise that I will soon be big enough to come with you and John and Leofric will say that I am ready."

We left before dark. My wife held my children and I leaned down to kiss them both. "Aelric and Edgar will command while I am away and John son of Leofric will keep me informed of the situation here in the north. I promise I will return as soon as I can manage."

"I know. Take care, my husband."

William said, "I will ask Edgar to continue my training!"

"Good!"

The sound of the hooves clattering through the bailey would have woken all in my town. It could not be helped. I saw waved farewells from some of the young girls in the town as they saw their young men riding to war. It was ever thus. I hoped that all would return rich men and with tales to tell to their pretty ladies but I knew it would not be. Some would fall and some girls would forever mourn their dead warrior.

We did not unfurl my banner, now complete with a wolf on the blue background with the two stars, until daylight when we were heading through Northallerton. It told the world that the Earl of Cleveland was going to war. The column was strung out over a large part of the road. There were sumpters as well as destrier at the rear. We had tents and cooking pots as well as food to sustain us. I hoped that we might find hospitality from lords along the way but I knew that our route would pass few castles. We would be travelling over the bare backbone of the land. We would cross the high moor. Even in summer it was a cold and sometimes inhospitable place. It was another reason for speed. There was little to be gained from a leisurely journey over the moors. It was still cool and the high ground would be even colder. It would be a good test of my new warriors so recently arrived from the east. That and the fact that they had to contend with horses would make their first few days a rude awakening to campaigning in England.

I rode with my knights in the van. Aiden and two archers ranged ahead. I did not feel that there was any danger but it was a good habit to get into. Riding with my four knights gave me the chance to refine my ideas for the coming war. I had fought in the county of Cheshire and the north Welsh borders before and knew that the land could turn against us in but a few miles. It went from flat plains to thick forests to impossibly steep valley sides filled with rocks and gullies. It could prove a death trap for our horses.

"I intend to strike quickly as soon as we arrive. It will frighten the Welsh, give hope to those within Chester and will be our best opportunity to make easy kills."

Sir Tristan asked, "You do not intend to raise the siege?"

"Unless I miss my guess there will be many Welsh around the walls and they will outnumber us. I do not doubt that they have prepared their own defences well but there will be one weak point. There always is. Aiden will find it. We will attack quickly and cause as much damage as we can. We then cross the Dee. There is a hill fort, an old Saxon structure at Broughton. It is protected by a marsh but, more importantly it controls the main road along the coast from Gwynedd and Anglesey. It is the easiest way for this

Owain to supply his men and transport his booty. I intend to use that as our stronghold until the Earl of Gloucester reaches us."

"And how long will that be, my lord?"

"I am guessing, Edward, five days after we arrive. Our journey is shorter than the Earl's and less hilly. Once we have crossed the moor the going will be easier. It is flat and will make good time. We will annoy the men of Gwynedd so much that they will be forced to attack us."

"How so my lord?"

I waved a hand at the four of them. "Each day you will set out and raid as far as you can to give heart to the men of Cheshire and to take as much from the Welsh as you can. You have good horses and with four conroi you can cover a large area. Owain will think we have an army. It will do your young warriors good to fight together under your banners. They will compete with the other conroi for the most honour and booty."

Edward nodded. He was experienced enough to know how it would work. "But when Owain does come he will have the advantage for we are horsemen and we will have to fight on foot."

"And yet we have fought on foot many times and successfully too. Besides we now have a secret weapon; the men who follow Erre. Along with Wulfric they will form the heart of my defence."

"It sounds a risk, my lord."

"I am merely planning for the worst that could happen. I hope that the Earl of Gloucester will reach us before that happens." I laughed, "However, Harold, think of all the booty we shall win while we await our leader."

There were finer details we had to manage. I had learned, over the years, that failure to do so led to more confusion than was necessary. It was another reason why I had chosen these four. They were closer to me than any other knights. Perhaps Hugh of Gainford would have fitted in too but I was happy with those who were with me.

We reached the Mersey on the evening of the fourth day. We had done well. We made camp in the forests they called Wirral. It was the lands used by the Earls of Chester for their hunting. Now that we were close to our enemies we made a defensive camp with sentries and traps to warn us of any incursion. I gave instructions to Aiden. He would leave before dawn and scout out Chester. I had confidence in him. He would bring back detailed information of who we faced and an accurate count of their numbers.

That evening, after we had eaten, the camp was filled with the sounds of swords being sharpened on whetstones. My men were going to war and they would be ready. There was a confident air in the camp. Success breeds success and we had been successful thus far. I did not expect to be worried by the Welsh warriors.

It was just a handful of miles from where we camped to Chester. When we rose, we made ready to fight. Those who were guarding the horses were protected by Erre and his men. Each conroi gathered around its banner. We waited for the return of Aiden. We did not have long to wait.

"My lord, they have over two hundred men along three sides. A further hundred are on the fourth. They have Welsh archers and spearmen but only five knights. I saw many Vikings and the wild Irish. They have ringed the town with a ditch."

I nodded. That was unexpected and might cause a problem. Vikings were like dismounted knights and they were fearless. They were as tough as the Varangian Guard but,

41

thankfully, less disciplined. They were an unexpected element in this equation. "And where are they weakest?"

"To the east of their defences they have a camp with tents and their horses. It lies outside their defensive ditch." He smiled, "I think, from the animals I saw on their fires, that the knights have been hunting in the land of the Earl of Chester."

"Good. Then we have our opportunity. Aiden, lead Erre and the pack animals towards the ford over the Dee. Wait for us on the other side." I had already told Erre what he would be doing. At first, he had taken it as a slight but he now saw the wisdom. We would be using our horses as weapons. It was not in Erre's experience and he was a professional enough warrior to realise that.

Aiden led them off. "Dick, command the archers. When we attack I want you to shower their defences with arrows. When we have raided the camp then follow us and stop any pursuit."

"Aye, my lord."

"Wulfric, you command the men at arms. The knights and the squires will lead the attack." I patted the neck of my jet black destrier, Star. "Let us see if they can stand against our warhorses."

Leofric brought me my lance and John unfurled my banner.

"We ride!"

We had little order as we rode through the forest. We had been here before and we knew the way. As the trees began to thin we caught the faint whiff of wood smoke. It became stronger and I slowed the column down. I saw the camp in the distance. We were too far to the west and I led the column of men through the trees to the east. We emerged from the trees in a small dell. We were hidden from the camp. I lifted my lance and the other knights

42

formed on me. Behind me the squires formed a line with my banner in the middle and then Wulfric cajoled the men at arms into their lines. Dick had plenty of time to organise his men once we had charged.

I led the men from the forest and we trotted. I could feel Sir Edward's foot next to mine on one side and Sir Richard's on the other. It kept us tight. Our horses were not moving hard enough to thunder yet but when they did then the enemy would see us. We crossed over a hundred paces before a sentry spotted us as we left the hidden dell. He was pulling up his breeks having relieved himself. His shout made every head turn towards us. It was too late for those within the camp. We were within charging range. We were but three hundred paces from them. I spurred Star and he began to move a little faster. I kept my lance upright.

The men of Gwynedd sounded their horns and began to turn to face us. I saw the spearmen racing for their spears and the archers stringing their bows. It would be too late for them. I had time to see that there were no Vikings in this camp. It was the knights, the squires and perhaps thirty of their spearmen and archers who had occupied this part of the siege works.

At a hundred paces I lowered my lance and kicked Star on. He leapt forward. I tucked my shield tightly into my body and looked for my target. I saw a knight with a red shield. It had a single leopard upon it and he had a war axe. I saw him shouting orders. He would be my target. Others were gathering around him. They were brave men. Star's hooves crashed and smashed into the skull of an unlucky spearman who did not get out of his way. I stood in my stirrups as I pulled back my lance and, as I neared the knight I punched forward. He tried to swing his war axe at the head of my lance but my hand had been too fast. The head went into his open mouth even as he was cursing me. His head snapped back and I relaxed my hand to let his body slide from my lance.

We were now like foxes in the henhouse. We were a wall of horseflesh and metal which ploughed through the disorganised Welshmen who had barely had time to arm themselves. I was aware of arrows falling to my right. Dick and the archers were doing as I had bid. I saw a squire brace himself against the ground with his spear. He intended to skewer my horse. I wheeled Star to the left and struck down with the lance. The head went into his shoulder and, as he fell, it broke. I let go of the ruined weapon and drew my sword.

I wheeled Star to the right around the wounded squire and leaned forward. An archer was aiming at Wulfric and the men at arms. As the Welshman's arm drew back I slashed my sword across the back of his neck. The sharpened blade bit into the flesh and the archer's head flew across the ground. It struck one of his comrades on the leg and he turned. Before he could bring his bow to bear I had hacked into his side and he fell in a heap at my feet.

I reined in Star. He was not yet tired but I knew not what lay ahead. I conserved his energy. I lifted my helmet and scanned the field. The warriors who were facing Chester's walls were beginning to organise themselves. We had achieved what I wanted. I turned and saw John, where he had been ordered to stay, close to my horse's flank.

"John, signal our men to hold." Harold and Leofric drew up next to me. "Tell the squires to collect the horses and head for the ford."

"Aye my lord."

I saw the men at arms moving around the field finishing off the wounded and gathering the booty. It was mainly from the dead knights. Dick and the archers had mounted up and I saw them approach. Edward and my other knights appeared at my side. "Have we lost many?"

Sir Richard said, "I saw one of Sir Edward's men fall. They took his horse with an axe and then slew him. The men at arms finished them off."

"Good that is less than I expected." Dick approached. "Have you thinned them?"

"Aye my lord, but there are still many remaining. Those Vikings in their mail shirts are certainly hard to kill."

"Cover us as we withdraw."

Heavily armoured men from Dublin were now heading purposefully towards us in their classic wedge. There was no flesh to be seen and they sheltered behind their enormous shields. There was little to be gained from trying to fight them on horses which had become tired. It was time to leave. I was aware of men on the walls of Chester cheering and waving banners. We had achieved our purpose. Chester would not fall any time soon and it would take a day or two for them to reorganise their camp.

"John, withdraw!"

As the banner signalled my orders I wheeled Star and headed south and east to the ford where, I hoped, that Erre and my men would be waiting.

Chapter 4

Erre showed how reliable he was. When we approached the ford, I could see that they had their spears ready to repel any enemy who tried to take the ford. The horses and baggage were protected by the servants further up the bank while the Varangians stood close to the water's edge. He raised his helmet and waved as he recognised us.

I dismounted next to him as the column crossed the ford. I waved over Aiden. "Go and make sure that the hill at Broughton is unoccupied."

Erre grinned, "I see you succeeded my lord. Perhaps we should have stayed with you and we might have relieved the siege."

"There are Vikings here, Erre, many of them. You know their worth. Can you imagine trying to dislodge them from behind their ditches?"

He nodded, "You need to catch them in the open."

"And we can only do that when they are hungry enough to come and seek us. And when they do so then you and your brothers will be the wall upon which they will break."

"You are a true strategos, my lord. I can see why the Emperor tried to tempt you to his service."

As we neared the vital hill I noticed the burnt-out farms which dotted the plain. The Welsh had been busy. I wondered how many families had been taken west to their island of their mountain as slaves. I began to be assailed by doubts as we approached Broughton. Suppose the Welsh had fortified and defended the old hill fort? We did not have enough men to assault it; at least not enough to assault it and then hold it. An attack on a well-defended position was always expensive on both men and horses. I was relieved when Aiden met us. His demeanour told me that there were no problems.

"There is no one there, my lord. It looks much the same as the last time we were here."

"Well done."

He was right. The ditches had not been deepened; indeed, some were still half filled with fallen leaves, rocks and broken branches. The walls which had fallen had not been repaired. The Earl of Chester had been remiss. He had left his back door not just open but broken. It was no wonder he had been surprised. Had this been my land I would have rebuilt the castle and garrisoned it. I pointed to the top as the servants arrived. "Set up the tents at the top. Prepare food. Our men have earned it."

Wulfric dismounted next to me. "I will set the sentries, my lord."

"Good. We were lucky there Wulfric. We caught them by surprise."

He shook his head, "We make our own luck my lord. I will have the men gather the loot together."

"You will organise it into five equal piles. On this raid we share equally."

Dick rode up to me but did not dismount. "We will scout the woods and see if there are either men or game hereabouts, my lord."

Dick and half of his archers were Sherwood woodsmen. It was second nature for them to forage first and rest later. They knew the value of a full stomach. The labour was a fair division. The men at arms would make the camp defensible and the archers would provide food.

We barely had time to set up the camp before darkness fell. Dick returned with two deer and a report that the land close by was clear of all signs of the Welsh. His grim face spoke of the dead he had found. The farmers of Cheshire had paid for the indolence of the Earl. "There is no one alive for many miles, my lord. There were few bodies. I am guessing the rest of the people and their animals have been taken."

Next morning my four small conroi each left the camp to head north, south, east and west. They would find the Welsh and cause havoc. The camp seemed emptier when almost two thirds of our men left. "Wulfric let us make this a harder nut to crack."

"Aye my lord." He shook his head. "The men feel slighted that they have to work in the camp while others go to war."

"Then tell them that tomorrow will be our turn. Our four conroi today will disturb the enemy and tomorrow they will look for us. We have the biggest conroi." I wagged a finger at him, "Let me do the planning, Wulfric and the men will all profit."

"It was not me, my lord but…"

"I know. Now clear the ditches and replace the fallen stones. We will not build a Miklagård but we will make it harder for them to dislodge us."

I waved Aiden and my squires over. "Aiden, I want you and Leofric to ride and find the Earl of Gloucester. He needs to know where we are and my plans. Keep hidden. Once you pass our men and the Welsh lines it should be easier." I smiled, "I would tell you where to go but I am certain that you know how to suck eggs!"

Aiden grinned, "Aye my lord." He turned to Leofric who had once been one of the boys who held his falcons. "Come Leofric let us see just how well and swiftly you can ride."

49

My men worked hard and as the morning turned to afternoon you could see the difference they had made. The walls were remade so that we could fight from behind them. It was an ancient fort and so there were no towers for my archers but Dick and his men improvised a step to give them some height. The ancients had used twists and turns in the ditch to guard their entrance and Erre and his Varangians made that into a death trap. We did not have the tools to deepen the ditch but by clearing it we made it into an obstacle once more. We also fired some sharpened stakes and put them in the ditch. I had men dig another ditch directly in front of the open gateway so that any enemy could not run directly in. They would have to turn. It was only a small ditch but it would slow down an enemy.

Harold was the first to return. It was in the late afternoon. He had been to the west and the road to Anglesey. His small conroi had been augmented by five pack animals. Two of his men bore wounds; one of them looked serious enough for the attention of our priest.

"Father John, would you see to the wounded?" Harold dismounted. I felt like a proud father as I saw the look of joy upon his face. He had fought alongside others before but this was the first time he had been entrusted with a solitary command. I clasped his arm, "It went well?"

"Aye, my lord. My time in Sherwood stood me in good stead. I found a bank and some trees which overlooked the road and we waited. This column of horses was escorted by ten men. There were but five warriors. We slew two quickly with arrows but the other three fought hard. The servants fled west; they will know we are here."

"And what were the rewards?"

"A sumpter with arrows, a second with spears and the other three contained grain." He held up a small bag. "We found some coins. I will give them to my men. They fought well. It was intended for Chester. Your strategy has paid off my lord. We are choking them."

I noticed his squire talking animatedly to John. "And how did your squire?"

"He was calm and doughty. He never wavered when we attacked."

"Good. This is all good experience for them."

As the day turned to dusk the others returned with varying degrees of success. We had suffered wounds and slight losses but our sudden appearance had caught the Welsh napping. Their losses far outweighed our own. We had another six horses as well as many swords, shields and coins. My men had not sighted any knights. These had been small groups of foragers looking for settlements which had survived the initial raid. I was pleased that young Harold had had the most success. The successful conroi was the centre of everyone's attention. Dick was delighted with the arrows for although they were not of the same quality as the ones our fletcher made, they would enable our archers to be more profligate with their precious missiles.

After we had eaten I gathered my knights, Wulfric and Dick, to give them the instructions and orders for the next day. "Some men escaped Harold's ambush and headed west. I will head there tomorrow with my conroi. They will have a better idea of our position and I would prefer to meet them on my terms. The rest of you will continue to fortify the camp. I will leave Erre and the Varangians here."

Wulfric shook his head, "He will not like that, my lord!"

"He will obey orders!" Wulfric nodded. "I want you to send out your archers tomorrow but they should stay hidden. I want this Owain to waste time tomorrow seeking us. They will find us eventually, but each day they don't brings the Earl closer to us."

"They just watch, my lord?"

"No Dick, they can ambush but I want them to remain hidden. I want them as the outlaws of Sherwood, invisible. Their job is to be our eyes and ears."

Edward threw the bone he had just gnawed into the fire. "Should we not be finding where their leader is? It was obvious that he was not at the siege."

"I do not wish to spread us too thin. Our first instruction was to relieve Chester. Our presence here has done that already. If we do not find whoever leads their army today then I will raid their lines again tomorrow and see if we can force them away. If they have not reinforced them then that may be possible."

Sir Richard stroked his beard; a sure sign that he was thinking, "Who is it that leads them?"

"The Earl thought it was Owain the son of their king. I know nothing of him save that he has two brothers. If the Earl is coming north then he must think him a formidable foe else he would have left the Earl of Chester to deal with him."

The next morning we rose early. I did not take Star; I took Scout instead. I did not think I would need a warhorse. I was also a little mindful of facing Vikings with their axes and savage disdain for horses. I used Dick and his archers as scouts. We headed west along what must have been a Roman road many years ago. It had not been maintained. It had a reasonable surface for horses and men but wagons would have struggled to cover long distances upon it for there were many of the cobbles missing and the ditches had not been cleared.

We headed just ten miles down the road. We used the remaining Roman marker stones as guides. The Dee lay to the north of us. I wondered if they might use the river to supply their men. I knew the Welsh did not but Vikings used their drekar the way we used horses. As we watched for signs of movement along the road I sent Griff of Gwent and Wilson to see if there were any ships in the river. I had not wanted to go too far down the road in case we were needed back at our improvised camp. Griff of Gwent and Wilson were only away a short time.

"My lord, there are ships coming up the river but they are the Viking dragon ships. There are three of them."

My immediate reaction was one of dismay. They were being reinforced and then I realised I was looking at this the wrong way. They now had more mouths to feed. I could not see them having spare food in their own lands in Ireland at this time of year. It was Anglesey which was the bread basket of Wales. They would be using their valuable source of supplies for their allies. Cheshire had not been conquered yet. The Welsh king was gambling on taking the fertile land for his own. "How many oars on each one?"

"One had thirteen and two of them nine."

"Were they heavily laden?"

"No, my lord, there were high in the water. I saw weed."

"You have done well."

Griff of Gwent asked, "Why is it good, my lord, that they ride high out of the water?"

"It means they only have one man per oar. They only have sixty men aboard the boats. We killed almost that many the day before yesterday. These must have been summoned before our attack."

"My lord, riders! They come from the west."

John's voice made me turn and spur Scout back into the trees. The place we had chosen for an ambush had a dip on our side of the road. I now used that to our advantage. I nudged Scout forward so that I could peer through the thin foliage. There were two knights on horses. They were followed by ten armoured men at arms leading a column of marching men. They were armed with spears. I saw the light glinting off some helmets. This was not the fyrd. I tried to remember the maps of the area. They could have come from St. Asaph. I knew there was a castle there but more likely it was from Flint which was just ten miles down the road. I could not make out the numbers but it mattered not. We had surprise on our side.

"Dick, have your archers ready. I will take the men at arms and charge up the road. You attack them in the rear with arrows."

"Aye my lord."

"Wulfric follow me."

I rode back down the road to a point about forty paces from the line of trees. I formed up with Wulfric, Roger of Lincoln and Jack son of John. With John my squire behind me the other ten men at arms made a solid wall of iron.

We had long spears, captured from the Welsh, with us. Our lances I would keep for the day we met a large body of knights. I estimated when the Welsh would appear and, when I judged the moment right, I spurred Scout. We trotted forward and then cantered. I saw the banners appear above the skyline and knew that they were within twenty paces of the rise. I lowered my spear and the other three followed suit. We saw each other at the same time. The difference was that we were going at a canter while they were moving at the speed of a walking man.

As soon as we were seen I heard the Welsh voice give the alarm. Dick's arrows began to descend upon those at the rear of the column. I later found that the men there were leading pack horses with fresh supplies to replace the ones we had taken. Although Dick only had nine bows they could release almost as fast as they could blink. I pulled back my arm, aware that I was not riding Star and Scout was not as big a mount. I punched upwards at the knight on my right. He, too, had pulled back his arm to strike me with his spear but I was faster, Scout was faster, and my spear was deadly. It struck him in his right side and tore through his mail links. As I withdrew it the head came away bloody. Roger of Lincoln, riding to my right, pulled him from the saddle and I heard his scream as my men at arms rode over his body.

The enemy men at arms had tried to make a hurried shield wall but the speed of our advance caught them in mid formation. I spurred Scout who leapt a little in the air when I urged him on. His front hoof flailed making two of the men at arms raise their shields for protection. I had an easy hit on one of them, striking him just above his belt with my spear. Roger of Lincoln took the other in the thigh. Then the four of us were into the disordered spearmen. Dick's arrows were still causing chaos and I saw the men leading the horses ahead of us turn and try to flee. I thrust my spear into one of the spearmen who clutched at the haft as he fell. I released it and drew my sword.

"Come on Scout! On!" My steed responded to my spurs and my shout. He was far superior to the sumpters ahead and we soon made up the ground. As I raised my sword to strike the men they threw themselves to the ground.

"Mercy! We surrender! Do not kill us!"

Wulfric and Roger reined in next to me. Wulfric growled at them. "Then throw down your weapons!"

I turned and saw that most of their men at arms lay dead or wounded and the surviving spearmen had all surrendered. I shouted, "Dick, bring your archers and take charge of these horses and the prisoners." I dismounted and nudged one of the Welshmen in the ribs. "You, stand."

He did so, "Please do not kill us. We have families."

I saw immediately that this was not a warrior. He was little more than a villein. "Then speak the truth and answer my questions."

"I will."

"Where have you come from this day?"

"The castle at Flint, my lord."

I pointed to the dead knights. "Was one of these a lord of the castle?"

He shook his head, "No, lord. The Lord of the manor is Cynan ap Iago. That is his younger brother Rhodri ap Iago."

"And is there a garrison at Flint?" He hesitated. "I was beginning to warm to you Welshman. It would be a shame if I had to slit your throat because you were too slow in answering."

"Yes, my lord. This is half of the garrison."

I smiled. "What is your name?"

"Gwynfor of Caerwys."

"Then you and these other eight shall live. You will return to your master and tell him that the Earl of Stockton, who leads an army of King Henry of England and Normandy demands that he surrender his castle. I will come tomorrow to receive his answer." I saw him glance behind me. I laughed, "This is not my army!

These are my oathsworn out for a pleasant ride." He nodded. "When you have delivered your message, I would go back to Caerwys and take up another occupation." He nodded and began to move albeit slowly. "I have given my word. Go."

After they had fled down the road Wulfric asked, "Why did you let them go?"

"A number of reasons. Firstly, we do not need extra mouths to feed and men to guard. Secondly, because I want the lord of Flint Castle to send a message to the other leaders in the valley. If they think we intend to attack then they will prepare for a siege of their own castles and are less likely to reinforce Chester but most importantly because there is no need. These were not warriors. These were like Tom the Fletcher who was slain for no reason."

He pointed to the other prisoners; the men at arms, "And those?"

"They are different. They are warriors. We will guard them and then decide how we may use them."

Arkwright and Jack son of John had both been wounded. Annoyingly it was in their legs which would mean they could not ride. My men at arms used their legs to guide their horses as much as their reins. We were short of men at arms. However, it was fewer than we might have expected. We headed back to the camp.

Our arrival prompted much discussion. We had two more fine palfreys as well as the sumpters with even more supplies. We would not starve that was for certain.

"Did your scouts bring in any news?"

Edward had taken charge in my absence, "They have columns of scouts out seeking us my lord. They rode in pairs on small ponies. Six of them will not report back but there were others who fled when they saw the bodies of the dead scouts."

I nodded, "And they have been reinforced with more men from Dublin. We are safe from attack from Flint. It is St. Asaph which might cause us problems. Harold, on the morrow, take your conroi and scout St. Asaph. Be cautious. Do not try any foolish heroics."

He laughed, "Then I shall try not to emulate you, my lord."

He left early while we questioned the six prisoners who remained. Arkwright and Jack son of John were more than happy to guard them and their bad temper at being camp bound was taken out on the hapless prisoners who were too petrified to move. It seemed that it was Cadwallar who commanded the men attacking Chester whilst Owain and his other brother, Cadwaladr, were in the Cheshire plain around Nantwich and Middlewich.

Dick commanded the scouts who ranged, this time to the north, east and south of us. Harold was to the west and would warn us of any danger from there. Once I was certain that there was no danger from St. Asaph's garrison I would attack the besiegers once more. I wondered why Robert of Gloucester had not arrived nor sent a message. The last time we had been in Cheshire he had used me as bait. I did not think he would do so again but I felt very vulnerable. At least I could beat a retreat this time. I would not have to fight my way out through the whole army of Gwynedd.

I was examining the swords of the knights we had killed when one of Sir Richard's scouts galloped in. "My lord, they have raised the siege. There is an army coming towards us!"

Chapter 5

I did not panic. I had expected this and we were prepared. "Dick, organise your archers. Sir Tristan, have your men disguise the stakes in the ditch." I turned to Erre, "Now is the time for you to show your worth, Erre. I want you and your men to be the gate. My other men at arms will fight from behind the walls."

Erre grinned, "It is about time we showed these horse soldiers how a real warrior fights."

The other archers galloped in and reported the same thing. There was an army coming. By piecing together all of their information we discovered that there were almost eighty Vikings and Irish warriors along with forty Welshman. The good news was that there just six knights and their leader was one of the Princes of Gwynedd. Seven knights could be handled; especially if we used the ground to our advantage. Although the Welsh had fine archers we knew that they had to be short of arrows. We had all of the ones that had been sent to them! We also had the benefit of height. The hill fort was on a small rise. It would slow down any attack. We also discovered, when all the scouts reported, that half of the men from Dublin had mail. That would somewhat negate the effect of Dick's arrows, at least until they were at close range.

"Dick, concentrate on the ones without armour. If we can thin them out they may become demoralised." I looked to the west. I needed Harold and his men. Even with them it would be a hard fight but without them we were in danger of defeat. The reinforcements from the dragon ships had made all the difference to our enemy. Even as I looked to the west I realised that it had been the reinforcements which had allowed Prince Cadwallar to attack us. Perhaps we had been lax and his scouts had spotted us or, more likely, we had been seen by the dragon ships.

I saw the rippling snake that was our enemy as it wound its way towards us. They knew we had horses and they were maintaining their solid lines to negate a charge. I did not intend to charge. I suspected that their leader would attack on a broad front. That way he would have overwhelming numbers all the way along our line. That was where Dick and his twenty-eight archers would come into their own. When Harold returned, if Harold returned, then we would have thirty-six. Perhaps thinking of my former squire made him appear for I heard Tristan shout, "My lord, it is Harold. He has returned."

He had come just in time. He threw himself from his mount. "There is a garrison at St. Asaph, my lord, but it is not a large one. I scouted Flint too and it could be taken."

I smiled at his enthusiasm, "Thank you, Harold, but we have a rather large army approaching us. We will deal with that first before we reduce a castle eh? Send your archers to Dick and bring your men at arms to Wulfric."

We stood behind Erre and his men while Wulfric distributed the new men at arms along the line. He did it carefully for he was looking for a balance. He knew the men at arms well and he sought perfection in our defence. There would be no random choices from Wulfric. The extra spears we had captured meant we could afford to give every man at arms two. In an initial attack we would be able to keep the advancing men at a distance and the longer we did that then the more time we had for the archers to weaken them.

"John, plant my banner here behind Erre. Then join the other squires. I want the five of you mounted and ready to fetch us our war horses when I give the command."

He looked disappointed. "I am not to fight in the line?"

"Follow my orders and you shall fight."

60

As he went Erre chuckled, "I like that young cockerel. He has spirit. He would face these wild men from Dublin even though they have more skill than he has."

Wulfric said, "Aye Erre, but not more heart. I have seen that boy fight and he is fearless."

The enemy were now two hundred paces from us. Dick had placed ranging rocks so that he knew the distance. Normally he would have waited until they were closer before he released his deadly missiles but the enemy had accommodated him well for they came in a solid block and given us the opportunity to send many arrows their way. At a hundred and fifty paces the arrows flew. Although my own archers were the best in my small force all of them were more than competent. They were an elite band. The enemy shields were slow to come up. A handful of men fell. The ones at the front also brought theirs up too even though no arrows were loosed at them. It made them take their eyes from the uneven ground and my men at arms laughed as some of them fell.

Dick kept releasing arrows. I saw him target the knights and their horses. It might seem cruel but archers knew the value of dismounting a knight by killing his horse. Two horses were killed before all the knights dismounted and took shelter in the wedge which moved relentlessly towards us. I heard a command given first in Welsh and then repeated in what I assumed was Norse. The line began to spread out to a wider formation. This time the men in mail were the subject of Dick's arrows. I saw a trail of bodies which marked the route towards us. I watched as Dick aimed deliberately at a Viking warrior who was encased in mail and had a masked helmet. The only flesh which could be seen was his lips and nose hidden behind a huge beard. As he raised his head and opened his mouth to shout an arrow plunged into it and silenced him forever. Another took his place.

The line was now forty paces from us and they would soon charge.

"Ready Erre?"

"I am always ready to fight, my lord, and I have picked out the trinkets I will claim when we have defeated them!"

It seemed they had not seen the first ditch and three of them were pushed in by the weight of numbers behind. I heard their screams as they fell onto the fire hardened stakes. They began to spread around the sides of the ditch. They looked eager to get at what looked like a handful of men in the gate. Once again, their sheer weight of numbers caused at least three more men to fall into the ditch. I saw their leader exhorting his men forward.

"Ready! They will charge soon!"

Having endured the barrage of arrows and the trap filled ditches the mercenaries from Dublin were keen to get at us and they came like a wild torrent as soon as they saw the clear entrance to the six Varangians who stood before them. Wulfric and his five best men were behind them and then I stood with my knights and my banner. The eighteen most powerfully armed men in my conroi were ready to face this horde. They were attacking the strongest part of our defence. I heard a wild feral scream from the entire enemy and they hurled themselves at Erre and his men.

Suddenly spears appeared above the shoulders of my Varangians as they thrust their long weapons forward at head height. They were strong men and the powerful blows easily penetrated the mail of the Dubliners. The slope had meant the Vikings did not have the speed they needed and they did not have numbers behind them to give them more power. The first six Vikings fell. Two of my men had broken their spears and they grabbed their second one. The next attackers arrived piecemeal and were despatched just as easily. I heard commands shouted and the whole of the enemy line ran towards the wall. It was not a high wall and it looked easy to scale. The ditch provided another barrier to them and more fell to be killed or wounded on the fire hardened and dung covered stakes.

The enemy gathered together again at the gate. I knew we had to rely on the archers and my other men at arms if we were to win. Wulfric saw the sudden attack and, as the next twelve Vikings rushed towards the gateway he shouted. "Push!"

His timing was perfect and my twelve men ran forward, aided by the slope, and slammed into the advancing Vikings. Three were knocked into the ditch where they writhed in pain. My best warriors now outnumbered them. No mercy was shown and they were slaughtered.

It was at that moment that I judged the time to be right. "John! Horses!" I had waited for the Welsh Prince to commit all of his men to the attack. The centre of the enemy line was now the weakest. I grabbed a spear and leapt on to Star's back. The smell of blood always excited him and he stamped the ground, eager to be away. We did not need a solid line and, as soon as I was mounted I shouted, "Clear the gate!"

Wulfric had been waiting for the command and they parted like the Red Sea for Moses. Half pushed to the left while the other half to the right. They cleared a path for my six knights. I rode to the left of the gate and jabbed my spear into the face of a surprised Welshman who was hurrying to aid his allies. I twisted as I pulled it free and then looked for the Welsh prince. I could not see his face but I saw the lions on his shield and surcoat. I galloped directly at him. He had no horse and was at a disadvantage. The knights around him hurried to form a barrier before him as Star thundered down the slope towards him. They say a horse will not step on a living man. That is not true. Star trampled and smashed the bodies of many dead ones that day and threw himself at those who were before him. The Welsh who had sense threw themselves away from his black hooves. Some did not; they lay crushed and broken on the bloody green hillside.

I was aware of horses coming behind me. My knights were eager to support me. The result was that we struck them like a giant arrow. Richard and Edward flanked me. My spear smashed as it struck the shield of a warrior trying to protect his prince. Star did the rest. He raised one huge hoof and smashed it down on the falling knight. As I drew my sword I kicked at the Welsh Prince. It distracted him enough so that his sword struck fresh air.

I whipped Star's head around and, despite his size and his speed he did so remarkably quickly. The Prince turned to face me and he tried to stand on my shield side so that I could not use my sword. I dropped my reins and, standing in the stirrups, swung my blade down on him. My sword struck him a blow on his helmet and then slid down to hit his shoulder. I heard something crack and then he screamed. I turned again. His shield was hanging down. I raised my helmet and shouted, "Yield! Surrender your men!"

"Never! I fight on!"

I lowered my helmet. I had given him his chance and he had spurned it. He was a brave young man but a foolish one. I rode at him and feinted. He tried to get on my shield side but his wound had slowed him up. I swung my sword sideways and it hacked through his coif and into his neck. He fell dead.

As soon as their paymaster died the Vikings turned and ran. Had the prince been their jarl then they would have fought to the death but he was not and they fled. Star had done enough and I leaned forward to pat his neck. I took off my helmet and turned to see if we had suffered. John was behind me. He had a huge grin on his face.

"Signal Dick to join me." I saw Sir Richard some paces up the slope and he was kneeling next to his squire William. He had been wounded. At the gate I only counted five of my Varangians. We had been lucky. Having the slope with us and being mounted had made all the difference. Our speed of attack had caught the Welsh unawares. They had thought we would sit behind our walls and fight them beard to beard. Had we done so they would have won for they outnumbered us.

Dick rode up, "My lord?"

"Take my archers and see where they go. Risk no one. You have done well this day as have all of the archers."

"Edward, take charge here. I fear I have lost one of my men." All the time I had been speaking I had kept an eye on my men. When Father John only made a brief visit and then left I feared the worst.

Erre heard my approach and stood. "It is William the Tall, my lord. He has died well and will be with your father and the other Varangians." I saw that William had many cuts and wounds. He stood a head taller than any other warrior and would have been a big target. There was a line of bodies where they had fought. I could see that our charge down the hill had not only disorganised the enemy it had left my six men exposed. They had suffered the attack by those who were close to them.

"Take whatever you wish from the dead, Erre. You and my oathsworn have merited that honour."

"Thank you, my lord."

I saw that we had a couple of dead men but the walls had given us the advantage. Others were wounded and I was glad that we had brought the priest. With his help and God's, they would be healed and fight another day. I dismounted and handed Star's reins to John. I will ride Scout."

As I rinsed my face with water I heard the cries as the enemy wounded were despatched. It was a kindness. The only ones who could have been healed were the wounded who were fleeing Dick and his archers. Drying my face, I saw the men at arms and archers searching the bodies in the ditch and on the approach to our camp. They would take their pay from the dead. John and the other squires would divide the booty from the knights. Our accurate archers meant we only had three extra horses but that did not matter. We had won.

It was almost dark when Dick returned. "They have departed in their dragon ships my lord." He grinned, "They could barely crew them they had lost so many. We caught up with a couple as they fled. They are now dead. The Earl of Chester came to his walls. He asked to speak with you in the morning."

"Thank you, Dick."

We burned the stripped bodies of our enemies. Their pyre lit up the sky and illuminated our camp. The smell of burning flesh was a familiar smell after a battle. It no longer bothered us. The men ate well and drank the ale from the skins the enemy had brought with them. Vikings liked their beer and knew how to brew it.

Richard of Yarm's squire had a serious wound. Like my two men at arms he would struggle to ride. Richard kept looking at his son while we ate. He had been his father's squire before William. I knew what he was thinking. It could have been his son who was hovering between life and death. I had promised my own son that he could come with us next time we fought. Had that been a wise promise to make?

I wandered over to my men at arms who had found the skins with ale amongst the men from Dublin. Wulfric sat next to Erre. I joined them. Erre proffered the skin. I shook my head, "Thank you, but no."

I sat. Wulfric nodded, "I was just telling these lads that they saved us this day. I have never seen such ferocious fighters."

I smiled, "I knew, Wulfric, from my father and from what I saw when we fought for the Emperor that they could do what they did and more." I put my arm around Erre's shoulder. "You may not be a rider, Erre but none of my mounted men at arms, save Wulfric could have done this day what you did."

"It was good to fight today, my lord. William died with a smile on his face." He gestured towards the pyre. "They were enemies I recognised. Fighting Thracians is not the same. They are wild tattooed barbarians. This is England and today, I felt I was fighting for England. I never fought for King Harold. Today it felt like I was."

My hand went involuntarily to the hilt of my sword and the blue stone. As Athelstan might have said, '*Wyrd*'.

We broke camp and headed back to Chester. There was still no word from the Earl of Gloucester. I had expected it before now. Our Welsh prisoners carried litters with some of the wounded while we used two horses to make one for William of Yarm. We reached Chester at noon. The Earl of Chester's men were still searching the siege works for booty and any enemy who had not fled.

"Wulfric, make camp yonder where we first encountered the enemy. The land is flat. I suspect we will not be here long."

I led my knights and squires into the castle. Men cheered as we passed through the gates. My banner had told them who we were. The castle still looked much the same as it had the first time I had seen it. The Earl needed to improve it. Had we not arrived then I fear the reinforcements would have swung the balance in the favour of those besieging. My castle was stronger and had better defences. This siege might just be the spur the Earl needed.

Ranulf de Gernan, the Earl of Chester, approached me. His smile told me of his happiness. I had met him before. Slightly older than me, he had less experience and that had showed. When I had campaigned in Wales with the Earl of Gloucester he had not been with us.

"Thank you for your help. I fear it would have gone ill for us had you not arrived when you did."

"It was Robert of Gloucester, your father in law, who summoned us."

He nodded, "When you rode away I wondered why, but now that I see how few you were in numbers I understand your strategy. Where is the Earl?"

"I know not. I sent riders to him but they have not returned. I discovered from prisoners that their leader is Owain, the Prince of Wales and he is south of here." I pointed to our camp. "I will join him on the morrow. Will you accompany me?"

"Aye but I can only take a few men. There is much work to be done here and we are too close to Dublin to leave this back door to England unguarded."

I nodded, "I have some wounded whom I will leave here. Some of them can fight. I also have some prisoners your men can set to work repairing their damage and we captured some grain. I expect that you are running short of supplies."

"We are! Come. Let us go into my hall and I will entertain you."

"First I must see to my men. John, ride to the camp and have Wulfric send over half of the food we captured, the prisoners and the wounded."

Ranulf's wife was the daughter of Robert of Gloucester. Maud was lively and vivacious. She had something of her Aunt, Matilda, in her. Her laughter and her smile seemed to light up the room. They had laid on a meal for us. It was not as grand as they might have hoped but with our extra supplies it was bearable.

68

Warriors always enjoyed food after a battle. Even the plainest of fare tasted good when you had been close to death. After we had finished the two of them questioned me closely about my exploits.

"My father speaks constantly of you. He entertained us royally with the story of how you have rescued the Empress twice."

I nodded, "Sir Edward here was with me both times. We are both Knights of the Empress. It is a great honour." I subconsciously fingered the medal she had given me. I still bore it around my neck. Like my blue pommel stone, I believed that it protected me. I am certain that Father Matthew would not have approved of such pagan beliefs. I told them, as modestly as I could, how we had saved her.

Maud clapped her hands, "My lord, you tell a story well. You could have been a troubadour!"

When the interrogation had finished Ranulf de Gernan asked. "What do you think has prevented Maud's father from coming to our aid."

Maud said, defensively, "If he could have reached us he would!"

I smiled, "Fear not, dear lady, I too, know that it was not carelessness which prevented his arrival. It is why I have ordered my men to break camp and to leave before dawn. We needed this day to recover from the battle but I have succeeded in the first part of my task, I have relieved Chester, but now I must ride to the aid of the Earl. If he has not come then he must have found trouble. Owain is the dangerous one."

I saw the look on Maud's face. It was a mixture of relief and gratitude.

"I wonder how the King of Gwynedd will take the loss of his son."

We all looked at Edward. "I do not know, Sir Edward, but it is not the old man we need to fear. Owain ap Gruffudd is the real power in Gwynedd these days. If they had been conducting the siege of my castle then I fear it would have fallen. He is a ruthless man and he is loved by his men. He is a dangerous foe."

"All the more reason why we will leave early." I rose as did my knights. "I will take my leave my lady." I kissed the back of her hand. "My lord, I will see you on the morrow."

"We have rooms for you and your knights, my lord."

"Thank you, my lady but, when I can, I share the hardships of a campaign with my men." I shrugged, "It is my way."

Chapter 6

When we left to find Robert, Earl of Gloucester, the Earl brought five household knights and ten men at arms. They had suffered too many casualties for more. The Vikings and the Irish had constantly attacked their walls during the siege. We left my wounded men at arms and William of Yarm. He was recovering and Lady Maud promised to keep a special eye upon him.

We headed south and east to try to meet up with either the Earl of Gloucester or discover the whereabouts of the rampaging Welsh army. I remembered the last Welsh incursion. The salt and the cattle on the Cheshire plain always seemed attractive to the Welsh. I sent Dick and four archers out towards Nantwich to see if they could pick up their trail. As we rode I asked the Earl why he had not fortified the lands to the south and west of his castle.

"There are still Vikings in Man and in Dublin who raid my west coast. I have knights patrolling that area. We had thought the Dee was a barrier. The castles along the border did not seem a priority. I can see now that they were."

I nodded and pointed to my two young knights who rode ahead of us. "I have given these two manors which protect my land to the west and the south even though they are safe areas. Sir Richard has a castle which also guards the crossing of the Tees. Rivers make good barriers but determined men can cross them. A castle is a better deterrent."

"But it costs."

"Stone is cheaper than the lives of your people. I use my gold to make my home stronger."

We spent the next few miles discussing how he might raise revenue without raising taxes. He seemed pleased with my advice.

It was two hours into our ride that Griff of Gwent galloped in. "My lord, we have found the Earl. He is being assailed by the Welsh. They are on a hill some few miles from Nantwich. There looks to have been an old hall there."

I was just turning to ride to the aid of the Earl of Gloucester when Dick, Aiden and the rest of my riders galloped in. Dick shook his head, "My lord, you are too fast for us. We rode to the camp but found you gone. The Earl has need of you. He is at Deofold."

Ranulf said, "That was where Harold Godwinson had a hunting lodge."

I felt a sudden shiver up my spine. It felt as though the past was reaching out to me. "And is that the same place that Griff of Gwent spoke of?"

"It is."

I was tempted to gallop off and go to the aid of the Earl but I did not have enough information. "How many men surround him?"

Aiden was a good scout. "They are mainly on foot. He has some Vikings but the majority appear to be his own warriors. They have fifty mounted men and I would estimate almost three hundred on foot."

I turned to Ranulf. "We must make this Owain think there are more of us than there are. And I would drive him south and west towards Oswestry. We will ride north and then east so that we approach this hill from that direction. If you have your men on the extreme left of our line, Sir Edward and my knights can be on the right and I will occupy the centre with my men at arms." I turned, "Dick, ride on our flanks. I want him to think you are men at arms. When we charge… if we charge then I want you to close and harass them with arrows."

Aye my lord.""

Ranulf said, "You will trick him?"

"If I can I will defeat him but if he sees us coming from the north east and fears he will be caught between our two forces he may withdraw south and we can rejoin the Earl of Gloucester. Aiden, keep ahead of us and warn us of danger."

I did not wait for further discussion but rode towards the north east. I used Aiden to keep us in the right direction. He had travelled through the land and knew the best route to take; we had to avoid observation. It worked well for he knew where they were and we would avoid an early confrontation. I saw the hill to our right as we rode down the greenway. The hedges and trees obscured our view for most of the way but the occasional glimpses showed us the banners of Robert of Gloucester. Aiden stopped and we joined him. "There, my lord, the Welsh!"

I followed him to a gap in the hedge line and saw the Welsh advancing in solid lines towards the hill. His knights and men at arms were gathered behind his rear line of spearmen. He would use them to break through when the line had been weakened. The problem I had was that I would have to take my force through the gap and then form them up. We would be seen. There was no alternative.

"John, signal the battle to move forward!"

I kicked Scout on and moved up the slope to the top of the field. We were half a mile from the right flank of the Welsh. I reined in and John joined me. The Earl of Chester took his men left and Sir Edward, right. With the Earl's men we had about sixty men at arms and I hoped that our thirty odd archers would make us look more than we were. Our destrier and baggage would have to be guarded by my Varangians, Father John and our servants. I was throwing the dice and our fate was in the hands of God.

73

I saw the enemy horse reacting. They turned as the word spread that a new force of Normans had arrived on their flank. It would have been a shock but they reacted calmly. They were well led. "John, signal the advance!"

We walked forwards with banners fluttering in the breeze above us. I was sending a message to the Earl as much as I was to the Welsh prince. When a shaft of sunlight shone on our armour making it sparkle I knew that the Prince of Gwynedd would think that my men at arms were knights. It would not be until we were much closer that he would realise who they really were. I watched as they formed into a line. At the same time, I saw that the men on foot had stopped their advance. They had not yet turned to face us but the Earl was, temporarily, safe from attack. He would be able to organise his defence.

"Trot!"

John signalled with the standard and we began to move faster towards our foes. The knights and the men at arms all held long spears which we had captured from the Welsh. I saw that only some of the horsemen who faced us were similarly armed. They too formed into a line and began to walk towards us. They were bravely led for our numbers would appear to outnumber them.

"Gallop!" We were just three hundred paces from them and I knew that we would close very quickly for their line had also begun to trot.

I knew I had to judge this perfectly. At a hundred paces I shouted, "Charge!" It coincided with the enemy beginning their gallop. I barely had time to lower my spear as the two lines of steel clashed. I struck a knight who bore a green dragon on a red background. I punched as I leaned forward and my spear hit him hard upon his shield. He must not have tilted much for he was thrown from his saddle. His lance had been aimed at my head and I watched as it moved from before my face to rise and fall with the

74

knight. I knew that some of my men would not be successful but I had to keep heading towards the group of knights who were gathered around the Prince's standard.

Behind me I heard the clash of weapon on weapon, the screams of men being hit and the cries of stricken horses. Without looking I knew that Dick and his archers were raining death upon them. They might not kill many knights but their horses would pay a fearful price. I concentrated upon the Royal Standard of Gwynedd. Glancing to my left and right I saw that I had men at arms on either side of me. They were my men. It gave me added confidence. I knew that John and Leofric would be hard behind me. I guessed we were an equal number to the Welsh ahead. Their first attack had failed. Would the Prince risk a second charge at us? When a horn sounded and they began to move south and west I knew that their leader was not willing to risk our reaching him. I slowed Scout down. There was little point in exhausting him. We had started the game and they would run. It mattered not that we were not riding hard. We had our spears in their backs.

Suddenly horses and riders began to overtake us as the Welsh knights and men at arms raced to join their leader. The infantry too began to move south and west. I saw standards on the hillside begin to move towards the fleeing Welsh. I edged Scout closer to the Earl of Gloucester's men. We could not catch the Prince but we might be able to catch some of his infantry. As I did so I saw Dick and his archers galloping to our right. They halted some fifty paces from the Welsh, dismounted, and began to loose arrows. They sent six flights before the Welsh managed to get out of range. They remounted and galloped again. It was a tried and tested tactic. Dick was a master at it. They had tried to release arrows from the back of a horse but it did not work. This did; ride hard, dismount, release arrows, mount and so on.

Soon my remaining men at arms and knights had joined me, as had the Earl of Chester. He forced his horse next to mine. "Your trick worked, Alfraed."

"God was on our side."

We pursued the Welsh for three miles until we came to more broken country and our horses tired. I reined in close to a stream and shouted, "Halt. We have done enough."

My men were all experienced enough to dismount and rest our weary beasts. My men led their mounts to the stream. I looked up at Ranulf and wondered why they did not do the same. Before I could ask him the Earl of Gloucester reined in. He leapt from his horse and embraced me. "Once again I am in your debt."

I gave a slight bow. "My men found me but they did not have enough time to explain what happened."

He laughed, "Better you hear of my mistake from me than your men. I divided my forces. I know now that was a mistake. I sent half towards Wrexham. I believed that the Prince was there and I intended to trap him. He turned the tables on me and attacked me as soon as my men had gone. I expect them to return soon but they are not led by Alfraed the Earl of Cleveland." He seemed to see his son in law for the first time. "I see you had the siege lifted."

"That was the Earl's doing."

"And how is my daughter?"

"She is safe."

Robert of Gloucester pointed his spear at a dead Viking who had been slain by Dick's archers. His body lay at our feet. He turned the body over. "This is a disturbing development."

I nodded, "Perhaps your father should invade Ireland and end the threat once and for all."

"Perhaps, although he is still in Normandy."

The Earl of Chester asked, "And what now, my lord?"

He looked at me, "Your archers will pursue them?"

"They will follow until they stop and then they will return here. If you wish to go back to Chester where we can gather our forces I will wait here for my men."

He shook his head, "I would keep us together now. It is lucky that they headed south west."

The Earl of Chester laughed, "It was not luck my lord. The Earl here chose our direction of attack to create their movement."

I shrugged, "I did not want to give them the chance to go to Chester and to cause mayhem there."

"Then I am decided. We will retire to Deofold and await your men there."

The old hunting lodge still stood. It had been long abandoned but it had a roof and kept out the draughts. When our pack animals were brought up we shared out the little food we had. The Earl of Gloucester had had to move so quickly that he did not have much food left.

As we ate I asked, "Who commands the other half of your army, my lord?"

"Sir Ralph Warenne. He is a doughty warrior and can hold the line but he lacks imagination. He will return here when he finds no one at Wrecsam."

"Let us hope he does not encounter Owain ap Gruffudd then or we could be in another difficult situation."

I could see that the thought had not occurred to the Earl who stood and walked to the door as though watching for his men.

He suddenly started. "Your archers return, Cleveland, or at least some of them."

That did not sound like Dick. He would have returned with all of his men unless prevented from doing so. Had he suffered a reverse? I joined the King's son as he walked to the edge of the wood to meet Dick.

"Well?"

The Earl was impatient. I nodded to Dick. "We followed them for ten miles and then they met up with a force of Norman knights and men at arms heading east. There was a confused battle. The Welsh drove the Normans from the field. We followed them as far as Wrexham. I left some of my archers to be the rear guard. I brought the news as soon as I could for I deemed it important."

The Earl clapped him about the shoulders. "It is indeed and you are a fine fellow. Was the battle led by Sir Ralph Warenne?"

"It was and he is wounded." Dick hesitated and I nodded for him to continue. "Four knights were slain as well as eight men at arms. Many of the fyrd fled."

"Then Owain has slipped away again." He reached into his purse and took out a coin. "Here is for your troubles, my friend. I am grateful."

Dick took the coin and went back to his archers.

"What do we do now then gentlemen?"

"Simple, my lord, we go to Wrexham."

"And fight?"

"We may not need to." I waved a hand towards the Welsh corpses which still littered the plain. "They have been hurt badly here and even if Sir Ralph was knocked about his men would have hurt the Welsh." I turned to Dick who still stood by the open door of the hunting lodge. "Did Sir Ralph's men cause casualties?"

"Yes, my lord. At least twenty warriors were either slain or badly wounded."

"There you are. We have both been hurt. If you pursue him he will not have time to lick his wounds and send for more men. Besides it keeps him on the defensive."

"But we are in no condition to fight."

I went closer to him and spoke quietly so that only he and Ranulf could hear. "If you do not then some of our men may decide all is lost and leave. You know yourself, my lord, that men are better when attacking." Even as I said it I knew that none of mine would leave but I had seen the hang dog look of those who followed the other two Earls.

"Very well. We leave before dawn and march to Wrexham."

"With your permission, my lord, I will see to my men. I have not spoken with them since the battle and I know not how they fared."

That was something of a white lie for John had already told me that none of my knights nor squires had fallen and that my men at arms had suffered only minor wounds. I was keen to reassure them that all was well. The camp had a despondent air as though we had been defeated. Even as I went down to the camp I saw the weary warriors of Sir Ralph de Warenne as they trudged into the camp. Such ill feelings could easily spread.

I found Sir Edward. I had to smile. My men had sent Aiden and Leofric hunting. I caught the smell of a game stew made with various animals and wild herbs. They knew how to forage. Their faces were a relief for they were in direct contrast to those of the other conroi. The other soldiers sniffed enviously at the air which was heavy with the smell of cooking meat. My men were relaxed; they knew we were far from beaten and that we had sent the Welsh running.

"Stew, my lord?"

"No thank you, Edward. I have eaten although not as well as you."

Wulfric wandered over. He was only a man at arms but he had fought alongside Edward for many years and could talk as easily with knights as with his fellows. "And what of tomorrow, my lord?"

"We follow the Welsh!"

Wulfric rubbed his hands. "Excellent. I still have much room in my purse for gold coins."

"I am surprised the Welsh had much upon their person."

He shook his head, "No, my lord. It is these men from Dublin. They all like their arm rings. Some are silver and one was gold. They also adorn their swords with pretty stones. The Welsh are not worth searching but the men from Ireland are. Michael the archer told me that there were still twenty or thirty of them with this Welsh King."

"He is a Prince."

"No matter, my lord. We will take whatever he carries about his person but I was hoping for a crown."

My men were irrepressible. They felt that they could conquer the world. I was lucky to lead them.

The Earl had been impressed with my archers and it was they who formed the van. Our numbers were not as bad as one might have expected. Sir Ralph and his wounded were sent to bolster the defence of Chester. We had just twenty-five knights, including the three earls. With fifty men at arms and just my archers the bulk of the army was the fyrd raised by the Earl. Although there were over a hundred and twenty of them they would not be reliable as a fighting force. I knew that the Earl of Gloucester was dubious about their quality for he kept his own men at arms close behind them. If they chose to flee they would have to risk the wrath of the Earl's men at arms.

When we reached Wrexham the gates were, as we had expected, closed. I waved Dick over. "Take my archers and stop any leaving from the rear gate. I suspect the Prince will send for help."

"Aye my lord."

As they galloped off Robert of Gloucester asked, "What is that about?" I told him. "This looks like a difficult place to take, Cleveland."

"I doubt they have many supplies in. There is little growing in the fields and we saw cattle and sheep as we passed. We can collect those. They will soon be hungry and we will not."

"You are suggesting that we do nothing?"

"I am suggesting that we wait and we eat the Welsh animals. Our horses will recover and we will eat well. The Welsh will starve and grow nervous. They will soon tire and either attack us or talk."

"And if they fight?"

"Then we have the superiority in cavalry. Most of their knights lay dead on the field at Deofold and we made great slaughter of their horses. We may have fewer men but we have more knights and mounted men at arms."

"Very well." He turned and shouted, "Make camp!"

The Earl had done this sort of thing before and he organised a closely guarded camp. He ordered his men to capture some of the cattle which still grazed, unprotected in the fields. When they were skinned he had them roasted over huge pits. The prevailing wind took the smell towards the Welsh. It would make them hungry. This simple act rejuvenated the rest of our army. A full stomach makes for a braver warrior.

I sent Aiden to find Dick and tell him to make camp beyond the town. The men on the walls watched us. Had I been Owain I would have sallied forth and tried to drive us hence while we were busy setting up our defences but he did not. That told me that he did not have great numbers. I took heart from that. After we had eaten I walked around our perimeter and our sentries to reassure myself that we would not be surprised. I stood, just beyond our furthest sentry watching the lights from the town and trying to imagine what the Welsh might do.

"You never stop do you, Alfraed?"

I turned and saw the Earl of Gloucester by my side. I shook my head. "I worry too much, I know that my lord."

"I meant it as a compliment. Your diligence and your scrutiny have saved us more than once." We both stared out towards the Welsh. "I tried to make up for my error the last time we fought the Welsh. I tried to draw the Welsh to me. It seems I succeeded too well."

"I think this Welsh Prince is a formidable foe. His men retired in good order. That speaks well of their commander." I gestured back towards the camp. "I spoke with Ranulf. The defences around Chester are not what they should be."

82

"I know. I have the land in the south of their land well managed and controlled by castles. I think perhaps he should visit with you and see your defences."

"I constantly strive to improve them for our enemies are always looking for ways to breach them."

"Perhaps when we have killed enough they may accept the inevitable."

"There are always young warriors who seek to gain glory and fame. We have them too but we manage them a little better than our foes."

"You are wise beyond your years. My sister always says that." I turned when he spoke of Matilda. He lowered his voice. "She is at my castle at Gloucester. She tired of the Tower."

"She has not returned to her husband then?"

"No. My father writes weekly urging her to do so but she is strong willed. I think the castellan at the Tower tired of her complaints. She can be a harpy at times."

I thought of the Matilda I knew. The Earl did not know his sister. She was no harpy.

I heard a horse in the distance. I looked at the Earl who nodded. It sounded like trouble. We hurried to the camp. Aiden was dismounting. He dropped to one knee and spoke, "My lord, Dick has sent me. The Welsh have opened the northern gates. He thinks they are sallying."

The Earl of Gloucester looked at me, "He is your man. What think you?"

"I will take my men at arms, my lord and support him. If I need any help then I will send Aiden back."

"Very well." I heard a grim laugh in the dark. "This Welsh prince is an annoyingly resourceful foe."

"Wulfric, mount our men. Erre keep your men here. We need swift riders this night." On campaign I rarely took off my mail. John brought Scout to me and Leofric my helmet and my shield. We were mounted in a short time. "Lead on Aiden."

We rode into the dark. Aiden had the eyes of a cat and led us unerringly along what seemed to me an invisible greenway. He held up his hand and slowed. He was listening. I heard, too, the sounds of combat. I drew my sword and the others followed suit. The town was less than a mile from our left. I saw the first Welsh body and it had an arrow in it. Dick was close. I heard Welsh voices. One sounded as though it was giving commands. I waved my sword to the left and right. My men spread out in a line behind me.

We came upon the Welsh column almost immediately. Their white faces turned as they heard our hooves. I shouted, "Stockton!" At the top of my voice so that Dick and the others knew that help was at hand. Then we were amongst them. It was a unique experience. We rarely fought battles in the dark. A face loomed up and you had seconds to decide if it was a friend or a foe. We had the advantage for we knew that we were all mounted. However, when a horse suddenly appeared before me, I realised my error. It was a knight and he swung his sword towards me.

We were sword to sword and I barely had time to block his blow with my own weapon. He was not a tall man but he was incredibly broad and powerful. Our horses spun around each other as they, too, fought. As I was taller I used that to my advantage. I stood in my stirrups and swung my shield before me. It allowed me to bring my sword down towards his head. He could not bring his shield around and he blocked with his sword. I punched at his helmet with my shield. He leaned into me and I felt myself overbalancing. I sat down and Scout continued his turn. He was well trained.

I was aware of the battles around me as men fought and died in the dark. Now that we were side by side again the knight swung his sword at my neck. I thrust my sword up and they rang together. It would be the strength of our weapons which decided this and when I saw the slight bend in my opponent's sword then I knew that his was a weaker weapon. I went on to the offensive and swung my own sword down hard. He met it with his own and the bend became more obvious; more than that it became harder for him to wield. It became unbalanced.

Once more I risked standing and I hit him again with my shield. This time he reeled and I stabbed forward with my sword. His weapon was now a hindrance and its shape, as he blocked, allowed my blade to slip between the sword and his saddle. It slid into his mail. I felt the links as they sheared. The gambeson gave some resistance but when I leaned into the blow it sank into flesh. I heard a grunt and I turned my hand and pushed harder. My tip was stopped by the cantle on his saddle and I withdrew the blade. He tumbled from the side of his horse.

I turned quickly to see how we fared. John and Leofric guarded my back. I saw a dead Welsh warrior between them. Dick and Wulfric rode up. Wulfric raised his helmet and pushed back his coif. He believed the encounter was at an end. "They are all dead my lord." He looked at the dead knight. "It looks like he was the only knight with them. Most had no armour. I think they were relying on speed." He pointed to Dick. "But for Dick here they would have succeeded."

Dick shrugged modestly. "They were no woodsmen and we heard them. We kept withdrawing and then releasing arrows. Had it been daylight we would not have needed help but they were like insects in the forest."

85

"You have both done well. Wulfric, keep the men at arms here and I will return to the main camp. The Earl will be worried. I doubt that they will risk a second sortie but it is better to be safe than sorry. Give me the head of the knight. It will be evidence for their prince in case he doubts our word in the morning."

Wulfric dismounted. He took off the knight's helmet and examined it. "Too small!" He threw it to the ground in disgust. Taking his axe, he made a swift strike and the head was cleanly severed. The man was already dead and there was little blood. He picked it up by the hair; the Welsh liked to wear it long and he handed it to me. I saw that it was an older warrior; older than me. That explained his skill.

"I will see you on the morrow. Leofric pick up that helmet and keep it for William. John, come with me too. Aiden, you can stay here."

It was a slower ride back for I did not have Aiden's skills. I knew I was close when I smelled the cooking meat on the wind. It made me hungry too. The Earl was warming himself by the fire when I rode in. "Well?"

I held up the trophy. "Some tried to escape. I think they were going for help. None will be coming. I left my men at arms to guard the northern gate. This may come as a surprise to the prince when you negotiate tomorrow."

"Just so. And you must rest. From what my son in law has told me that the Welsh may well know you. I believe they will remember you from our last visit. What we lack in numbers we will make up for in reputation."

I was exhausted and as soon as I lay down I was asleep. When I woke I found that I had been covered with a blanket. My squires were close by. I did not disturb them when I rose. I suspect that they had watched over me during the night. The two Earls were up and eating some of the beef which was still warm from the previous night. I joined them. "We have no bread but this will suffice." The Earl gestured to the walls. I doubt that they will have eaten well. We will visit with them at noon." He laughed. I have sent one of Ranulf's men as though he rides to Chester for aid. It will set the Welsh to thinking."

In the end we did not have to initiate a truce. The gates opened and three riders emerged. One bore the flag of Gwynedd. The Earl said, "Ranulf, ride and see what they want. If they want to speak, then agree to it."

As the Earl and two men at arms rode off, Robert of Gloucester said, "An interesting development."

"Perhaps the rider you sent to the north frightened him."

"This Prince Owain does not seem like a man easily frightened. Come we will take that big fellow of yours, Wulfric. He would put the fear of God into anyone."

He waved his squire over and asked for his horse. I went to Wulfric. "Get yourself ready. We are to ride to meet the Welsh."

"Should I take my axe?"

I laughed, "I think the Earl will be disappointed if you do not. If you could stroke its edge whilst we talk then that might help." He laughed and nodded.

Ranulf rode back after a brief discussion. "The Prince Owain wishes to speak with you, my lord. We have agreed that the meeting shall take place a bowshot from each of our camps."

Just then an arrow sailed from the walls and stuck the earth. The Earl nodded to Sir Edward who had some of his archers close by. Thomas of Whitby pulled back and released his arrow. I mounted Scout which had been brought by John. I noticed the sack which hung from the saddle. My orders had been obeyed. Wulfric and I followed Robert Earl of Gloucester to the area between the two arrows. When we reached it the gates opened and three men rode forth. Parity of numbers minimised the opportunity for treachery.

The two Princes were of my age. The one who looked to be slightly younger had an angry look upon his face. The elder spoke. "I am Prince Owain ap Gruffudd and this is my younger brother Prince Cadwaladr."

The Earl said, "I am the Earl of Gloucester and this is the Earl of Cleveland."

"What is it that you wish?" We remained silent. I could see that the Earl had confused him. The Prince frowned. "Why are you here?"

"You asked for this truce. We assumed you came to give us the terms of your surrender."

The younger prince became angry, "Surrender! To a rag tag army like yours?"

"Peace brother." Prince Owain gave an apologetic shrug. "My brother is outspoken but he is quite correct. Your army is too small to take our town. In fact it is smaller than when it followed us." He leaned forward. "You should know that I have sent to my father for more warriors. If I were you I would leave now before they return."

The Earl looked at me and nodded. I turned around and took the sack. Opening it I grabbed the hair of the dead knight and held it before me. There was a gasp of horror from the young prince. "Would this be the knight who led the warriors seeking help? If so they all lie dead."

Prince Owain's shoulders sagged. "And your rider has already gone to Chester." The Earl nodded. "We have supplies enough to sit out a siege."

The Earl waved a hand at the land around. "And we enjoy eating Welsh cattle. When you are encircled by a ring of steel then we shall see if you have enough supplies. When you have to resort to eating dogs, cats and rats we shall see if you have enough supplies. When my men have ravaged the country hereabouts then we shall see, eh Prince Owain ap Gruffudd?"

I saw resignation in his face. "What are your terms?"

"Surrender Wrexham to us and pay an indemnity of a thousand head of cattle."

Prince Cadwaladr shouted, "Never!"

Prince Owain turned to his sibling and said, "Brother this is negotiation. The Earl begins with a ridiculously high figure." He looked at the Earl. "The animals you have already eaten and a hundred more besides."

"My men have healthy appetites; we would wish at least five hundred head of cattle… and Wrexham."

"You may have the five hundred head of cattle but Wrexham is not to be bargained. If you demand Wrexham then we shall sit behind its walls and decide this matter by feat of arms."

The Earl nodded, "Then you vacate the town and take your army back to Anglesey."

This was the crucial moment when it would be decided if we fought or left. "I have your word that you will not occupy it when we have left?"

"You have my word."

"Then I agree to your terms." He nudged his horse forward and the two men clasped arms. "This is not over, Robert, Earl of Gloucester."

"I know."

Then the Prince turned his attention to me, "And you, Alfraed Earl of Cleveland should know that my brother here has sworn to kill you for the death of my brother."

I nodded. "He is welcome to try. Would you like to test my mettle now Prince Cadwaladr?"

For a moment I thought he would accept and then he thought better of it. "I can wait. Vengeance is best served cold and I am too angry now."

"I killed your brother fairly in combat."

Prince Owain said, "I know but my brother here feels that family honour has been impugned."

The Earl of Gloucester pointed to Prince Cadwaladr, "Let me give you some advice young man. Become a great warrior if you wish to fight the Earl. He has defeated many men in single combat including those close to the Holy Roman Emperor. He is not a man to be beaten by an untried boy."

I know that the Earl did not mean it cruelly but I saw the young prince colour. He now hated both of us.

Prince Owain said, "I will send men for the cattle and we will head home."

"We will leave this land when the cattle are delivered."

As we rode back to our lines the Earl said, "They must have had even less supplies than we thought."

"They did not expect us to react as swiftly as we did. I think that Prince Owain should have reduced Chester first then he would have had something with which to bargain but I think he is a dangerous foe, my lord."

"I agree." He reined in. "Wulfric go and bring the rest of your lord's men from north of the town. Their work is done." When Wulfric had gone he turned to me. "Come with me back to Gloucester. I would hunt with you and I am certain that my sister and her Swabians will be pleased to see you."

My spirits rose. "But what of the Tees, my lord?"

"Sir Edward can take your cattle hence and he and your other knights can watch over your land. Besides you only need a few of your men with you. The rest can return to your castle."

I did not need much persuasion and I nodded my agreement.

Chapter 7

Half of the cattle were given to the Earl of Gloucester whilst the rest were divided between my knights and the Earl of Chester. As soon as two hundred and fifty cattle arrived Sir Edward and my men took our share and drove them north. I retained my squires, Aiden, Griff of Gwent, Ralph of Wales and Roger of Lincoln. If I was not safe in the land of the son of the King of England then the country was, indeed, in a parlous state. I took only Scout for I would not be going to war. Leofric led the sumpter with our supplies.

I took Sir Edward to one side. "Watch over the valley for me."

He nodded and then, speaking quietly said, "My lord, I am your loyal servant, as you know but I beg you not to do anything you may regret."

I think Edward saw, in that instant, into my heart. I smiled, "I will heed your advice. I would not risk the honour of the Empress nor would I betray my wife."

He looked relieved and swept a hand at the cattle. "The knights you did not bring will be more than a little unhappy that they do not share in this bounty. Our young knights are rich men already." It was not just the cattle which had made them richer. We had slain many men and all of my knights had shared in the bounty. Soon they would all buy better metal, helmets and weapons. Each would hire a couple more men at arms. It was a slow process but soon we would have the best equipped nights in the land.

As they left I could not resist a chuckle. Edward had been a working man at arms for many years and his one aim had been to acquire money and land. He could not rid himself of that avaricious trait. I had never wanted for aught and I needed no extra cattle to make me happy. As I walked back to the Earl I wondered what I did need.

It took over ten days to gather in all of the cattle. The Earl of Chester had left with his just four days after my men. Eventually we had them and we headed south. The Earl of Gloucester left his cattle with his men and we rode ahead. I was pleased. The thought of riding at the pace of two hundred and fifty head of cattle did not appeal to either of us.

We rode swiftly and did the journey in three days. The Earl had built himself a strong castle which, like mine, utilised the river. Despite the lands to the west which his father had conquered this was, to all intents and purposes, the border. Here the sentries on the walls wore mail and scrutinised every visitor.

His Steward greeted us. "We have guests, John. The Earl will be in my quarters. Put his squires and men in the warrior hall."

"Yes, my lord."

"Is my sister within?"

"No, my lord. She and her guards went for a ride this morning."

The Earl frowned. "I hope they steered clear of the river. The Welsh would love to have a hostage of her high status."

His Steward smiled. "Sir Rolf was adamant, my lord. He led the Empress east."

The Earl laughed and, as we went indoors said, "Those Swabians are damned reliable fellows. I can see why she keeps them around."

"They are the best men to have behind you. They never fail and they never run."

I was led to a guest chamber. I saw Judith and Margaret the Empress' ladies. They were in the chamber opposite. They curtsied. "Congratulations, my lord, on your new title. Is Sir Edward with you?" Both of them enjoyed flirting with Sir Edward. After the men they met at court it was good to meet a real man.

"No, he is heading back to my castle. This is just a visit so that I may hunt with the Earl."

I noticed a sly look on Margaret's face. "I am sure my lady will enjoy the time you spend here."

I felt myself colouring and so I bowed and went into the chamber. There was a knock on the door and, as I opened it, I was ready to speak harshly to them when I saw Leofric with my bags. He smiled innocently, "I thought you might wish to change, my lord."

"A good idea." I allowed him in.

"Should I see if I can get water for a bath, my lord?"

"Aye, even if it is only a bowl. I would rid myself of the smell of blood. It might offend the ladies."

"Your lady sent down some of the perfume we brought back from Miklagård. She thought you might need it."

I was reminded, at that moment, of just how thoughtful my wife was.

I stripped when Leofric returned with hot water in a jug and a large bowl. He helped me to wash. He took my soiled surcoat and undershirt. "I will get these washed. The Steward has been told to do all he can to make your stay a pleasant one."

My wife had packed my fine silk surcoat and under shirt which I had bought in Miklagård. The surcoat still needed a wolf upon it to match my new seal but it would do. When my hair was brushed and oiled I felt ready to meet the world. Leofric stood back. "The Earl said to take you to his Great Hall. He will join you there."

As we went down I asked. Are you and the men comfortable?"

"Aye, my lord. John and I share a corner of the hall."

"And the horses?"

"It is a fine stable. They are content." He hesitated. "I still prefer our castle, my lord."

I laughed, "Between you and me so do I."

The Great Hall was empty save for a servant who hurried over to me. "Wine sir? Or beer?"

"Wine."

He gave me a goblet. "I will tell the Earl that you are here."

I knew that the Earl would have a good cellar. I sipped the wine and found it heady and strong. It was perfect for me. Others might add water but not me. I sat by the window to look west to Wales.

Without looking around I knew that someone had entered. I sensed a perfume I had not enjoyed for a long time. When she spoke then I knew who had entered.

"My lord. This is a pleasant surprise."

I turned and saw Matilda, Empress of the Holy Roman Empire although her title was now Countess of Anjou. To me she would always be the Empress. She had grown even more beautiful.

95

"My lady." I took her proffered hand and kissed it. I felt the slight squeeze from her fingers as I did so.

The servant reappeared, "Countess, would you like some chilled white wine?"

"I would, Cedric."

He scurried away. She came close to me and held my hand in hers. "I have not long to speak with you."

"I am your knight, as ever. How can I help you?"

"My marriage is a sham. My father has sold me into bondage for a piece of land. I cannot be married to the child."

"What would you have of me, my lady?"

"Take me somewhere; anywhere where I do not have to endure my husband's loathsome presence."

"There is nowhere."

"Constantinople! You know the land and the Greeks like you do they not? I hear you impressed the Emperor. We could live safely there and you could be one of his generals."

"They do but the Emperor is now an ally of your father. I think that taking the heir to the English throne would not make me welcome there."

She released my hand and turned her back on me. "Heir to the throne? That is a nonsense. The Barons may have sworn allegiance but they will never allow my husband to have aught to do with England. They will choose someone else." She turned again. "I beg of you. Take me away from this living hell to which I have been sent"

"I will give it some thought but I cannot see a solution to this problem; at least not one with a happy outcome."

We heard footsteps coming down the corridor. She leaned and kissed me on the lips and then said, "Come to my chamber tonight." She spun lightly away to a chair and was seated when Cedric returned with the wine.

He was followed by the Earl and the Swabian knights. Rolf rushed up to me and picked me up in a bear hug. "It is good to see you!" As soon as I was deposited I was picked up by Gottfried and then by Karl. My ribs ached after their enthusiastic welcomes.

The Earl loved this and he roared with laughter. "You four would make a formidable weapon! None would be able to stand in your way."

Rolf nodded, "And if Sir Edward and Sir Guy de la Cheppe were here then we would be invincible!" He clapped me on the back. "How long do you stay?"

I gestured to the Earl. "We go hunting and then I must return to the north. We have to be ever vigilant!"

The Earl said, "Tonight we feast and tomorrow we hunt the wild boar."

I did not drink overmuch and I was, generally, silent. I listened to Rolf and the others as they spoke of life in Anjou. Although they did not criticise outright I could hear in their tone that they were unhappy with the behaviour and attitude of the Empress' young husband. The Earl frowned but he did not say much. When I rose to retire the Earl followed me out and spoke to me in the corridor where we could not be overheard.

"You are close to my sister, I know that. If you get the chance I beg you to persuade her to return to her husband. My father is not a patient man. If the marriage fails then it will be the nunnery for my sister. He wishes his lands to be in firm hands after he is gone."

"I will do my best but I am not certain what I can do."

He peered at me and it was though he was seeing into my heart. "You have the power over my sister, Alfraed, and we both know this."

As I went back to my chamber then I knew why the Earl had brought me here. It was not to hunt. It was to make Matilda return home. I undressed and sat looking at the pommel of my sword which hung from the head of the bed. Had my father's spirit sent me to fetch the sword to make me focus on being a warrior and to forget the entanglements which had been placed in my path? I know not how long I stared at the blue stone which sparkled in the candlelight but I heard a soft tap on the door. Returning the sword to its scabbard I went to the door and opened it. There stood Margaret, the Empress Matilda's servant.

"My lord," she spoke so quietly that I had to bend down to hear her. "My lady wishes a word with you in her chamber."

I lifted my head and shook it. "I am sorry, Margaret, I cannot do that. It would not be honourable for your lady is married as am I. I am a knight and I have taken vows. As much as my heart wishes me to do as your lady asks then I must be strong."

She smiled, sadly, "You are a good man and my lady is a good lady. You are right but it will break my lady's heart." She curtsied and left.

I did sleep but I know not how. My heart was not in the hunt the next day and it was left to the Earl himself to make the best kill; a fine tusker who killed two of the Earl's hounds before he was killed. The Earl was in good humour. After bathing I joined the Earl and his knights in the hall. As I entered he toasted me and then gestured to the fire. I joined him. He smiled, "You are a good fellow, Alfraed. My sister has told me that she returns to her husband tomorrow. I knew that I could rely on you. I told you that you had power over her."

The feast that evening was in honour of the Empress. She glanced at me, frequently, and smiled each time. I knew that I had done the right thing but that did not mean that I was happy about it. If I was Wulfric or a man at arms then I would have been able to obey my heart. I was a knight and I was a gentleman. I had responsibilities as well as rights.

I stayed another two days after the departure of the Empress and her knights. I had done my job and the Earl said, "I have secured the border and with my knights returned here we can both leave. I will now follow my sister and accompany her to Anjou. I want to make sure she gets there. You, my friend, need to show yourself in the north. Word of our victory will have spread and your presence on the border will discourage any attempts by our neighbours to encroach upon our lands."

"What of Carlisle and Durham?"

"I have ordered that the castellan at Carlisle builds a larger keep. It should be safe enough for a while. The river protects the castle as does the Tees for you. Durham?" He shrugged, "Until my father appoints a new Prince Bishop then you must watch that closely. Do you have doubts about their loyalty?"

"It is my closest neighbour. I would be happier if I knew that the lord who ruled as Bishop had a strong arm."

"And that is the problem my friend. We need someone unique. They must be acceptable as a leader of the church and yet a strong warrior. As they cannot marry it is not necessarily an attractive appointment. Men wish to leave something for their children. You know that as a father. I must confess that if I were the King I would have chosen someone before now. The trouble is that the Palatinate is a powerful piece of land."

I was not unhappy about returning home. The Earl's words had made me realise how important my family was. In addition, I could throw myself into being a lord of the manor once more. As there were just a handful of us we made excellent time and caught up with Sir Edward and the captured animals close to Northallerton. William of Yarm had recovered and he and the wounded men at arms were with Sir Edward. My closest friend was not in the best of humours. "I pray we reach home soon. If not then I fear I will slaughter every animal here! They stink and they move so slowly that an old man could move faster."

I laughed, "But think of your people when they receive this bounty and think of the men you can hire with the profits."

"Perhaps but I am yet to be convinced." He gave me a searching look, as we headed up the old Roman Road to the north. "And how is the Empress?"

"She has returned to Anjou. Rolf and the others asked after you."

I realised that I had been both clumsy and curt but Edward merely nodded, "That is good. And what of us? Has the Earl more plans?"

"We are to show ourselves along the border. I will leave the three of you to stay with your manors and take Sir Hugh with me. It will do him good and I am sure Sir Hugh Manningham will enjoy a show of strength."

"The Lady Adela may be unhappy at your brief visit."

I nodded, "I know. Perhaps I will take William. That will please my wife."

As we rode the last few miles I pondered Sir Edward's words. I had not been unhappy to obey the Earl's commands. If I was at home then I would mope but if I was on campaign then I would have too much to think on to worry about my family. I was being selfish and I knew it. My wife would be sad at my absence but she would smile and bear it as she always did. She was long suffering.

All of my people were pleased to see me. The sight of the captured cattle and the treasure we had taken from our enemies meant prosperity for all. Although I had not been away for long my town and my castle looked a little stronger. William the mason had been busy as had my men at arms. We did not rest upon our laurels and were ever vigilant. The better our defences then the less likely we were to be attacked.

I had been lucky in the campaign. I had lost none of my men and those who had been wounded could still fight. Although two of them would not be able to ride to war they would still be able to guard my home and that was an equally important task. As we waited for the ferry to come across the Tees I turned to Wulfric, Dick and Erre. "I would have the three of you ride to York and see if there are archers and men at arms for hire. Choose only the best."

Dick nodded, "And if we cannot find them there, my lord?"

"Then head for Sheffield, Nottingham and Lincoln. You have a month to bring them back."

The ferry bumped into the wooden jetty. Ethelred's ferryman, James the Elder bowed. "Welcome back, my lord."

"And we are glad to be back, James."

Wulfric asked, "Will you not need us for a month, my lord?"

"Your task is more important. I have to make a procession to the north but others can deputise for you. It will be good to see which of them can be leaders."

"You would replace us, my lord?"

"No Wulfric but none of us are immortal. I shall be taking William with me to begin his preparations. I am preparing for the day when I am too old to fight and besides when we go to battle it is good to have others who can command."

I saw the relief on their faces. Sometimes my men surprised me. Did they not know that they were as valuable to me as the stones of my castle?

Erre asked, "Why me, my lord? I do not mind but there are unlikely to be warriors such as us in this land."

"There may be more than you would think and I wish more warriors like you. You have proved your worth more than once. Now that we have lost William the Tall I would bring your number up to ten, including you. You will know the qualities you need to spot."

He nodded, "I will seek out others such as me but I am not certain we will succeed."

I looked up as I heard a cry from across the river. It was William and he was waving wildly. My wife held Hilda and they too waved. The moment I stepped ashore he raced up to me and threw his arms around me. I saw that his head came to just above my waist. He was growing.

"Did you kill many men, father?"

"I did. And look," I turned to Leofric and held out my hand. He brought the helmet we had taken from the small dead Welshman. Although still too big for William he would grow into it. "Here, my son, a helmet from a dead Welshman. When you have burnished it then we will make a leather lining for it."

His face lit up. When he put it on his head half of his face disappeared. My wife shook her head. "It is too large, my husband."

I winked, "He will grow into it."

As I walked into my castle she told me of the happenings in the town and what Hilda and William had been up to. It was as far removed from the slaughter at Chester as one could imagine and was nothing like the intrigues of Empress Matilda and her husband but the mundane nature of my life in my castle and town brought me comfort. I was home.

John, my steward and clerk, brought me down to earth when I entered my Great hall. "My lord, there are many cases and disputes for you to settle. With so many new people living in the manor we, needs must, have a session each quarter."

I sighed, "Then I will hear all of the cases next week." I was a lord of the manor once more.

Chapter 8

The sessions helped me to spend a little time with my family and allowed me to break it to Adela that I had been tasked with scouring the border. She had a remarkably understanding attitude.

"It is a great honour husband that the King trusts you to control the border. I am proud of you."

"I will take William with me. It is time he began his training as a squire."

Her face fell. "He is too young! His life will be in danger."

"I promise you that he will be safe but he will be the lord of the manor one day. My own father began his life as a warrior when he was little older than William. Leofric will always be at his side. Besides, there should be little enough danger. I am only sent to show the Scots that they are not forgotten. They will have spies who will know I was in Wales."

I persuaded her. I believe that she was afraid that if I made William stay at home he would blame her.

I sent word to Sir Hugh of Gainford and asked him to bring ten of his men along with me. I intended to use Sir Hugh Manningham's conroi for the bulk of my force. I would take just ten men at arms and ten archers from my retinue. It would be a chance for Roger of Lincoln and Aelric to lead and I could watch them. Some men might be a good warrior and yet be a poor leader. I did not mind that but I had to know. Wulfric and Dick were natural leaders. I dare say that given different circumstances they could have been knights.

Star was left behind again as was Aiden. The hawks had been neglected and I wished him to discover how many animals we had on our lands. I did not wish my people to hunt the deer and the boar to extinction. Although we enjoyed the meat there were always plenty of rabbits. I wished my son to enjoy the fine hunting I did.

We rode up the coast road for I wanted to see how De Brus was faring. Hartness was prospering. Since the new lord of the manor had taken over it had been a well-governed and defended piece of land. Sir Hugh and I did not stop long for I was keen to spend the night at Hexham. The nights were lengthening and we made the sanctuary that was Hexham before night fell. The land was well ruled by Sir Hugh Manningham but the woods and forests had the potential to be the lairs of brigands and bandits. Young Scots still liked to venture south for the opportunity to capture and ransom those who ventured alone.

This was the second time I had taken William north and I noticed a marked change in him this time. He asked more questions of Leofric. He was attempting to learn more on this journey. He was growing. I had done the same when my father had shown an interest in my development as a warrior. I was pleased. I listened to their conversation as we rode up the north Tyne. "Why does John carry the standard, Leofric? Is he a better warrior?"

I heard John snigger. Leofric was a thoughtful squire and he would not be upset by the question or John's laughter. "No William. John is a bigger warrior. The standard will fly higher in his hands. It means I fight more frequently than John for he must listen for your father's commands. It is the standard which tells our men what they must do. If you have to hold it then you have a great responsibility. It also means you will find it hard to defend yourself."

There was a silence as William took that in. "When I become a squire, Leofric, what will I do?"

"You will do whatever our lord asks. When Sir Hugh was the squire of your father, John and I spent much of the time when they were fighting holding Star and the destrier of the other knights. A squire must be skilled in many things."

"And will you be a knight, like my father and Sir Hugh?"

"That depends upon our lord. If he chooses to knight us then perhaps but we have much to learn and far more skills to acquire."

"You are not ready now then?"

I heard John answer, "It will be some years before we even consider trying to gain our spurs."

William's voice was filled with disappointment as he said, "Then I will have even longer to wait."

Both of my squires and Sir Hugh's laughed at the sad little voice he adopted. I turned in my saddle, "Which is why you need to learn as much as you can from these three squires. Watch and learn. Tonight, John will show you how to put an edge on a sword."

He brightened, "Your sword?"

"No, my son. You can sharpen John's sword for him. When he is satisfied with your skill then you can watch him sharpen mine and we shall see if you are ready for that responsibility." That seemed to satisfy him.

As we approached Hexham I saw that Sir Hugh Manningham had improved his defences considerably and I knew that any attacker would lose many men in an attempt to take it. He had done it gradually and whilst it was not made of stone it was strongly made. My messenger had warned him of our imminent arrival and he had quarters prepared for my men. This was another reason I had brought so few of my men. It cost my knights when I had to stay with them. The giant who protected the Roman Wall for me grinned when he saw William. He liked my son.

"I see you have brought another powerful knight to my home. Welcome young William!"

My son stood a little taller and then bowed. "Thank you for your hospitality, Baron."

Sir Hugh waved his arm, "Pray enter!" As they passed by he said to me, "Your message was brief, Earl. What is it that we do?" Sir Hugh followed us as we entered.

His hall was darker than mine for it was made of wood and only lit by candles and the fire. It seemed oppressive after my airy home. "The Earl of Gloucester wishes us to show a presence along the border. Although our neighbours have been quiet of late he worries that the Welsh incursions may encourage them."

He snorted as he waved over a servant with some wine. "If they have any sense they would head further west. Sir Barnard does not seem worried about raids."

I saw my former squire, Hugh of Gainford look uncomfortable. Baron Barnard of Balliol was his closest neighbour. I asked, "You have heard something?"

He shook his head, "No but Sir Barnard seems to be absent often. As my closest manor I oft times visit." He smiled, "I learned from you, Earl that close ties make for better defence."

"Aye you are right there! I know that Morpeth and the New Castle are stout allies. If their defences were breached or their loyalty compromised then I could not hold the road south." he nodded towards me as he drank some of the wine. "And until we have a new Bishop of Durham then the situation betwixt us is parlous."

I liked Sir Hugh for he was plain speaking. He had voiced my concerns. The Palatinate was the jewel in the crown of the north. Whoever controlled it could rule the north. Since the death of Bishop Flambard then there had been a succession of temporary castellans. The Archbishop of York had placed a reliable priest to manage the cathedral and the religious side but it was the walls of stone which worried me and not the walls of faith.

"Then when we have processed we will ride home that way and visit with the Baron." I shrugged, "I do not like to use my title but this seems a good time to command some service."

He feted us well and it was good for the men at arms to get to know each other. We rose early and headed west.

Sir Hugh brought most of his men with us as we headed north to the old Roman Wall and the road which ran along its southern side. There were trails, tracks and greenways to the north of the wall but the position of the solidly made Roman Road meant we would be seen clearly as we headed west. We were making a show for the Scots. I would not need to visit the castle at Carlisle. The Earl had assured me of its loyalty. It was the area to the east of that castle which posed the threat. With those who lived in Ireland eager for the promise of raids in England that route was the easiest for them to take. They could land on the north bank of the Solway and flood eastwards with nothing to stop them save Hexham, then Morpeth and then the New Castle.

There were one or two small manors which bordered the walls but the knights who lived there were little more than farmers having but a couple of men at arms. Although they had castles they were small. Any attacker could reduce them in a day. They were defences against brigands and animals only. We took tents for the three of us and our squires. Our men would sleep under the stars. We would not be on the road for long.

I used Sir Hugh Manningham's scouts to keep watch to the north. They rode along the old wall which afforded a fine view north. I saw that, in places, trees had begun to grow. "I would have some of your men cut those down at the end of summer. The timber will be useful but I am more concerned about the cover it would give an enemy."

"You are right, my lord. I should have seen that. You have an eye for such things."

"Perhaps. When I studied in Constantinople I was drilled by my teachers about lines of sight and defences. The Romans built well but they intended the wall and the road to be maintained." I pointed at the surface across which we rode. "This too will need repairs soon. I will write to the King. It is not right that you should bear the expense. This artery is vital."

We reached Haltwhistle and the manor of Robert de Lapaigne. He was a young knight with just four men at arms and six crossbowmen but his castle was well sited. He was embarrassed that he could not offer us accommodation.

"It is not a problem. We are here to show the Scots that we are ready should they wish to steal from us."

"And I am glad that you have come. There have been rustlers taking cattle and sheep from those who farm to the north of us. Many of the farmers have fled south."

I nodded, "One or two have reached the Tees." I noticed that Sir Hugh was becoming a little distracted and he kept peering north. "Is there a problem?"

"Two of my scouts have yet to return. I had sent them to the north and west of this manor. Owain and Alan are reliable men something may have happened to them."

I had learned not to ignore such problems. "Aelric, take the archers and ride to the north and west. See if you can find Sir Hugh's scouts."

It was dark and we had eaten when they returned. The two bodies draped over the rear of two of my archers' mounts told their own story. Aelric dismounted. "We found the two men to the north west, my lord. It was the foxes fighting over them which alerted us." He shook his head. "They had only just begun their work but it is not a pleasant sight. Their heads were taken. If they had not worn the livery of Sir Hugh we might not have known who they were."

Sir Hugh nodded his head, "Where did you find them?"

"There was a village or some such a mile or so beyond where they were slain. It was on a hill. We smelled wood smoke and when Griff of Gwent went to spy upon it he said there were Roman ruins hard by."

Sir Hugh nodded, "Booth Castle. It was a Roman camp. The Scots raided and took it last year. I would have fortified it and built a castle myself but…"

"But the King had us fighting in the east; I know. There is little point travelling through the night. We know not the tracks and I would not risk losing more of your men."

"And horses!" Sir Hugh Manningham and I knew that horses, in this part of the country, were as valuable as men. The ones who had slain Owain and Alan were now mounted.

We prepared to ride before dawn. I worried about taking William. I could not afford to leave Leofric behind to watch him. He would have to ride with us. His mother would not be happy but what she didn't know would not worry her. My son, for his part, seemed quite happy about the prospect. We reached the site of the attack by dawn. The trail the killers had left was clear to see, even for me. We headed towards the settlement Sir Hugh knew lay ahead. I was not worried about an attack; we had three knights and over twenty men at arms as well as my archers. It would take a strong force to cause us problems.

As we followed Sir Hugh's scouts I pondered the problem. Who had risked Sir Hugh's wrath to kill his men? Although we were some distance from Hexham he was known as the King's man along the wall. Had the Earl of Gloucester had some intelligence about this? It seemed a lucky stroke that we happened to be in the area when the attack had occurred.

Hugh of Gainford pointed to the ground. "Horse droppings, my lord. They came this way."

"Aye." I turned in my saddle. "If there is trouble William then you stick close to Leofric and do all that he tells you." I would not need to give advice to Leofric he would protect my son, with his life if necessary.

The arrow when it came was badly made and badly aimed. It smacked into my helmet. The angle of the side deflected it off behind me. I heard no other cries. I had known men hit by such accidents. It was an ambush. I drew my sword and pulled my shield up. I heard Leofric instructing William. I risked a glance behind me. He looked so small on his pony. Then I concentrated on the attack. My archers had dismounted. Two held the horses while the others strung their bows and found whatever shelter they could.

Sir Hugh shouted to his knights. "Hexham! Ride to the right!"

"Hugh, Roger, follow me!"

I swung Scout to the right as another two arrows thudded into my shield. I could see nothing although I knew that whoever was attacking us was hiding in the trees above and ahead of us.

111

They were hoping that we would not be able to follow them in the forest. Trees did not stop my men. Hugh of Gainford brought his horse next to mine. Without turning he said. "We were lucky then, my lord. They took us by surprise."

"It is where we miss Aiden and his nose. He would have smelled them before they could have loosed."

Suddenly an arrow flew from behind me and a half-dressed archer fell to the floor some fifty paces from me an arrow sticking from the side of his head. Aelric and his archers were watching our backs. They had dismounted and were running through the trees almost as swiftly as we rode. I leaned over Scout and peered ahead. The Scots were hard to spot for they were dressed in brown cloth and were almost invisible in the trees. I caught a glimpse of something shiny and I leaned further forward sliding my sword to the side. The warrior jabbed his spear which hit my helmet. The head broke from the spear and I rammed my sword into his unprotected middle. Scout's speed tore the sword from the wounded man and he slumped dead besides the path.

I reined Scout in. "Hold!" I realised that this was not going to result in many more dead Scots for they were hard to see. We would be wasting our time. "Reform and head for the settlement."

I heard my orders repeated ahead of me. Hugh and I turned. As we neared the edge of the woods I saw that John had also remained with William. He looked at me apologetically. "I thought is best to stay with Leofric."

"You did right, John." As I sheathed my sword I said, "The pickings were poor anyway. These were not warriors; these were brigands or farmers."

Roger of Lincoln drew next to me, "I counted four of them dead, my lord. I think another three escaped west."

Aelric and his archers waited for us just beyond the woods. "That was a well-aimed arrow Aelric."

He nodded, "I saw his hand and guessed where his head would be.

As we neared the overgrown Roman road I saw Sir Hugh and his men. "We killed six, my lord."

"Did you lose any?"

He nodded, "Peter of Blythe fell from his horse. His arm is broken."

I knew the fellow would suffer more from his friends than from the wound. It was seen as foolish, in the extreme, to fall from one's horse.

"Aelric, take the archers and form a screen ahead of us. I doubt they will try another ambush but let us take no chances eh?"

The land rose towards the old Roman fort. The road which led to it had not been used for over eight hundred years and it was barely recognisable as a road. The fort itself was in a state of disrepair. They had used some of the stones to form a low wall and then added the wattle and daub to the sides. It would be less draughty inside such a building. Apart from a handful of fowl and a couple of sheep the village was empty. Even so we rode in cautiously.

"Search the buildings. See if they left anything worth taking."

I dismounted. While my men and Sir Hugh's searched for danger I joined William and my squires. My son's face was aglow. "That was exciting." I took off my helmet. He held his hands out for it. When I had given it to him he examined the place the arrow had struck. There was a mark but it had not even dented my well-made helm. "Did the blow not hurt, father."

"It matters not if it hurts. So long as it has not buried itself in your body you fight on. It is a bruise and nothing more."

He handed it back to me. "Is it over now?"

I shook my head. "The women and the children will not have fled through the trees. The men did that to distract us and allow their families to escape. They were brave men. We will follow them. They cannot outrun us."

"And what will we do with them when we catch them?"

I pointed to Sir Hugh of Hexham who was leading the men at arms towards us. "Sir Hugh will make them slaves. It is payment for the men he has lost."

"I would not like to be a slave."

Leofric laughed, "You are the son of the Earl of Cleveland. You might be held for ransom but you will not be made a slave."

He looked at Leofric curiously, "And you, Leofric; would you be held for ransom?"

"I wear your father's livery. They might take me and try to make the Earl buy me back."

"Would you buy him back, father?"

I shook my head, "It only encourages such action. I would take my men and give Leofric his freedom by force of arms." I saw the surprise on William's face. "Remember that, my son, you have a responsibility for the men who serve you. They will trust you and you should honour that trust." He nodded and I saw, in his eyes that he understood.

Sir Hugh reined in. "My lads saw them heading north east. They will be heading for Gilnockie Tower. It is stone and can be easily defended. It is sixteen miles from here."

"Then we can catch them." I turned to Hugh of Gainford. "Have your men slaughter the animals and then fire the huts. We will leave a message for these invaders. You should be able to catch us up."

"Aye my lord."

We travelled through a mixture of farmland and forests. It seems that this land was wilder than that south of the Tyne. There were only greenways which twisted and turned. It meant we could be ambushed. Aelric and my archers were vigilant. After an hour or so I heard a shout from the scouts. "They are ahead of us!"

I spurred Scout on and saw a long line of villagers. They had men at the back and the women were at the fore driving the animals. "Sir Hugh, send your archers to head them off. We will tackle the men."

As we formed our lines I saw that they had seen us and a rider galloped off driving a line through the women. He was on one of the two horses they had stolen from the dead men. He would escape but the others would either be dead or be slaves within the hour. I knew that he was going for help but I could do nothing about it. the women, children and the last of the men lay before us.

I did not bother to command Leofric. He knew what to do. I drew my sword as we descended upon the band of fleeing villagers. I noticed that there were more warriors with this band. At least six had shields and over half of them had helmets. Their weapons were a mixture of spears, swords and wood cutting axes. The twenty men turned to form a rudimentary shield wall. It was a valiant attempt but it was doomed to failure. Unseen by the warriors the archers were already galloping ahead and their families and animals would be secured.

Roger of Lincoln and Wilson rode to my right while John held the standard to my left. The others were to his left. It was not an even line for the ground was not easy to negotiate but we kept the same speed and, to the Scots, we would appear as a solid wall of horse flesh and armour. Some of Sir Hugh Manningham's men had spears and I saw Sir Hugh urge them on. It was a clever move for their spears reached the brave souls at the front of the shield wall. As the spears of the three men and arms and their horses hit them two Scots fell. Their centre broken, we poured through the gap. I saw Wilson slice down with his sword and split open the helmet and skull of a Scot. Roger brought his sword up under the chin of a second. It emerged through the back. The survivors ran.

I chose one, younger than the rest, and brought Scout close to him. I swung the flat of the blade across the back of his head. He crumpled in a heap at my feet. I reined in and watched our men finish off the warriors. As Leofric and William joined me I dismounted and handed my reins to my squire. I turned over the youth. He was no more than fourteen summers. I saw in him, William, my son, in a few years' time. I had laid him unconscious for I wished to question him.

Hugh of Gainford and his men joined me while Roger of Lincoln led my men at arms to follow Sir Hugh towards the women and animals now some way ahead and hidden from view. I took off my helmet and gave it to John.

Hugh of Gainford dismounted and joined me. "That did not take you long."

"I know. I wanted a prisoner because I do not understand this attack. They must have known that killing Owain and Alan would bring retribution. Why risk our vengeance?"

Nodding he waved forward his squire, Ralph, "Disarm him."

As he did so the youth began to come to. I took out my sword and held it gently against his chest. His eyes opened and then widened rapidly when he saw himself surrounded by his

116

enemies. "Do not struggle or you will die. Answer my questions and I may well allow you to live. Do you understand?"

There was a moment of defiance in his eyes. I pressed my sword lightly against his chest and he nodded.

"Good. Why were our scouts killed?" He hesitated. "Every other man in your village is dead and the women of the village are captured. I want to know why your headman ordered such an action. It means the end of your village."

"It was not our headman. It was the lord from the west, the Baron of Dumfries, he told us to kill any Normans who ventured north of the wall. He promised gold for every head."

That explained why they had had their heads taken. "Where does this Lord have his castle?"

He pointed vaguely to the west. "It is a day's hard ride in that direction."

"You have never been there?"

"We came from the north two summers since and I only know the land around our home."

"What is his name?"

"He is a lord that is all that I know."

He knew nothing more and I sheathed my sword. "Do you have family to the north?"

"Aye, my lord. My grandmother lives there still."

"Then return hence and stay away from England. You will live longer."

He rose and looked nervously at the men at arms. "You will not ride me down for sport?"

"No, I will not. Now go." He began to run along the greenway. He kept looking over his shoulder. He darted into the forest some half a mile from where we stood and he disappeared.

"Was that wise, Sir Alfraed?"

"He may return to fight us but I saw in him, William, my son, in a few years' time. I would hope for mercy for him should he be in a similar situation."

We heard the sound of animals and keening women as Sir Hugh Manningham returned with the villagers and animals. As he reined in next to me I said, "We will camp at Booth Castle." I pointed to the sky. "It is getting late."

"Aye." He pointed to the horse his squire led. "We have Owain's horse, at least and the slaves will come in handy. Some of these young boys will grow into strong backs."

I rode at the head of the column and we made our way south again. Hugh of Gainford looked around at the land which had been taken by the Scots. "I can see why the Scots took this land. It would take more men than Sir Hugh's to control it. There should be a castle."

"And when King Henry returns to England I will suggest that to him. We have done what was asked of us and this time I cannot be reproached for laying waste to the land. We dealt with murderers, that is all."

"You will not seek a confrontation with this Lord of Dumfries?"

"There is little to be gained and we have not enough men. We will let Sir Hugh take the slaves back to Hexham and we will head west and then return along the Roman road by the wall. We have done as the Earl wanted. The man who left will have reported my banner. The Scots know who is here now and, I hope, will heed the warning."

He nodded, "It is coming to high summer and soon the men will be needed to work the fields."

"That was my thought too. We will be home again in four days." I turned to William. "Have you learned much in this little expedition and campaign?"

"Yes, father but I thought fighting would be harder."

Hugh laughed, "That was not fighting William. We were hunting men that is all. When you face a foe who has armour and is well led then it is a different proposition."

Each day brought a change in my son. This was his school room. I had learned to be a knight in Constantinople where I had learned the theory. It was only when Athelstan had begun my training proper that I had understood the real meaning of knight. William would learn by watching us.

Chapter 9

Sir Hugh wanted to send some of his men to accompany me but I waved his offer away. "We have done as we were asked. The Scots know I am not in Wales. We have bloodied the nose of the Earl of Dumfries. Besides this makes our force look twice as big for with you heading east and me heading west we can make a larger show."

He saw the wisdom of that suggestion. "I will send your share of the profits to Stockton."

Normally we would have divided it into four parts; half for me and the other half for the other two knights. "You lost the men and the horse, Sir Hugh, you take half. We are satisfied."

He did not argue. He had had little other opportunity to make money. "I will make sure I keep armed men along the road to Carlisle then."

We headed east. I was making for the gap in the wall at the deserted Roman fort which lay close to the steep part of the wall. The land to the west was within twenty miles of Carlisle. I thought that would be safe from attack. Aelric and my archers formed a screen ahead of us. The land began to rise towards the wall. It became less cultivated and wilder. In places you could see the natural rock protruding through the soil. I could now see why the Romans had built their wall here. I think I began to relax. The land through which we passed was empty. No one lived here. The ground to the north was better for farming.

The Roman road down which we rode had been abandoned for many years and was like the one we had used before. It was overgrown. It also passed through forests which had spread towards the ditch. Soon, unless it was repaired, the road would be consumed by the forest and it would be as though man had never been in this land.

Hugh of Gainford's men formed the rear guard and one of them, Alan of Reeth, rode up to his lord and me. "My lord, we are being followed."

I knew better than to ignore such things. "Aelric, send two archers to the rear. See if we are being followed."

"Aye my lord."

As the two men passed us I said, "Prepare yourselves!"

My men at arms all adopted a closer formation. Our swords were drawn and shields pulled tighter. The road was wide enough for four abreast but Hugh and I rode together so that Ralph and John could protect William and Leofric.

There was a shout from behind and I heard Ralph of Wales shout, "Ambush!"

I knew that there were men to the rear of us, Ralph's shout had told me that but if I were laying an ambush I would have men ahead of us too. I saw, ahead, the sky lightening as the forest ended and more open ground appeared. "Ride for the open but keep a tight formation!"

Our horses leapt forward and that must have taken the enemy by surprise for they were slow to emerge from the trees to attack us. My archers could not use their bows on horseback but they had all practised with their swords. Two men galloped from the forest to my right. One was a man at arms. They had four others running behind. The danger was the man at arms. He had his shield towards me and that was my only advantage. I would have the first blow. I would need to rely on John, behind me, to despatch the second rider.

I veered Scout towards the man who was taken aback by my aggressive move. He made the mistake of turning to his right and I swung my sword hard across his shoulders and back. His manoeuvre and the force of my blow sent him tumbling from his saddle. His head cracked into a tree and he lay still. I felt a punch in my shoulder as the next horseman thrust his spear at me. My mail held. I jerked Scout's reins to the right and he spun around allowing me to stab at the horsemen. He had no armour and my blade pierced his chest aided by the speed of his horse. As he fell from the horse my sword was released.

As I viewed the scene I could see that we were outnumbered. Our only chance was to make for the gap which was still some way away. "Roger, form on me. Make a shield wall."

It was a risky strategy. If the Scots decided to attack our horses then we would be vulnerable but our shields would be locked together and, with our armour, we should be safer. It took some moments to gather and I felt arrows striking me. I heard a cry as one of my men suffered a wound.

Roger shouted, "Ready my lord!"

Hugh of Gainford shouted, "I have your rear, Earl."

"William, draw your weapon. Today you fight!"

I held my sword behind me as we swept towards the gap. I counted on the fact that we had horses and most of those who followed us did not. I did not worry about Aelric and the archers for they were woodsman all; they would look after themselves. We were almost at the gap when a huge warrior hurled himself forward and swung his two-handed weapon at Leofric's horse. The blade bit into the shoulder slicing through to bone and the brave steed crashed to the earth, dead. Leofric was thrown from its back and he landed heavily. The huge warrior pulled his axe from the body of the horse and raised it to slice down on the unconscious squire.

To my horror William leapt from his horse and, with his sword in one hand and his buckler in the other ran to protect Leofric.

I was forced to whirl around and break the shield wall of men and horses. I could not let my son die without trying, at least, to help him. Even as I turned I saw that he had used his head. As the Scotsman swung his deadly blade my son ducked and ran hard at the man. He held his sword before him. He must have been terrified but he ran bravely at his foe. He ran straight into the man's middle. His momentum forced the blade into the man who screamed in pain. He used his left hand to smack my son in the side of the head and he fell, stunned, next to Leofric. I did not break stride as I swung my sword around at the man's neck. My well sharpened blade sliced through as though the flesh was butter.

Reining in I looked for enemies. John appeared next to me and, after handing him Scout's reins I jumped to the ground. William opened his eyes, "Is Leofric safe?"

"Never mind Leofric I will see to him." I lifted him on to Scout's back. "John I charge you with the protection of my son. Let nothing stand in your way!"

Before I could get to Leofric four warriors or five ran at me. In a bunch they were hard to differentiate. They were eager to finish off a dismounted knight who stood alone over the body of his squire. A spear was thrust at me and I deflected it on my shield as I spun around to my left. I brought my sword across the bare back of the warrior. I cut through to the white of his backbone. I felt a blow on my helmet as a sword was smashed down upon it. I briefly saw stars and I tried to continue my spin. God smiled on me that day for the axe which would have hacked through my mail struck, instead, my shield. My move had opened up the warrior and I stabbed my sword into his unprotected middle. I pushed until the hilt hit his flesh. He spat blood and a curse at me as he died.

Withdrawing the sword I turned quickly. There were three of them left. The rest of the skirmish seemed to be far away but perhaps that was my imagination. Suddenly a horse burst next to me and Hugh of Gainford galloped into the three men. They had concentrated so hard on me that they had failed to see the horse and knight galloping at them.

Hugh's horse bowled one of the men over and was trampled beneath the hooves of his mount. One of them staggered towards me and I brought my sword down diagonally across his body. It ripped it open to the ribcage. Hugh backhanded the last warrior across the back of the neck.

Edgar and Wilfred appeared and formed a defensive half circle with Hugh. I knelt down and took off Leofric's helmet. There was heavy bruising to his head but he was breathing.

"Edgar, pick up Leofric and put him on your horse." As he did so I saw him begin to come to. I looked at the scene of the ambush. There appeared to be just a couple of combats continuing and they were going the way of my men. I looked up at Wilfred. "Ride to John and guard my son." He galloped off. Hugh's squire appeared. "Ralph, sound your horn! We need to rally!"

The strident notes of the horn echoed through the forest and, one by one, my men appeared. Roger of Lincoln led a horse. "My lord, Alan of York will not need his horse any longer."

I nodded and mounted. I saw that we had suffered grievous losses. Three of my men at arms were dead and I could see wounds on two of the others. Sir Hugh's men had also suffered and two of his men at arms were also dead.

Aelric rode up, "I have let you down again, my lord. I should have spotted the ambush."

"No, Aelric. I was complacent. Did you lose any archers?"

"Tom the Bowyer fell."

I nodded. We had lost six men. Even if Dick and Wulfric had been successful in their search for more men at arms we would be no better off. "Find any horses you can and bring any treasure you can find. Roger, bring our men and we will bury them." I pointed to the open area. We will find somewhere close to there."

We passed Will's son who was kneeling over a Scot. He stood. "These men were sent by Sir Walter Comyn. It was he who gave orders to the villagers at Booth's Castle. This man was the one who rode for help." He pointed to the horse which I recognised as one of Sir Hugh's. He wiped his dagger on the dead man's kyrtle. "He told me all, eventually."

"You have done well. Bring the horse. We have need of it."

John and Wilfred flanked my son who looked shaken. I put my arm around him. "You were brave, my son, but you should not have risked your life for Leofric."

Leofric who was behind me said, "He is right William. You should have left me. I am grateful that you tried to save me but you are more important than I am."

William looked confused. "But you would have done the same for me."

I shook my head, "Nevertheless Leofric is correct. You are my son. Perhaps I was wrong to bring you. Your mother was right. You are not yet ready to go to war. It is too dangerous."

I thought for a moment he was going to burst into tears but he stiffened his jaw and said, "It was not my turn to die and it was not Leofric's! I am your son! I would do the same again."

I nodded and saw that both Wilfred and John smiled their approval. Inside I was proud of his courage and his skill. Wilfred handed him the Scotsman's axe. "Keep this as a reminder of how close you came to death."

I almost laughed out loud when my son tried to hold the axe. It was a heavy weapon. The blade and the decorated handles showed it to be a fearsome weapon. The blood of Leofric's horse still stained its edge. We buried our men and covered their graves with rocks. I said words over their bodies for there was no priest but they had died as warriors. They would soon be in heaven with Athelstan and the other dead oathsworn. It was getting on towards dark but I did not want to risk another ambush and so we headed for Carlisle. My original plan lay in tatters amidst the ambush on the road. We reached there before the sun set and my banner was recognised. We were admitted.

Sir Gilbert de Bois was the castellan. He was not there permanently. He had been charged by the King to oversee the completion of the castle. I had met him once and he was a dour, unimaginative man. He would defend the castle well but he could not think of the wider picture.

"What were you doing north of the wall? That is full of Scotsmen."

I sighed, "It is still part of the King's lands and I was charged to show myself."

He grunted, "I do not know why anyone would want that land. There is little there of value."

"There are people, Sir Gilbert de Bois, for they were there before they were driven hence by the Scots. I would have you send patrols north of the river just to show the Scots that they are not forgotten."

I was an Earl and he could not gainsay me. He nodded.

That evening after he had quaffed a fair amount of wine he loosened up a little. I was somewhat distracted for I was concerned about the blows to the head which both Leofric and William had suffered. Although Sir Gilbert's healer had looked at them I was anxious to have Father Matthew look at them.

"You are well known in these parts, Earl."

"Hmn?"

The Scots use your name to terrify their children. They call you the Wolf from the Wall." He laughed and I realised he was a little drunk. "It is your standard of course." He leaned in. "I have heard that Gospatric has put a price on your head."

"It is a sad man who cannot defend his own honour. Gospatric is a bloated carcass who has others do his killing for him."

"You are probably right. I do not know the man. I will be glad to get to a warmer clime where the wine is drinkable."

"You are from Normandy then?"

"Aye. My elder brother has the estate." He laughed, "And he has not yet had the good grace to die. He has no children and so the manor would be mine. Still this is not a difficult task I have been given."

"No, I expect it is not." A thought came to me. I had had an itch in the back of my mind which I could not scratch. Perhaps, in his cups, Sir Gilbert de Bois might give me the answer I sought. "Do you see much of Sir Barnard de Balliol?"

"He has passed through here once or twice. He has a cousin in Scotland. He likes to hunt there."

"A cousin?"

"Yes, one of the Comyns, William I think."

I became more attentive. "He is in Dumfries then?"

"They have land all over Scotland but I believe that Sir Barnard does visit Dumfries regularly. To be honest, Earl, I would have thought you would have had regular contact with him. After all he is a near neighbour of yours."

I smiled, "I have much to occupy me, Sir Gilbert. I have recently returned from a Welsh campaign and then this foray into Scotland. I shall be pleased to get home and enjoy my manor."

As we headed east, the next day I confided in Hugh. I trusted him and I worried for him. "I have heard disturbing news of Sir Barnard de Balliol. It may be nothing but he is a friend of William Comyn."

"Is he the brother of Walter, the one who tried to ambush us?"

"I do not know but I am guessing that he is. I would like you to keep watch on him, surreptitiously of course. But you need to be careful around him. Watch your words and keep your ears open."

"Why do we not tell the King or the Earl of your suspicions?"

"Because they are just that, suspicions. I am learning that we have to play a game. We know not who our enemies are and who our friends are. I know whom I trust and you are one of those. You are young but I am confident that you will make the correct choices." He nodded and looked thoughtfully to the north. "I am sorry that you lost those men at arms. I know that they are hard to replace."

"I have their armour and their weapons. You said that Sir Gilbert de Bois said that your name is becoming known. It works for us. We have many soldiers of fortune who cross the Tees and seek employment. I will hire more."

We made it to Gainford before dark and I stayed with Sir Hugh. Although I was eager to get home it would have been rude of me to leave quickly. Sir Hugh had shown himself to be a calm and confident leader. He had demonstrated loyalty and I would reward that loyalty.

When I reached Stockton, my wife was surprised. Wulfric and the others had not returned from their expedition and she had thought I would have been away longer. When I told her of the ambush I expected a different reaction but she was unexpectedly calm. "Our son has survived and he looks to have come out of the ordeal well. But I pray that both of you are more careful on your next campaign."

Both my son and I were relieved.

After a fine meal and a pleasant evening, I felt replete. I was home in my castle. It was not as strong as some but it was certainly better than most. I had seen that on my travels. My family were safe within its walls. I felt full of energy the next day and relished the prospect of being a lord of the manor for the next few months. I sent for John my steward and my clerk.

"John, I need to write a letter to the Earl." It did not take long to dictate the missive. Neither the Earl nor I went in for flowery phrases. I gave him the bare bones of the events. When I had finished John said, "Sir, if I may speak without offending you?"

"Of course."

He sighed and laid down his scribe. "It is just that the treasury is shrinking. You have many expenses and with new men to equip and to pay I am not sure that we have enough. You have brought cattle and treasure to the manor but we have more mouths to feed. Your work on the castle and the church are not cheap." He held up his hand, "I know they are necessary, my lord, but they are expensive."

I smiled. I had chastised him for holding the purse strings too tightly. I could hear, in his voice, that he did not wish to upset me further. "What do you suggest, John, son of Leofric?"

"Taxes, my lord." I cocked my head quizzically. "I know that the King has his taxes but we only get a small part of those. You provide protection for the people and they prosper. We need to tax that prosperity."

"But I do not wish to lose their support. They are vital to us."

He nodded, "The tax I propose is not going to be a burden. A penny a month for each house which is within the walls of the town and one halfpenny a month for those with a mile of the walls."

"Can the people afford that?"

"Look at the homes of some of the burgers, my lord and how they dress. They can afford it."

"Even so that will not bring in a fortune."

"No but we now have many visitors. We tax Ethelred for every person who uses his ferry and tax them if they stay in the town or castle."

"I hope that would not deter visitors."

"I do not think so and it is the reason I stopped short of taxing ships any more than we do. They are vital."

"Is that the limit to the taxes?"

"Well sir I did think that we could use the farmers to supply the food for the men at arms and archers. If each contributed a little then our bills would shrink." He saw me frown. "I promise you sir, that once we have the finances under control we can cease the taxes. You will be going on campaign again, will you not?" I nodded. "And hopefully that will bring in more treasure than the recent one to Wales." He shook his head, "The Welsh are too poor. We need a campaign in Normandy. That is where the real money can be made."

He was irrepressible. "Very well but the Lady Adela knows the mood of the people. If she tells me that they are unhappy then we will revoke the taxes."

"Believe me sir I have spoken with many in the town and they appreciate that they are safe. It is over a year since we were raided. They prosper."

After he had gone I decided to take a walk around the town. Adela and I had done so many times in the past but we had got out of the habit. Adela was keeping a close watch on William. She did not let him accompany me. I went alone. I wanted the opportunity to view my manor closely and without unnecessary questions. The gate house which led to the town was almost complete. The double gates were a solid barrier. I patted the stone approvingly as I passed through them; nodding to the sentries. Alf and the other burghers had made stone walkways through the town. They gave a sort of structure and order to what, in many places, was a random huddle of huts. The homes within the wooden palisades varied from Ethelred's magnificent hall to wattle and daub dwellings. Ethelred's hall acted as a home and a warehouse. I did not mind its ostentation. It could hold most of the town if danger came. The majority of the homes were the huts which had been around since before the Romans. They were round and made of wattle and daub. Some had stone bases but they were all just one room. The exception was Alf who had an oblong building. Half was his home and the open half was his workshop and smithy.

I walked east first towards the tannery. It was the place which had the most unpleasant aroma in the whole town but it was necessary. The tanned hides brought in a good income and I shared in that income. The smell meant that few homes were in this part of the town. The gate at the eastern end was wood but it had two small towers and the tanners were the defenders of that gate. The north gate was also made of wood. This was the place where those who worked close to the river could be away from the smell. They all had a greater income. These would easily be able to afford John's tax. The exception was Hilda the ale wife who still lived close to the castle and the river. She was almost as rich as Ethelred and it was said that Wulfric had his eye on her as a bride. Although I suspect he would just have used her as a convenience. Wulfric would not want an encumbrance of a wife.

The west gate was made of stone. Eventually I would have all of the wooden palisades which surrounded the town replaced by stone but that would have to wait. The west gate had been chosen as the first to be made of stone because it was the closest to my castle. Even as I examined it I began to plan for the wall which would join the gate to my castle. That would need stone and that in turn meant more income.

It was when I returned to my castle that I realised we needed more accommodation. With more men at arms and archers we were growing short of space. In addition, I needed chambers for those like the Earl and the Dean of Durham who sometimes visited. Perhaps John was correct; we did need taxes.

My three warriors returned three weeks later. They had done well. I saw a column of men approaching the ferry. I was eager to see what they had gathered for me. I saw at least six archers and six men at arms. Erre stood with three axe wielding warriors and I knew that he had done as I had asked. We had lost three men and gained fifteen. John son of Leofric might be unhappy but I was not. We would have the autumn to train and prepare them to fight under my banner.

Erre was more than happy, "We found these three straight from the boat. They had come all the way from the Muslim lands to the south of Aquitaine. They were glad to be away from that disease-ridden land and they came cheaply!"

In contrast to Erre Wulfric was unhappy when I told him of the losses we had suffered. He was a plain outspoken man, "Some of the other lords should bear some of the dangers, my lord. It is always you."

"I am Earl and it comes with the title. Roger and Aelric did well." I waved a hand towards the new arrivals who were busy examining their new home. "Are you happy with them?"

"Oh aye my lord. There were thirty or forty we could have brought but we wanted the best. They have heard that you pay well and are a noble knight. It made our task easier. I suggested the others sought employment with Sir Edward, Sir Richard and Sir Harold."

"Sir Hugh needs men also."

"Do not worry, my lord. I let them all know they would be welcome." We heard a shout as William practised with Leofric. "I heard your son did well in his first battle."

"He killed a Scotsman who was as big as you." I saw the look of doubt on his face. "I finished off the man but William stopped the axe from hitting Leofric."

"Then I will lend a hand with his training. Leofric himself has much to learn."

"You are right. We have the autumn to make the men into one conroi."

"We fight in winter?"

"I do not know but I have a feeling that we may do. There are questions I need answers to."

Chapter 10

It was not war which took me away from my home it was another summons from the King. Now that Matilda had returned to her husband every knight was summoned to London to swear allegiance once more to Matilda. The King was taking no chances. The last time we had sworn the Empress had been a widow. Now she was married. It was typical of the King. He was thorough.

It was the Earl of Gloucester who would accept our oaths. The King would remain in Normandy. We did not need war horses and we did not need a large retinue. I took my squires, Roger of Lincoln, Edgar and, of course, my son William. He now felt part of my retinue. My wife was happy for there would be little danger on the road to London. We left the Tees towards the end of November. It was strange how the King always chose December for such ceremonies. Perhaps he was superstitious; his father had been crowned in December. Even though we did not have our retinues we were a large number of men. There were over twenty knights in our party. Along with the men at arms, squires and servants we made a formidable force. I was happy that both our homes would be safe and that we would not risk an attack on our journey.

I led the column and I led them hard. We made almost sixty miles each day so that we reached London in five. I remembered my father saying that King Harold had marched further in five days on foot and then fought a battle. It was no hardship for we stayed in castles along the way. King Harold and his men had slept in fields. We also knew where we would stay whilst in London. The Earl of Gloucester had sent word that we were to be housed at his hall. I had stayed there before and knew that it was close to the Cathedral. As the Earl was still on the road it was left to his castellan to inform me of the events which would take place.

Henry d'Abbeville had fought alongside me and we trusted each other. He was one of the Earl's most loyal of knights. That was important for there were many knights I did not trust. He took me to one side when I arrived. "I am pleased you and your men have arrived. The Earl and the King know of your loyalty. Your presence will be a show of force."

"There are traitors in London then?"

"Let us say there are some who do not wish the County of Anjou to have the opportunity to grow at our expense."

"But it is the Empress who is named heir and not Geoffrey of Anjou."

"And if she dies? She has, as yet, no child. I know the King is keen for her to bear an heir for him. Until she has a child then the situation is dangerous. Her death, whilst childless, would plunge the country into chaos and anarchy. And then there are others who might seek to take power for themselves."

"You mean the brothers Blois?"

"I do not dishonour either of the brothers but there are rumours. They are that, however, just rumours. There are always enemies. So long as the King's brother lives then there is a danger that someone could put him on the throne and rule through him." He smiled, "The King has placed his closest ally, Roger of Mandeville in charge of the Tower. Now that the Welsh princess is back in Wales it is a prison no longer. It is the strongest keep in the land. So long as the Tower is held then the country is safe. You should keep your eyes and ears open while you are here in London. Come we will join your knights." As we returned to the others he said, "The Earl knows that you keep the north safe and that he keeps the west free from danger. The two protected borders guarantee that the Empress will become Queen and will rule."

I saw the doubt on his face which belied his words, "But until she is with child there is danger."

Nodding he said, "There is danger. As we know from the death of the King's son one heir is never enough." He smiled, "You should have a second son. You will have plenty of manors to leave to your heirs."

As we joined the rest I contemplated his words. I had not even thought about heirs but he was right. I needed to plan for the future. By my reckoning I would be thirty years old when the year changed. I had come to the land of England as a callow youth and now I was a powerful Earl who commanded Barons. I had but one son. Edward had only recently married and he had one son and a second child on the way. I had been remiss. When I returned I would need to look at my own circumstances. I had rejected the advances of the Empress. I did not regret that decision but I knew that it was irrevocable. I should look now to my home. Adela loved children. A third child would be good for us all.

When the Earl arrived he too gathered his closest advisers and leaders. We met in his hall and, with guarded doors, he confided in us. As the doors were closed I looked around. I recognised a few of the fifteen men in the room. Most of them held manors in the south and west of the country. Ranulf de Gernan, the Earl of Chester, and I were the only two earls from the north. I wondered at that.

"I know that many of you wonder at the need for a ceremony to swear allegiance to my sister yet again." He spread his hands. "The fact that you are the handful of men whom I have summoned should be evidence enough for the need. Many do not wish to swear. There are some who vacillate. My father has yet to produce another heir and with each passing month that seems more and more unlikely. Now that my sister has been reconciled with her husband my father wishes to make a statement that the Empress Matilda will become Queen of England. The ceremony will take place tomorrow. I intend to have my clerk make a note of those who are absent. I will visit with the absentees myself and discover the reason for their absence." The stern tone of his voice made it clear that any who did not attend would be dealt with. "All of you need to return to your manors and be vigilant."

Roger of Mandeville snorted, "When the Lady Maud becomes Queen she can safely rest behind the walls of my tower. We can laugh away any attempt to overthrow her."

We all smiled for Roger was a warrior through and through. He was as close to the king as a brother.

The Earl smiled, "The problem is, old friend, that the Empress resides in Anjou. We need to look closer to home for danger."

I ventured, "You mean the brothers Blois?"

The Earl frowned briefly. We had had words on this matter before. "You seem obsessed with Sir Stephen and his brother. They are in London and they will be at the ceremony. They will swear the oath."

I knew the brothers and I did not trust them. "And what if they are foresworn?"

There was an audible gasp from the room. That was unthinkable. The Earl shook his head, "When we doubt oaths then all order in the world is gone. Let us deal with the world we know." He pointed to Ranulf de Gernan and me. "I have especial intelligence for you two lords. Although the Welsh are subdued it seems that their friends from Ireland are casting covetous eyes on Cumberland and the land to the north of Chester."

Ranulf frowned; his father in law's words came as a surprise. "How do you know, my lord?"

138

"I have an understanding with the King of Gwynedd. I have given him free rein to pursue his ambitions in Powys. He thought to give me that information as thanks. I think he was disillusioned when his mercenaries fled after you had retaken Chester. I believe he called them, *'ungrateful snakes'*."

Roger of Mandeville asked, "Is that not dangerous; allowing the king of Gwynedd to become more powerful?"

"The land he covets is mountainous and unproductive. He seeks it to become King of all Wales. For the moment we will allow that. My father knows all. I have exchanged letters with him. Wales is a minor consideration at the moment. Should it become necessary I believe we can defeat him." He gestured towards me. "The Earl of Cleveland showed that. The men of Gwynedd have few knights. Their only power is their archers and, outside their mountain aeries they can be defeated." He nodded to the two of us. "When you return home be vigilant around the borders. Sir Gilbert de Bois is here in London to take the oath. Although he has few men Carlisle should be the rock upon which the men of the west will fall."

"The castle is still unfinished, my lord. I was there recently."

"Then I will send coin back with you, Earl, so that the work can be accelerated."

After the Earl had finished I sought out Ranulf. "What do you make of Gilbert de Bois?"

"I have had little to do with him. I have been completing my own repairs. Despite what my father in law says I am still worried about the Welsh."

"You are wise to do so. The land to the west is well within my reach. I can be at the west coast in two days if I just bring horsemen."

139

"You have more mounted men that I do but I can be there in a day but it would be more likely to be two."

"Then we need Sir Gilbert de Bois to be vigilant. We will need to speak to him as soon as the ceremony is over. The Earl is right. If it is the Irish and their Vikings who come over then our castles will hold them for they are made of stone. However, the wild men of the west move swiftly and they could devastate the rich farmland which lies south of Carlisle and north of Chester."

Ranulf nodded, "And they are dangerous men to fight. Their axes can gut a horse and split a man in two."

"I know. My squire's mount was hacked in just such a way by a Scotsman."

The ceremony was unenthusiastic. Save for those loyal to the Earl of Gloucester the rest of the barons looked like children dragged to a church. I saw Stephen and Theobald with their younger brother Henry. They took the oath however I did not see Sir Barnard de Balliol and that worried me. The Blois brothers gave me a curt and cold nod as they passed. I smiled as I acknowledged them. I could play the game of the east as well as any.

Ranulf and I waited for Sir Gilbert as he left the ceremony. He bowed. We were both his superiors. "Sir Gilbert, the Earl of Gloucester believes that the west may well be attacked by the Irish and their Viking allies."

For the first time since I had met him he looked worried. "Carlisle?"

"I would hope for such an attack for your castle is strong and we would easily throw them back but I believe they will strike between Carlisle and Chester. There are few castles there and none are made of stone."

"You mean the Lune and the Ribble valleys?" He was the most animated that I had ever seen before.

Ranulf nodded, "And the Mersey too."

"Do not forget Cumberland. There are many who live there who have Norse blood coursing through their veins."

Sir Gilbert looked concerned, "There are no Normans in that land. They all speak a language I did not understand. Twixt Carlisle and Kendal is unknown to me."

"I think that is why they have been left to their own devices. It is a land which grows only rye and barley and hitherto they have not caused trouble. Allies from the west may change that."

"What would you have me do, my lords?"

"Send word to the lords whose manors are close to the coast. They should send messengers to you and the Earl of Chester at the first sight of enemies. You must send word to me. It is imperative that we all gather before they have spread out. I have no doubt that they will outnumber us but we will be mounted."

"Is the Earl certain they will come in winter?"

Ranulf nodded, "The land south of Cumberland is mild, even in winter. It is a short journey from Man and Ireland. They will come. I am just surprised they have not come before."

I laughed, "They are too fond of fighting each other. Their experience with the Welsh must have given them a taste of wealth."

Sir Gilbert stroked his beard. "Then I need more horses." He looked at me as though I could conjure them out of fresh air.

"You must use your own coin to buy them. I have money from the Earl of Gloucester to pay for the completion of the castle. Use the taxes the Earl has you collect."

He smiled, "I thought that was for me."

We both shook our heads. "The defence of the manor comes first. If you wish profit then go hunting!"

Perhaps my tone intimidated him or my reputation. Whichever it was he subsided and nodded his assent. "I will buy horses."

I smiled. "Good. Keep a good watch on the coast. You must send a rider to me if danger approaches. He can tell the lords along the Tees the news and they can prepare. A second should be sent to his lordship in Chester. Those two riders should have the finest horses you possess."

"I will do so." I knew that he would. It was in his interests to keep us informed. We might be his only salvation.

As my knights and I rode north, now with a sumpter and chests of coin for Carlisle Castle I took the opportunity of enlightening my knights. They all seemed happy about the prospect of fighting the Vikings and the Irish. They all knew of the wealth we had brought back from our last encounter.

"Will there be much profit, my lord?"

Sir Guiscard of Normandy was always on the lookout for more money. He had rich tastes. Unlike the rest of us his profits went into fine clothes and drink not men. "Perhaps but the enemy will be a dangerous one. Keep horses and men ready to ride at a moment's notice. It will be Gainford where we gather. Hugh, you should send a rider to Sir Hugh Manningham here when you receive the news." I looked at the Baron of Hexham. "You should make directly for Carlisle."

"Aye my lord. It will make a change to slaughter the Irish."

"Do not underestimate them, Sir Hugh. They are wild and ferocious fighters. They go for horses!"

His face reddened. "Then we shall kill them before they get the chance."

"Bring only mounted men. Your manors need defence and we need speed."

When we broke our journey in York we were told that there were many unemployed warriors who sought employment. None of us wanted to spend the time enlisting them but we decided to send our sergeants at arms back once we reached home.

It was a horrible journey north for the winter attacked us with a vengeance and, when I saw Stockton loom up out of the gloom, I was grateful beyond words. My home seemed warm and inviting after the grey wet world through which we had travelled. My wife looked as beautiful as a spring morning and my children were as jewels in a crown. I was happy. The long dark nights were to be relished rather than dreaded. My wife and I enjoyed each other's company as we had never done before. I had exorcised Matilda and I was free to love my wife.

Wulfric was pleased that there was some prospect of war. He had been more than unhappy at the missed opportunity to kill some Scotsmen. He had the men trained well and was keen to try them out. He and Erre rode back to York to enlist more men. Now that we had more warriors like Erre we could afford to take all of our horsemen. We had begun breeding our own horses and had foals which would soon be ready to ride. We had no destrier stallions yet but palfreys were what we used every day. William now had his own mail hauberk and he had grown into his helmet. The leather inner made a tight fit and I had had him made a bigger shield. He had applied himself well under the tutelage of John, Leofric and, most importantly, Wulfric. Adela had not been happy about the bruises and cuts he had suffered. I had told her that they were more valuable than armour. They were a measure of his experience.

I had also decided that this time we would take Aiden. It would save lives. He was more than happy to be part of an expedition. He enjoyed the challenge. John son of Leofric was also happy for the finances of the manor were now much healthier.

Wulfric and Erre brought back six men at arms. There were another three of the men who had served in the east. They, like the others, had come from Al-Andalus. I think they went there from Miklagård believing that they would like the climate. They found that they did not for the Moors were cruel and wished to convert all to their religion.

In the middle of February William the Mason finished the tower of the church of St Mary which lay in my town. Father Matthew asked for the Dean of Durham, Father Michael to consecrate it for us. We still had no bishop there. I, for one, was happy for I liked Father Michael. He would have made a good knight. He could have been a warrior monk had he so chosen. It was when the congregation spilled out into the cold that I realised just how much we had grown. When William had designed the church with me we had had far fewer people. Now we were larger than Carlisle.

As we waited for the priests to begin I spoke quietly to William. I did not have to bend down as far as last year. He had grown. "God's grace and favour are as important to you as your armour. Remember that and pray for his help."

"I will."

There was something about the interior of the church which made me think of a cave beneath the ground. With no outside light it was dimly lit by candles which threw, even in daylight, strange shadows. We all listened in silence to the Latin

144

spoken by the two priests. I knew the words but, apart from Adela, few others did. The 'Amen's' from the congregation came a heartbeat after the ones from us.

The Dean walked over to my family and laid his hands, first on Adela and me and then on William and Hilda. He blessed us.

Once outside we were greeted by the smell of roasting meat. I had given one of the Welsh cattle to be cooked as a celebration of the consecration of the church. As my men at arms mixed with those in the town I saw liaisons blossoming. Edward had told me that men at arms only looked to women for marriage when they were settled. I took it as a compliment that they felt settled in my manor.

It was a good day. Despite the wind and the dark scudding clouds, the rain held off and the hardy folk of my town enjoyed the slices of beef which were placed on freshly baked bread platters the flour for which I, too, had provided. In a time of shortage, it was a veritable feast and I was pleased to do it for my people.

I took the opportunity to speak with Alf and Ethelred. Despite John, my Steward's words I still worried about the effect of the taxes. I spread my arm in a circle. "Our town grows and, I hope, prospers."

Alf nodded. "The Church is a clear sign that God favours us. We are content."

"Despite the taxes?"

Although Ethelred frowned, for he was a mean man, Alf laughed. "Do not worry about Ethelred. He still has the first penny he earned tucked away somewhere. The taxes are nothing. We would pay double."

Ethelred spluttered, "Now, kinsman, do not be hasty!"

145

I laughed for I also knew him well. Alf shook his head and wagged his finger at the merchant and ferryman. "Before the Earl arrived we paid no taxes and we were poor. It was the Earl who allowed you to build your ferry. It is he who draws in the ships and the people." He jabbed his finger towards the large hall. "You were happy to live in a hut before he came and you now have a lord's house, servants and slaves. You should be ashamed of such an attitude."

"You are right. Forgive me my lord. It is ever thus. A man forgets whence he came." He chuckled. "Besides those who pass through pay even more taxes than we do and yet they come still."

We talked then of the changes we had made and those that we would make in the future. I enjoyed the time speaking with my burghers.

That evening, with the children asleep and Adela in my arms we lay, huddled beneath our blankets and furs and spoke of the future. I know you are to go away and that it will be at short notice but when you return I will have grown larger."

"A child?"

She giggled, "We lay together so many times on your return that I would have worried if it were not so."

I hugged her tighter. I said nothing but I knew that it would be another son. We planned, as all parents do for our three children and I fell asleep dreaming of my two sons riding to war behind me. It was a joyous picture. Those next days were amongst the happiest I can remember. We were like two children with a secret. No one else knew and that made our secret even more special.

Chapter 11

Seven days after the feast a rider galloped in his horse all lathered and sweating. He threw himself from the saddle and dropped to his knees. "My lord, Sir Gilbert said that ships have landed men in the Lune valley. They are spreading like ants in summer."

"You have done well. John, see to this rider. Ralph of Wales, ride to Normanby and tell the lords twixt here and there that we ride. Griff of Gwent ride to those to the north of us." They ran to their horses. As the rider from Carlisle rose I said, "You told my knights along the valley?"

"Aye my lord."

"Wulfric, Dick let us ride." All had been prepared. Our sumpters had the packs of mail and weapons already close by. Erre knew that he was to stay and guard my castle. He now had more men under his command. The servants who would accompany us had their orders. It took less than an hour for us to be ready.

Tristan and Harold were ready with their men as we passed their halls. They both had small retinues but I was happy that they left their demesne well defended. Tristan's father, Sir Richard, caught up with us as we passed Sadberge. The farmers along the way looked up in wonder when they saw the colourful array of knights and men at arms pass by. I knew, from my own farmers, that they worried at such movements. It meant danger and they were always vulnerable when we left.

We reached Gainford in the afternoon. I held a council of war with those knights of mine who had arrived. "As the attack is along the Lune then tomorrow we ride to Kirby Lonsdale. There is a castle there and it is held by the de Taillebois family."

147

Sir Geoffrey of Piercebridge said, "But that is over fifty miles hence and it is winter."

"And while we delay then the people who live there will suffer and die." I turned to Sir Hugh, "Have you sent a rider to Sir Barnard?"

"He is not at home. He visits with his cousins in Scotland."

I said nothing but, when I returned I would visit with Sir Barnard and explain his duties and responsibilities in such a fashion that he could not misunderstand my words!

It was a mighty host which crossed the Tees and headed for Hawes. It was a slightly shorter route than the one which passed through Barnard Castle but it was over the high moors of the West Moor Land. I decided to risk it. The roads were barely passable. There was little at Hawes but it was a good pass which led to the Lune. Once we made the pass we would have some shelter from the bitingly cold east winds and driving snow which found gaps in our cloaks and our armour.

I heard William excitedly asking Leofric about the land we would be visiting. This would be his first real campaign and he was keen. That was as it should be. Now that there was the prospect of another son I was less worried about William. He had shown himself to be resourceful and also lucky. Both were attributes which every warrior admired. Skill was one thing but if you were lucky too then others would fight close by you.

Aiden ranged far ahead with his hounds. I felt happier for his presence. There was little chance of us being ambushed. We could ride easier. Without Aiden we would all end the day with stiff necks from looking over our shoulders and ahead for danger. All had confidence in my former slave who had become as valuable to me as any warrior.

Sir Edward had become a father again and he told me of his second son, Henry. I kept the news of Adela's gift from him. It might be bad luck to do so. However, I enjoyed his stories for I anticipated my stories after my son was born at harvest time.

Aiden returned shortly before dark. "I have ridden to the castle my lord and told Sir Ivo of our imminent arrival. He had not heard of the raid. He has sent a rider to his father, the Baron of Kendal."

I nodded, "Is the castle far?"

"We will be there as the sun sets." He grinned as he pointed to the west, "We are heading in the right direction, my lord."

Sir Ivo was the second son of the Baron of Kendal. Named after his grandfather he was of an age with Tristan. His small wooden hall would not hold us and we camped in the cold outside his palisade. He did however, have hot food for us.

"How many mounted men can you bring with us, Sir Ivo?"

"I have but five mounted men at arms and my squire."

He sounded almost embarrassed, "That will swell our numbers and besides we should have riders from the north and the south joining us by late tomorrow."

"You intend to attack with the men you have here, my lord?"

"That depends upon their numbers. At the very least I hope to stop their depredations. I have fought Norse and Irish before. They are fierce fighters but they do not use horses. It may be that our presence alone makes them return home. They cannot have expected such a swift response from us. The King of Gwynedd's betrayal of them will come as a shock. Make sure you bring plenty of lances. If we can break them with lances we will have fewer casualties."

My own knights knew my philosophy but I could see the doubt in his eyes and hear it in his words. "Is there not glory to be had? We can face them sword to sword."

I heard Edward snort, "I can see you have never faced a wild Irishman wielding a double handed axe. Ask the Earl's squire what an axe can do to a horse. Take the Earl's advice young man and use a lance. It is cheaper to replace than a horse."

I saw Sir Ivo redden. He did not like being spoken to as a young man. "Sir Edward means no offence. He has fought since before you were born. He is a rough and ready soldier but his wisdom in the area of warfare is not to be doubted."

Mollified Sir Ivo nodded, "Thank you for the advice. I confess I have yet to face an army." He smiled, "I have done well in the tourney."

Sir Edward said, "Then you have naught to fear so long as you follow the banner of the Earl. He is the best general I have ever followed."

Sir Gilbert arrived during the evening. He brought with him Baron Geoffrey of Kendal and six knights. His twenty men at arms would be welcome but he only had crossbow men. I preferred the speed of the war bow. We would be reliant upon my archers once more. I was glad I had not left any at home. It seemed we would need them all.

I led my large battle towards the Lune. Aiden was aided by some of Sir Ivo's gamekeepers. They knew the land and could move silently. We did not need them to show us where the raiders had been. The burnt-out buildings and corpses told their own story. The bodies were those of men and youths who had fought to save their families. There were no animals to be seen. I took this to be a good sign. They would have to move more slowly and would need men to guard the animals and captives they had taken.

A rider came from the south and met us two miles from the tiny hamlet of Caton. He pointed south. "My lord, the Earl of Chester has sent me. He has found a large force of raiders along the Ribble. They are holding Preston. He begs you to come to his aid."

This was a problem. There was not just one force of enemies but two. "Tell the Earl that we must first rid the land around the Lune of the raiders and then we will join him." He nodded and rode off. I turned to my knights, "It is now even more urgent than ever that we strike and strike quickly. Dick, gather every mounted archer. I want a screen ahead of us and we now move like quicksilver." As he rode to organise the men I said, "Squires, bring our warhorses. They ride next to us. When we sight the enemy we change mounts."

We had twenty-one knights and sixty men at arms. With our twenty-four squires we had enough armour but did we have the numbers?

"Wulfric, I charge you to command the men at arms. Form them into one force. When we charge, I want them as two lines behind the knights and the squires."

Sir Gilbert asked, "You intend to charge them without knowing their disposition?"

"Perhaps but I want us to be ready to charge if the opportunity arises. I will not waste time giving orders. Watch my banner. When I signal I expect instant obedience. I know not half of the knights who follow me but you will have to watch my own knights. They know their business." I saw from some of the faces of Sir Gilbert's knights that I had offended them. I had not been diplomatic. This was war and I had no time for diplomacy.

We headed down the road in a four-wide column. The archers ranged ahead of us. We had not gone more than two hundred paces when Aiden galloped in. "My lord, we have found them. They are close by and they have a camp close to a bend in the river. There is a hill and they have occupied it. Their ships lie in the river yonder."

"How many warriors are there?"

"I counted over two hundred my lord but there were others in the boats."

"Are they moving?"

"No, my lord, it seems they have risen late. There are captives and I heard wailing."

He did not need to elaborate. I knew what the Norse and the Irish would have been doing. I knew that the rider from the Earl of Chester had not seen them or he would have said. That meant that they were returning to their camp after each day's raiding. They would spread further afield each day. If we struck quickly then we might catch them unawares. "Find Dick and bring him to me." Turning in my saddle I said, "Warhorses and lances!"

I dismounted and handed Scout's reins to William. "Your task, squire, is to guard Scout. Watch the battle and if Star falls then bring Scout to me. If my lance breaks then bring me a fresh one. Do you understand?"

"Yes my lord!"

I would have the advantage of two squires following me. Few of my knights had more than one squire. I had just mounted when Dick rode up, "My lord?"

"Divide the archers in two. Aelric commands one wing. You take the crossbows with you." I saw the look of distaste on his face. Archers hated the crossbow.

152

"Crossbows my lord?"

"Their bolts can pierce armour. Take them. I want the two of you to guard our flanks. Keep arrows falling while we advance and then when we withdraw. You will make them bleed to death."

"Yes, my lord."

I saw that my battle was ready. "Forward."

With banners fluttering and war horses snorting we rode the last mile to the hill by the Lune. The enemy could not fail to see us as we snaked towards the hill. We were like a huge metal snake. They had chosen their camp well for it afforded them a good view across the vale. When we neared I saw the movement on the summit. There was a great deal of action as they prepared to defend themselves against us. I saw that they had made a barrier of captured carts and such. That did not worry me. Their weapons meant they would have to stand atop their defences to fight. The worry was the hill which would sap the energy from the legs of our horses and slow down the final attack. We would be striking at a pace barely above a walk.

There was a gap in the dry-stone wall at the foot of the hill. I led my men through and, while they formed up behind and next to me, I examined the defences. The hill rose to its peak about six hundred or so paces from where we stood. The very top was slightly curved so that the enemy had a flat area on which to stand. They had a solid base from which to fight. I could see many banners but I recognised none. I also saw a few banners from which hung skulls. While most were animal skulls I saw one human one. These were wild men we faced.

I turned and saw that John and Leofric were behind me. William was with the other squires behind the men at arms. We had three strong lines interspersed with a few squires. Each line was separated by forty paces. It would be my knights who would strike the first blows and that was as it should be.

I stood in my stirrups so that all could see me. "Let us drive these savages back to their island. We take no prisoners! Forward for King Henry and England!"

We moved forward at the walk. I had had a leather extension fitted to Star's saddle so that I could rest my lance upon it. It meant I could strike with an arm which was fresh and full of power. Sir Edward rode on one side of me and Sir Richard on the other. If Sir Gilbert and his knights were put out that I took my own knights in the place of honour I cared not. We fought as one conroi and we knew each other. My line would not break.

When we were four hundred paces from the enemy line I spurred Star so that he trotted. Glancing down the line I saw that some of Sir Gilbert's knights were falling back slightly. As we neared the line of Irish and Norse I saw that the raiders had mounted the carts. Some were falling to arrows and bolts as Dick and Aelric rained death upon them from the flanks. When they raised their shields for protection I smiled. My strategy was working. At a hundred and fifty paces we began to canter. Annoyingly those knights who had lagged behind now spurred ahead and did not keep a continuous line. It was only my eleven knights and the four next to them who had any sort of order. It was too late now to address the problem and I lowered my lance and shouted, "Charge!" We were just fifty paces from them when John made the signal.

As soon as I spurred Star he leapt forward. I pulled back my arm and aimed my lance at a large Viking wearing a full byrnie. He was bringing down his shield to his middle for the arrows had stopped. If he thought he could hold my blow then he was wrong. He had no one behind him and he had not set himself. Star did not stop as I jabbed my lance forward with all the force I could muster. Later my arm would tire but at that moment I was still fresh. Star's hooves crashed into and demolished the cart. My blow with the lance was stopped by the shield but the crumbling cart and the force of my blow threw the Viking backwards. He fell

154

beneath Star's hooves. I reined him in and stabbed an Irish warrior in the chest with my lance as he raced at me. The head broke as he fell dead.

We had broken their first line. I turned my horse to allow Wulfric and the two lines of men at arms to attack through the gaps we had created. My own knights followed suit but I saw three of Sir Gilbert's men charge headlong into the enemy who were racing to fill the gaps. They were fools. Aelric and his archers tried to support them but I saw the three of them and their squires surrounded and butchered. We could not afford such losses.

Star snorted and stamped the ground as I waited for William and my lance. He was there so quickly that I wondered if he had ridden in with Wulfric's men. He handed me my lance and his face was aglow. "Well done, William, now withdraw down the hill."

"Have we not yet won?"

"We are not even close to winning!" I turned Star and shouted, "Reform!"

None of my knights had fallen and I saw that young Sir Ivo was still alive. Sir Gilbert looked chastened while Baron Geoffrey looked embarrassed about the behaviour of his knights.

"Keep together!"

Wulfric and the men at arms had not had an easy time of it. The successful attack on the three knights and squires had heartened the enemy and they had formed a three-deep shield wall. The ones at the front all wore mail byrnies and Wulfric and his men were struggling to make successful strikes. I saw Wulfric shout the order to reform. They fell back to reform behind us. As they did so a dozen or so wild Irishmen broke ranks and hurtled after them. Dick's archers cut them down to a man. It gave me an idea. As Wulfric passed me I said, "When we fall back then you do the same. I want them to think we flee."

He grinned, "Hastings?"

I nodded, "Hastings!"

It was a short line which attacked the enemy shield wall but our horses had had a brief rest and when we charged from fifty paces we must have presented a terrifying aspect to the Vikings. They were brave fellows. Only some were Christian and all would wish to die with a sword in their hands. As we neared the line I pulled back with my lance and, at the last moment, lifted Star's head so that his hooves rose. The Viking who faced me was brave but he still raised his shield to protect himself from my horse's hooves. I punched my lance into his middle. The head broke his mail and tore through his leather kyrtle. I twisted as I felt it slide into soft flesh and, when it ground on bone, I pulled it out. He fell back breaking the line. A second warrior stepped forward and smashed his sword through the shaft of the lance. I could see that most of my men had broken lances. "Fall back!"

As we turned I saw two warhorses without riders. Two more knights had fallen. As we approached Wulfric I saw him order his own men to turn. Over my shoulder I saw that many of the Irishmen had left the shield wall to pursue the defeated Norman horsemen. They thought we had broken. The Vikings who remained closed ranks. Our two companies of archers and crossbows sent flight after flight into them. More Irish followed their fellows after us.

I yelled, "Turn and charge!" This would not be a cavalry charge. We would be a ragged mass of men on horses but the ones before us had no armour and were alone.

Drawing my sword, I whipped Star's head around just in time to bring my blade down across the neck of an exultant Irishmen with lime spiked hair who had raced ahead of the others.

His red blood quickly stained his dead white head. We were like foxes amongst chickens as we turned and fell upon them. They were taken by surprise. I had to lean down to slash at them as they tried to hide beneath Star. That was a mistake for he stamped them with his hooves. Had they had armour they might have survived but they were without any protection. My long sword caused terrible wounds. It tore deep cuts into bare flesh. I saw bone through the flesh. Arms were severed and heads despatched. It was a slaughter. Behind me Leofric and John protected my back and flanks. My thin line of knights and squires led my men at arms back up the hill. Ahead the Norse still held their shield wall and I knew, from Star's labouring gait, that he would not be able to charge again. I slew the last Irishman who had failed to regain the shield wall and I reined in Star.

The Norse warriors were now a manageable number. Our archers continued to loose arrows at them. The bolts from the crossbows punctured any mail which was not protected by a shield and their line was shrinking. Had the Earl of Chester not needed our help then I would have let the archers finish them off but we had to leave as quickly as possible.

"Dismount! We fight on foot!"

John waved William forward. The other squires took the reins of the horses of their knights. John held Star's reins as I dismounted.

"William, stay here with John and guard the standard. Leofric, come with me."

I stepped forward and waited for the rest of my knights to join me. I saw that De Brus was not there. He must have fallen. Sir Gilbert, Sir Ivo and Sir Ivo's father were there.

"Wulfric, form a second line behind us. Wedge formation."

Leofric tucked in behind me between Sir Edward and Sir Richard. We moved up the hill. I did not rush for the archers were still causing damage and the enemy line was shrinking. I saw a Viking chieftain in the centre of the line and I made for him. If I could kill their leader then the rest might become disheartened. Of course, it could go the other way and the chief's oathsworn would fight to the death. I saw that he was smaller than I was but broader. His sword was broader too and had less of a point than mine. He would try to batter me to death. He had an open helmet and his neck was protected by a mail aventail. His bare arms were covered in warrior bracelets. This was an experienced warrior. His shield was enormous. That did not worry me for mine would function as well and was lighter. He did, however, have a boss which I knew he would use offensively. My father and Erre had told me that.

I saw anger in his face for he had had to endure the arrows and bolts of my men. He had seen his allies throw away the advantage of numbers and he intended to cut me into tiny pieces. I knew from Erre that the Norse despised Normans with our armour, lances and horses. It must have seemed like a gift from the gods for us to fight them on equal terms. I was not afraid. I had trained with Athelstan and he was a warrior without peer.

I feinted towards his middle with my sword. He had to hurriedly bring his shield from over his head, where he had been protecting himself from arrows, to block the blow which never came. I flicked the sword up and aimed for his unprotected throat. Although I took him by surprise he managed to move away from the fatal strike it should have been. Even so I scored a long cut along his neck. My sword came away red. He cursed me in Norse and then brought his sword over his head. There was no subtlety in the blow. He intended to break a bone or two in my left arm. He did not know that my shield was cunningly constructed so that it had a curve on it. I turned my shield as the sword hit and the heavy blade slid down the side.

The expected move from me would have been a stab at his middle but I did not do that. Instead I hacked at his right hand. Had I connected then his wrist would have been severed. He pulled his hand back and my sword rang against his blade. His sword was old and I saw it bend a little. Not much but enough to upset the balance. It was then he tried the punch with the shield. I had been expecting it and I spun around so that the shield struck fresh air. I turned my sword so that, as it came around, the edge of the blade struck the mail links on his byrnie. It was across his back and the links were severed for the length of my blade. The broken mail hung down like a sea anchor. He was forced to turn to face me but the combination of a wounded neck, torn mail and a bent blade made him a weakened warrior.

He swung his sword overhand. Rather than blocking with my shield I used my stronger sword. Sparks flew and the sound was like a church bell. The Norse blade bent even more. I swung my shield upwards towards his chin. He had not expected that and I saw his head snap back as it caught him beneath the chin. How he remained conscious I do not know but he was stunned and I took my chance. I stabbed at his middle. The weakened links at the rear had also made the front less strong and my sword entered the mail, and his leather byrnie and his middle. I ripped it sideways to eviscerate him. Even dying he tried to raise his sword but he failed. As he fell he yelled, "Allfather!" And he died.

Before I had time to gather my wits a warrior took off his helmet and hurled it at me. I barely had time to deflect it away before he ran at me wielding a double handed sword. He had gone berserker. An arrow plunged into his shoulder and he ignored it. I braced myself with my shield held before me. He was a powerful warrior and he would bowl me over; I knew that. As the sword swung over my head I ducked. At that moment John jabbed the point of my standard into his face. Although it did not stop him it made him slow down and I ripped my sword across his unprotected middle as I spun away from the sword which whistled above my head. My blow and John's made him stumble. He looked lost. He

159

was bleeding heavily from his stomach and his face was a mess. I turned and brought the sword down across the back of his neck. Even a berserker could not fight without his head. His headless torso tumbled to the ground. I looked around as cheers rang out. The enemy were destroyed. We had defeated them.

Even though I was aching and I was tired I knew we had not finished. "Dick, rescue the captives. Wulfric, Ride and destroy their boats!"

William galloped up with Scout. He leapt from the saddle, "Father, are you hurt? How did you kill that monster? He looked unstoppable!"

"I owe my life to John here. His timely blow gave me the time to slay him."

I sheathed my sword. I would clean it later. Surveying the battlefield, I saw that we had won but paid a price. I saw dead men at arms littering the field. I saw two of my surcoats. My men had fulfilled their oaths and died well. I would remember them. Sir Gilbert and the Baron of Kendal made their way over to me. Sir Gilbert bowed his head, "I am sorry, my lord. My men did not obey orders."

I nodded, "They have paid with their lives. I leave you two to clear the field and gather the treasure. Protect the captives and send our share of the treasure to Stockton."

The Baron of Kendal looked at me with an open mouth. "You will not stay?"

"The Earl of Chester needs my help and I never let down a friend. We ride as soon as my men return."

Chapter 12

The survivors managed to take two of the drekar and headed west. Sir Gilbert's men burned the others. Their blackened carcasses would remain in the estuary as a reminder to any other raiders that death was the only reward they could expect. We stayed only long enough to bury our dead and then we headed south. With luck we could reach the Ribble before dark. Sir Raymond's death saddened us. He was the first of my knights to die since Sir Hugh's father. I had sent his men at arms and archers back to Hartness with his horse and armour. He had a wife and he had a son. As much as I would have liked to keep his warriors his family would need them more. We had lost men at arms but, thankfully, no archers. We had twenty miles to travel and, with tired horses and exhausted men, I did not want to risk stumbling into an ambush. If the Earl of Chester could not hold out until dark then this was a huge enemy force we faced.

Sir Edward and Sir Richard rode next to me. Sir Richard shook his head, "When you ordered us to dismount, my lord, I thought you had lost your senses. What man loses the advantage of fighting on horseback? And yet you were right. They would have destroyed too many of our horses."

Sir Edward nodded his agreement, "And the Hastings retreat was a master stroke. If we did not have to ride to the Earl's aid then we would be celebrating now on the Lune rather than making our weary way south."

For my part I was glad to be away. Although we had just lost one knight the other conroi had not been as lucky. There were just three knights who had survived unscathed. Sir Ivo, his father and Sir Gilbert were the only ones unwounded. With five dead and two who were grievously wounded it had been a harsh lesson for the knights of Cumberland. Sir Ivo and his father had been close to

Sir Harold during the battle and had copied him. If they had not then they too might have remained on the field.

"I think we were lucky to be fighting the Norse now. I think that in their heyday, before Hastings, we would have suffered more. We might even have lost."

"They are tough warriors. Thank the Lord that they never learned to use horses."

Aiden rode back to us as the sun was just dipping towards the sea to our right. "They are not fighting, my lord. The enemy are still in Preston and the Earl has made a camp between them and their ships."

That was a clever move by the Earl. "Can we approach the Earl's camp without being seen by the raiders?"

"If we head further west then we can."

"Then we will do so." Although it would make for a longer journey I took us west and sent Aiden back to tell the Earl that we were on our way. It was dark when we trudged into the camp. The Earl had his two healers tending to the warriors who had been wounded. I waved Father John over to help them as I dismounted.

The Earl strode over to me. "Thank you for coming to my aid, Alfraed. My man told me you were fighting to the north. You won?"

"We won but the knights of Cumberland suffered heavy losses. It is just my knights and men that I bring. How went today?"

He led me to his tent so that he could tell me in private. I knew that my men would be organised by Wulfric. Leofric and John would see to William. He was now a squire and he would have to suffer the rigours of camp life with the other young men.

"We had to force the ford and cross the river. They hit us then and we lost some men. Our horses forced them back up the hill but they are wickedly efficient with those axes and we lost some of our palfreys. The slope leading to their camp made it hard for us. We charged them time and time again. I think neither of us could fight more. Your arrival might just tip the balance."

"I brought my men this way so that we would be a surprise for them." He nodded. A servant brought me a flagon of ale and some stale bread and cured ham. I ate and drank gratefully. The food allowed me the time to think. Athelstan had always said that a good warrior used his brain and thought things through. "The enemy ships, they lie in the estuary?"

He swallowed his ham and said, "They moved into the estuary and anchored in the middle. We cannot get at them."

"And have they men aboard?"

"A skeleton crew of boys with a couple of guards on each."

I rose and went to the fire, "Aiden?" John looked up, "Find Aiden for me." He ran off.

When I returned to the Earl he said, "You have a plan?"

"No, I have an idea." Aiden appeared. "Go to the river. I need to know if the tide is on its way in or out."

He grinned, "I can tell you that without a journey my lord. It has just turned. It will be low tide by the middle of the night and then it will return."

"Good. Rest for I have a task for you and Dick later on."

The Earl looked at me curiously, "The tide?"

"Your arrival meant that they could not do as they did on the Lune; they could not draw their boats on the beach. They can

163

ride safely in the middle of the estuary but when the tide ebbs then they will be perilously close to grounding. There will only be a narrow channel which is safe for them. They cannot leave for their crews are in Preston. If we can fire them then the ones in Preston will have to try to save them or risk being stranded here. I am hoping that they try to save them and attack us."

"It is worth a try."

"I will find my men and give them instructions and then we will rest. We have travelled far and fought hard this day."

Wulfric and the rest of my men at arms were camped with Dick and his archers. They were a closely-knit group. I saw Wulfric give a wry smile and a nod to Dick as I approached. "I amuse you Wulfric?"

"No my lord but I had just said to Dick that you would have a trick up your sleeve and you appear, as though by magic."

I laughed, "You know me well! I have a plan which may save lives." I explained my ideas to them. I was gratified when they nodded approvingly. These men were no fools and if they thought it could succeed then it just might.

I made my way back to my tent which my squires had erected. The three of them waited anxiously. They helped me to undress and John took my sword. "I will have to put an edge on this, my lord. It saw hard service this day."

"Thank you John and thank you for that timely blow with the standard. It bought me time."

He looked pleased that I had remembered to thank him. He nodded to William, "See, young William, a squire might not ride in the first rank but we each play a part. Now go and fetch your father some warmed ale to help him to sleep."

The two of them hurried off as Leofric began to oil my mail. "Your son did well today my lord. He never flinched. His sword was not needed but it was ever ready."

"And I am grateful that you watch over him."

"Sir Hugh did it for us when we were beginning. Your son is younger than we were but he has great courage." He worked in silence and then asked, "We fight again tomorrow, my lord?"

"We may but I hope not." I did not need the warmed ale to sleep but I was grateful for it. As I lay on the ground I saw John lie across the entrance to the tent. If anyone came in the night he would be the first to know.

I woke myself. I had trained myself to wake up at a particular time. My three squires all rose as I did. "Get back to sleep. I need you not." The three of them gratefully snuggled into their blankets. It was a cold, cold night.

I wrapped my cloak around me and join my men by the edge of the camp. Aiden waited. We said not a word for none was necessary. He led us through the undergrowth and down the river bank. The ten ships lay in two long lines in the middle of a shrinking river. Leaving Dick and the archers to make their way across the mud I went with Wulfric and his men carrying the rafts they had constructed earlier. They were small but each was covered in kindling and firewood. When we were far enough upstream we walked to the water and placed the rafts in the river. The current was fast for the tide was still on the ebb. Using his flint, Wulfric set fire to the kindling which covered the rafts and then the ten tiny boats were pushed into the river.

We hurried back to Dick and the archers. I hoped that with so few on each ship there would be panic when the fire rafts headed for them. The ebbing tide meant that the river was narrow. There was nowhere safe for the ships to go. They would find it hard to fend off the rafts and if they did they would merely fend them into another drekar. Dick and his archers would pick off any that they saw.

We heard the cries from the watch on the ships when the rafts were spied. I saw the men on the two rearmost ships begin to hack their anchors in an attempt to flee for they were the closest to the danger. Two of the crew fell to Dick's arrows. A pale hand tried to saw through the rope from the protection of the strakes on the ship. One of the ship's anchors was severed and it leapt down the river like a greyhound released. The man who tried to man the steering board fell to an arrow and the rear of the drekar slewed around; the bow must have grounded. The stern struck the next boat and its dragon prow became entangled with the sheets on another. The river became blocked by the three ships. All of them cut their anchors and the floating dam drifted down toward the others.

All of us had become so engrossed in the tableau before us that we had forgotten the fire rafts. Now fully ablaze five of them struck the stricken three drekar. Fire is a sailor's worst enemy and with good reason. The fire licked around the drekar and then whooshed up the bone-dry ropes which led to the sail. The three ships began to burn. When their crew tried to douse the flames an arrow would hurl them into the river. Two of the drekar which were closest to the mouth of the estuary managed to raise their sails and hurry away from the fiery floating inferno which sailed down the river. With five ships afire and the other rafts still drifting down stream there was no escape. We heard the cries as the crews were burned alive. I watched as two ship's boys leapt in the sea and attempted to swim towards the two remaining long ships. In my heart I prayed that they would make it. I saw that the current was too strong and flailing arms which disappeared beneath the waters told me that they were drowned.

As we returned to the camp I saw the Earl and the rest of the knights watching the drekar slowly sink beneath the river. Sir

Edward nodded and pointed towards the castle in the distance. "Well that should give them something to think about."

I nodded, "It should indeed."

I managed to get an hour of sleep before I was woken by the sound of a horn. My squires were up before I was and while John ran to see what was amiss the other two held out my hauberk for me to don. John came back and said, "It is the Irish and the Norse, my lord, they are coming from the castle."

I had expected a reaction. From the walls of the walled town they would have seen the fire the night before and now, as daylight illuminated the river they would have seen that their means of escape was gone. They would be angry and they would assume that they had before them just the men of the Earl of Chester. My banners were hidden and our horses and camp were below the bank. We now had the element of surprise. The Earl of Chester had only fifteen archers and ten crossbows. We now had treble that number and it was they who would break the back of this mailed mass of marauding men.

By the time I was dressed in full armour the Earl had gathered his knights and they were mounted. "Sir Edward, keep our men hidden. John, stay with William and keep my banner here. Leofric you shall come with me."

I mounted Star and joined the Earl. I could see, in the distance, the lines of Irish and Norse as they emerged from the walls of the wooden town. It would take them some time to form the boar's head wedge I knew they would adopt.

"Well Alfraed, what do you suggest? Do we charge them?"

"We do not need to do that. We now have archers aplenty. If we line up your knights and men at arms it will appear like a thin line which they will easily break. We put our archers behind us

167

where they are hidden and I will send Sir Edward and my men to the west. They can attack their flank."

He nodded, "I like the plan." As he formed his men I sent Leofric to give Dick and Sir Edward their instructions. John and William joined me. "Keep my standard furled until I give the command."

"Aye my lord."

I saw that they formed a double wedge. Two warbands of Norse formed the horns and the Irish the head. They began beating their shields and chanting as they descended. I looked along the line and saw that the Earl had just ten knights and thirty men at arms. It must have looked like a perilously small number to the two hundred enemies who descended the slope intent upon revenge. Their ships were precious to them.

Dick and the archers appeared behind us. The Earl's crossbowmen took up a position on our right flank. Archers could release their arrows over us. Dick said, "Ready when you command my lord!"

The order to release would be mine. I knew my archers and knew their range. The others might not be as good and so I had to allow for that. I would give the order when they were two hundred paces from us. They would not charge until they were fifty paces. In those one hundred and fifty paces they would have to endure over three hundred arrows and bolts.

This was a well-led band for their shields were locked. They would need a charge of lances to halt them. With just forty odd of us we would have a difficult task but I knew that Sir Edward would be attacking their flank with the best warriors in the whole of the north.

"Release!"

The sky darkened as the arrows flew. The crossbows were more effective than normal for the Norse raised their shields to protect themselves from the descending arrows and the flatter trajectory of the crossbows tore through mail and into bodies. As the slaughter continued I turned to Ranulf. "They are your men, my lord. It is your order we wait."

He nodded. When the Norse were a hundred paces from us he said, "Charge!"

We would not be hitting the Norse line at much more than a trot but our long lances would strike their leading warriors before they could strike at our horses. The bolts and the arrows meant that the wedges were not solid and there were gaps. The Earl struck the leading Viking but there was a gap before me and my lance punched into the shoulder of a warrior who was not expecting the blow. As he fell backwards he broke the head from the lance and I threw the now useless wood like a javelin high into the air. It clattered amongst those at the rear.

Pulling back on Star's reins my stallion reared and smashed his hooves at the warriors before him. It afforded me the time to draw my sword. As he descended he crushed the knee of a Viking who fell screaming to the ground. As I spurred him on, he trampled the man to death. The death had made the others recoil and I swung my sword at warriors who were just looking to protect themselves from my horse. My sword struck the neck of a Viking who was too slow to raise his sword. I was now through the armoured Vikings and into the wild men of Ireland.

I heard a wail from my left and, glancing up, saw Sir Edward leading my knights and men at arms sweeping towards the enemy flank intent on causing as much damage as they could. I could not help feeling proud at the immaculately straight line they maintained. As I swept my sword at a distracted Irish warrior I heard the clash and crack of wood on metal and flesh. The screams of the dying mixed with the thunder of hooves and the exultant shouts of my men. Warriors can stand and suffer great casualties so long as they know they have a retreat. The unexpected attack from the flank meant that they were cut off from the safety of Preston's walls and the Irish broke. They ran in the only direction they could, the river.

Ranulf shouted, "Follow them!"

It was a good decision. Sir Edward and my men could finish off the Vikings but the Irish had to be destroyed before they disappeared into the woods and forests of the land to the north of Chester. We had enough brigands and bandits of our own without adding foreign foes too. I reined in Star a little for he would run until his heart gave out and we were catching the Irishmen. Had they had more sense they would have turned to make it hard for us but they did not. Unprotected backs were hacked, slashed and stabbed as we made a path of bodies to the river. A dozen or so managed to make the river and they threw themselves in. The tide had turned and they flailed in the water. Gradually they slipped beneath the black water. I saw four of them struggle ashore on the other side. The Earl of Chester reined in and spoke to one of his knights. They would scour the land for the last survivors.

We walked our horses back to the battlefield. As we approached Preston I saw Wulfric leave the gates of the town. He rode directly to us. I could see that something was amiss from his face. He bowed his head and spoke to us both, "My lords, they have slaughtered every man woman and child in the town. There are none left alive. They have even killed the cats and the dogs." He shook his head and I could hear, in his voice, that he was close to breaking.

I turned and saw the last ten Vikings standing back to back and chanting their death song. I turned Star and rode towards them. "Dick, fetch the archers and the crossbowmen."

Their leader shouted at me in Saxon. "Come from your horses, Normans, and fight us man to man. We will die but we will go to Valhalla!"

"You are nithings! You killed women and children. You deserve nothing!"

"That was the Irish!" He seemed indignant as though it was nothing to do with them.

"Then in the next life choose your allies better." I turned to Dick, who had arrayed his men in a half circle around one side. Crossbow bolts which missed their target could travel for long distances. My voice was cold as I shouted, "Kill them!"

My archers were at such a close range that the Vikings had no defence. When they held their shields up the bolts from the crossbows punched through mail. Their leader was the last to die. His body was covered in arrows and as he opened his mouth to curse me a bolt smashed through the opening and he fell dead.

We had suffered. Many were wounded. Our horses had suffered too and we camped at Preston for a week to recover and to bury the dead villagers. The Earl of Chester decided to burn the old town down. "I will have a new castle built and this one will be of stone. My squire served me well and I will knight him. This will be his manor."

I saw the looks on the faces of the other squires when the news was announced. It gave all of them the hope that they, too, would be elevated through an act of bravery. The move was a clever one. Even as we left, at the end of seven long days, the men of the Earl of Chester were beginning to build the castle. The heads of the last four Irishmen would adorn the gatehouse when it was finished. It would not be a finished castle but its new bones rose like a phoenix from the blackened remains of the charnel house which had been Preston. It would become stronger and the raiders would not have such an easy time of it the next time they came.

We headed north to make sure that Sir Gilbert and the men of the north had scoured the land for the last of the raiders. We would head home. I would see my family again. This time I would not need to leave so soon and, possibly, I might be at home when my wife gave birth.

Part 2

The War Within

Chapter 13

As we passed the scene of the battle of the Lune we saw the blackened remains of the bonfires used to burn the bodies. In future years the crops would be good from the bones and ash of the dead raiders. Some good would, at least, come from their raid. I was still angry at the slaughter of Preston. It is easy to be critical in hindsight but the Earl of Chester should have erected a stone castle before now. The temporary one his squire would erect was a start but that was all. It took two days to reach Carlisle. We stopped at Kendal and spent some time with the baron.

"I am grateful, my lord, for the advice you gave my son. He is young but I now have high hopes for him."

"He is a fine knight." I spread my arm to the north and west. "What of the people here? Do they have Viking blood?"

"They do. Many were slain when King William scoured the north but there are many hidden valleys and caves. They survived but they are ever suspicious of us. Between Carlisle and here there is little hospitality."

"It is dangerous?"

"No, my lord. They are not so foolish as to attack us but they harbour legends and stories of heroes who will come to save them."

I was intrigued, "Who are these heroes?"

"They speak of a King Coel and his warlord, Lann, who drove the Saxons from this land and then disappeared beneath a cave in Wales. It is said they sleep there with Merlin the wizard and one day will rise from the dead to reclaim this land."

"You are Christian; you cannot believe such legends, surely?"

"It matters not if I believe it or not they do. They are Christian but they have some pagan beliefs. They speak of wolf warriors who prowl at night and can change into wolves."

"You have wolves here; perhaps they mistake them for warriors."

"King William appointed a young lord of the manor at Coniston in the north west of the land. It was said wolves howled and he and his five men at arms and squires were found dead."

"They were killed by wolves?"

"No, my lord, by blades, and my father found footprints there but even though he searched for weeks no trace of their killers was ever found. He hanged five local men but it did no good." I cocked my head quizzically, "The hangmen were found dead and the wolves were heard again. I leave that lake to the locals. We have had no trouble since."

As we rode north the next day I pondered his words. I did not believe the story of the men who could change into wolves. This was the work of men who could make the sound of a wolf. If I ruled this land I would hunt them down and end the threat. This was not my land and I had problems enough at home.

We did notice the land warming as we neared Carlisle. In the ten days we had been away spring had decided to erupt. It was a good sign. We were not destined to get home soon, however. In the short time we had been away the Scots had decided to make raids in the absence of Sir Gilbert. With so many of his household knights fallen he begged me to stay until he had finished the castle. I sympathised with him. The Baron of Kendal had shown me that the hold on this side of the land was tenuous. We stayed in the castle and I had my knights take their conroi north of the river to intimidate the Scots. I gave orders that they were not to attack unless they were attacked first. However, any stray animals were to be collected and brought back.

The stay gave me the chance to help Sir Gilbert divide the profits from the attack. The Vikings always carried their treasure with them and we had a fine collection of gold and silver arm bands as well as many precious jewels. The mail was always useful if only to be melted down and reused. With the treasure form Preston all of my knights, men at arms and archers were much richer. Even John son of Leofric would be happy. I was also keen for the horses to recover. We had treated them harshly and the spring growth allowed them to recover some of their vigour.

Sir Tristan was the one who engaged the Scots. While patrolling close to Booths Castle he was challenged by a young Scottish knight to single combat. It was a mistake for Tristan had been trained by both Edward and Wulfric. He returned with him and his warhorse while his squire went for ransom.

I took the opportunity of speaking with the young man, who was a cousin of Walter Comyn, the man who had placed a price upon my head. Sir Robert Comyn was a fiery youth who hated the Normans and wanted the traditional lands of Scotland to be ruled by King David. Even so we managed to speak for he respected me and my name.

"The land you claim was English. King William conquered it and I have read that in the time before the Romans it belonged to what is now England."

"It does not matter we held it before the Bastard came and we will take it again."

I could see that he would not be persuaded and so I spoke with him of the politics of the land of Scotland. "Does the King have support from all his lords?"

His eyes narrowed, "Are you trying to get me to be disloyal, my lord?"

I shook my head, "I have no doubt that you are loyal to your king. I can see that you are a true patriot. I am thinking of others who covet the throne."

He relaxed a little. "There are some. It is said the De Brus family who have lands in England and Scotland has ambitions to be the ruling clan. And then there is the Balliol family. They have some claims to the throne." He shook his head, "Not very strong ones but…"

"Sir Barnard is a friend of your cousin is he not?"

The young man was naïve and did not see beneath the question. "He is a different branch of the family."

Different or not I suspected that Hugh's neighbour was straddling the border with a foot in each camp. "Can your family afford the ransom?"

"We are not poor, they will pay!"

"I doubt it not but perhaps next time you will only challenge someone whom you can defeat."

I saw in his face that he was embarrassed that he had lost, "Sir Tristan looked young."

"He is but he has fought with me for many years."

"They say that you are the most dangerous knight in the north of England."

There was no answer to that, "Any knight can be dangerous as you discovered with Sir Tristan. Take my advice young man and become the best knight that you can be before you challenge others."

He reflected on that and a couple of days later, when the ransom arrived, he thanked me for my advice. "One day, my lord, I will be ready to meet you lance to lance and then you should watch out."

"I will, my fiery young friend. You may be an enemy but I admire your spirit."

With the castle almost finished and the border quiet we took Sir Tristan's ransom and began our journey home. We had been away for longer than I would have hoped but not as long as we might have. I looked forward to seeing my land burgeoning with new crops, animals and people. I stayed with Sir Hugh to break up the journey and left the next day with just Sir Tristan and Sir Harold for company. I did not cross the river at my ferry but at Yarm where Sir Richard had constructed a wooden bridge. The river was narrow and so long as only two riders crossed at the same time it was safe. If trouble came it would not require much work to demolish it.

When we reached Yarm, I knew that there was trouble ahead. Lady Anne had a troubled look upon her face. Sir Richard thought the problem lay with his manor. "What has happened?"

She came to me. "We had a message ten days since that the pestilence had come to Stockton. Your good wife sent a message that we were not to come close until it had been eliminated."

"And have you had word since?"

"No, we obeyed her and to be truthful we feared the worst."

"You were correct to listen to her. She is a wise woman. We will go home and find out the situation. Sir Richard I leave William in your care."

"I want to come with you! It is my mother and sister!"

"And I am not only your father but also your master. You will obey me."

Lady Anne smiled, "Your mother will be happier knowing that you are here, young William. Come."

Lady Anne was a close friend of my wife and was almost as an aunt to William. He did as he was commanded. "I will send word Sir Richard."

"It will turn out for the best."

I shrugged, "We are in God's hands now."

Those last few miles were torture. Neither Harold nor Tristan could offer me comfort. They were too young. My mind was filled with pictures of our people dying of the awful disease. It could come in many forms. Sometimes it was red pustules which covered the bodies. At others it was a heavy fever. It seemed like a punishment from God in whatever form it came. The contagion could spread like wildfire. I prayed that my wife had locked herself in the tower and sat it out. I knew that she would not. She was too kind.

I said goodbye to my knights some three miles from home and led my men towards the western gate. The land seemed empty. Where were they all? I saw that my banner still fluttered from the south west tower. That meant nothing. The gates of the town were open.

"Aiden, come with me. Wulfric take charge and keep the rest of the men out here." He looked to argue. "If the pestilence and the plague are still within then you have to protect us." He nodded. As Aiden and I rode forward I turned and said, "I bring you for you are the swiftest rider. If there is trouble then obey my commands."

I was relieved when I saw that smoke still came from the huts. Alf came from his hut. He looked pale but he walked. He held his hand up when he was twenty paces from me. "Thank God you have come, my lord. We have the plague."

"And yet you live."

"That was by the will of Lady Adela. When the plague came it was in the castle. She blocked the doors and told us to stay until she emerged. She charged me with sending a message to the other manors. I sent my son and told him not to return. We all became ill but few have died in the town. Had an enemy come then we would all have been taken for we could not fight both the disease and an enemy. Father Matthews insisted upon going into the castle."

"And have you heard from the castle?"

"There are still people alive within the walls but we have seen none on the battlements."

"I needs must enter. You say there is no disease here any longer?"

179

"No, my lord. We were sick and none ate for days. The tanner's daughter died over ten days ago and none have died since. Some did not even get the disease. They cared for the ones who did. I had the men clear the poisoned matter we produced from the town and pour it into the river beyond the town walls. The river will take it to the sea. It is only in the last three days that we have eaten."

"There were no deaths here then?"

"Only the old and the babies. That was to be expected. Death always comes to those first. Oh and one young girl, Alice the daughter of James the Tanner. We did not bury them but burned their bodies. We wanted to rid the land of the disease." He frowned. "We smelled burning bodies in the castle, my lord. I know not who they were."

"Aiden, fetch Wulfric. Tell him to care for the town. Alf, I need a ladder."

"You would enter even though there is disease there?"

"If it were your family Alf...."

"Then I would go too. I pray you wrap something around your mouth my lord."

"Fetch the ladder. If I am fated to die then a piece of cloth will do nothing for me will it?"

He fetched the ladder. I took off my helmet and my cloak. I turned as Wulfric and my men rode in. Alf held the ladder and I climbed it to mount the walls. I felt like an attacker yet my sword would not help me against this enemy. It was a disease and was invisible.

At the top I looked down into my bailey. It was eerily empty. I descended to the gate of the keep. There were no horses within the stables for we had them all. I wondered about my

180

falcons and the falconers. I almost struck myself. Why was I thinking of hawks when my family was in danger? I saw the ash from the bonfires they had used to burn the bodies. It seemed a pathetically small amount; perhaps few had died. As I walked across the silent bailey I wondered where everyone was.

"Hello! Adela!"

I heard a thin voice from the servant's quarters. It was next to the bottom floor of my keep. I opened the door and was struck by the smell of disease. Father Matthew was attempting to rise from a chair by the table. "Stay, Father."

"The Lord has answered my prayers and you have returned. I must speak with you for my time is short and I have not long to live."

"Where is everyone? Where is my family?"

"The ones who live yet are in the Great Hall. Most of those who died are burned." It was maddening that he did not tell me what I wish to know and yet I could not rush him. He had the smell of death about him. "It was your new men at arms who brought the disease; the ones who came from the lands of Muslim. Your daughter played with them and she became ill first and then the first of them, Will's Son, went into a deep sleep from which he never recovered. Your daughter died the same night." I felt my heart sink to my boots. My daughter was dead. He pointed to a small pot. "Her ashes lie in there. They should be placed in the church. There are niches at the side of the altar for urns such as this."

"You planned well for your church, Father."

"Aye and I hoped to see it filled with you and your family. Now it will just contain our ashes." He shook his head as thought to clear it. "The Lady Adela knew that drastic measures had to be taken. She closed the gates and forbade all from leaving. I joined

181

her. Others began to show symptoms. It was the new warriors and some of Erre's men who succumbed first. They had lived close by each other. Your falconers and some of the slaves were the next to die. One threw herself into the river rather than suffer. Your wife and I tended to them. I knew of a potion which made them sleep. We gave it to them all save your wife and me. None died after we gave it to them. I think God was able to care for them while they slept."

I did not think that God had done anything of the sort. It was my wife and the priest who had saved them. God had stood idly by and done nothing to save my daughter. My innocent daughter had died and yet those evil men like Stephen of Blois lived. There was no justice.

"Where is my wife?"

He hesitated, "She died three days since. I gave her the last rites and she is in heaven as is your daughter. She lies on your bed. I could not carry her down to burn here. I had no strength in my arms. It has taken me all my time to minister to the sick and to keep them asleep." He shook his head, "They will be waking soon."

I wanted to scream and to rant against God but the Earl in me made me ask other questions. "And the disease; will I now get it?"

He shook his head. "That is how I know I am to die. It took some days for the disease to take the men who had not been to the Muslim lands. Those in the town who became ill only had the briefest of contact with the warriors. I do not think I will spread the disease but you must burn our bodies and our clothes to be safe. If you want to be certain then do not go out of here for ten days. I became ill ten days ago."

"And yet you continued to help those who were sick."

"It was God's will. I have served the town and I have served you. God used me as his tool. I am content."

"But I am not for he took my wife and my child."

"Do not berate God. Your wife knew she was dying. There is a letter for you. It is in her hands."

His breathing became laboured. He grabbed hold of his cross.

"Can I do anything for you, Father?"

"You can pray for my soul for…"

He pitched forward and died. He was a good man. I am not certain I could have done what he had done. Could I have ministered to those with this pestilence? He had entered a castle filled with a deadly disease. He could have stayed outside the wall and lived. As much as I wanted to see my wife I knew I had a duty to the living. It was with a heavy heart that I went to the Great Hall. It lay just below my chambers and I could almost feel the presence of my wife.

My household, warriors, servants, Steward and slaves all lay on straw laid out on the floor. Some were asleep but I saw Erre prop himself up on one arm and try to rise. "Stay on the floor, Erre, I command you. You are still weak."

He shook his head, "I am sorry, my lord. This is my fault. If I had not brought those new warriors into the castle then none of this would have happened."

He was right, of course, but it was not his fault. He had only done what I asked of him. "It is not your fault. Father Matthews has just died. I will get you all some food but then those who can, will need to help me. We have to remain isolated for ten days." He nodded. "Keep everyone here until I return."

I went up the stairs with a heavy heart. I knew what I would find. It would not be a surprise but it would hurt me. I knew that with each step I took. I opened the door of my chamber and saw that she lay with her arms folded and her letter on her chest. The room smelled of death. Her body had lain here for some time. I took the letter and put it in my surcoat. I would read that letter later. I leaned over and kissed her cold dead lips. "Farewell my wife. I am sorry I was not a better husband. You were the best wife a man could ever have had. Look after our child, Hilda, in heaven and I swear that William will be loved twice as much." It was the silence and her cold hands which made me break down and burst into tears. It was not manly nor was it knightly but I was a man and I had loved Adela. I had left her for war so many times and she had never complained and now she lay dead.

I stood and beat the walls with my fists until they bled, "Why did you take her! There is evil in the world and she was pure and innocent! You are not a just God you are worse than the Devil! He does not give hope only to dash it away! From this day I renounce you!"

I was angry but at that moment I meant what I said and my life entered a dark and lonely period when I was not the man who had married Adela. I became something else. I became something I did not like.

I went down to the kitchen again. I moved Father Matthew from the chair and laid him in the passage outside. His body was already stiffening. I found the potion which Father Matthew had used and I found some vegetables. I chopped them and put them in a pot with water from the well. The fire was still glowing and I relit it. When the kindling caught I added more logs and put the pot over it. I emptied some of the potion into it. I had not been told the dose- I guessed. When it was bubbling away I took out the letter.

Dearest Alfraed,

If you are reading this letter then I am dead. I am sorry.

Our daughter is dead. God must have wanted her badly to take such a precious angel. I tried to save her but I failed. I hope that some of our people survive. I did my best and Father Matthew has been a saint. He could so easily have stayed without but if any are saved then it is due to his skill and care.

I know you will be angry with me but I believe that it is God's will that kept me here. If I had left then the disease might have spread. I believe that Stockton will be safe and it will just be those in the castle who die.

I pray that you and William will return safely from the wars. I know you will for you are the finest knight in Christendom and I was honoured to be your wife. I hope that when I am in heaven I can meet your father, Faren and Athelstan for I yearn to tell them of your glory. Our daughter and unborn child will watch with me from on high and we will wait for you.

Farewell my husband,

I will love you in death as I did in life,

Adela

I read it four times. My tears made some of the letters run but I knew it by heart by then. There was a movement behind me

185

and I whipped my head around. It was Erre. "What are you doing here?"

"I am well, my lord. I came to help."

I nodded, "You are right. I have made some soup. We will take it to those who are awake. Then we must burn Father Matthew and then my wife."

His face fell, "Lady Adela is dead?" I nodded, "I am so sorry my lord. I have caused more trouble than enough. I should leave."

"No Erre. You must stay for Lady Adela gave her life so that you and the others should all live."

I had but three of my Varangians left: Erre, Olaf Leather Neck and Sven the Rus. All my efforts to make us stronger had had the opposite effect. We were now weaker. I knew that I had to speak with Wulfric; he would be worrying. I was trapped in a charnel house but I was still Earl of Cleveland and I still had responsibilities.

"Watch over the others whilst I go to the gate."

I reached the gatehouse and saw Wulfric and Dick speaking with Alf and Ethelred in the town. There was visible relief on their faces when they saw me. Alf said, "Is all well within, my lord?"

Shaking my head I said, "No but the worst appears over." I hesitated for saying my next words would set them in stone. I would not wake from this nightmare. "Father Matthew and Lady Adela are both dead. The next fire you see will be consuming their flesh. Send to Norton and ask Father Peter to come. We have need of him. I want riders to go to Sir Edward and Sir Richard to inform them of this disaster."

Wulfric cocked his head to one side, "And you my lord, what of you?"

"Father Matthew said that in ten days I will either be dead or the plague will have died out. Until then I stay here. There are many still alive within these walls and that is due entirely to Father Matthew and my wife."

Alf nodded, "We will say prayers of thanks in the church." He pointed to the newly finished church. Father Matthew had not even managed to hold an Easter service in it.

"We are short of food. Bring baskets and put them before the gate. Erre and I will hoist them up."

Wulfric smiled, "Erre lives?"

"He does but only Olaf and Sven remain. The new men brought this plague from the land of the Muslim."

I saw all four of them cross themselves. Ethelred said, "Then I know how the plague came to the town. One of the new men lay with the daughter of the Tanner. I think they survived because of their work. That concoction to tan the leather would kill any disease."

"Then I will return to my Hall. Wulfric, Command in my absence." I saw Aiden. "Your falconers are dead but the hawks live."

His face fell. "They were good men. I would be grateful if you would care for them until I can tend to them. I will put food for them in the basket."

As I returned to my Hall I wondered if I could ever be happy here again. Erre came towards me, "They have all been fed my lord. Although they are weak they wish to help."

"Then they can prepare the funeral pyre."

"Aye my lord." I turned and went to the stables. The hay had all been taken for bedding and just the two hawks remained. I could see that they had been fed and watered. That had to be Father Matthew. He had been a kind man. He loved all creatures. I saw that he had left two dead mice for the birds. The two birds looked agitated and so I spoke softly to them as I had seen Aiden do. "There, there my beauties. Fear not the night is almost over and soon Aiden will be with you." I held the mice out and they took them with their beaks and then held them in their talons so that they could tear the flesh from them. It did not take long. When I had watered them, I stroked them on the back of the head as I had seen the falconers do. They seemed calmer.

As I left I understood Aiden a little better for I felt more at peace. The two birds were survivors. They would be stronger. Erre and the others would be stronger and closer too. The pyre was built and the bailey empty. They had worked quickly. I went to speak with them. As I entered my hall everyone stood and bowed. I looked at their drawn pale faces. These were my people. I could not give up. Adela would not have wanted it so.

John, my steward, approached, "We are all sorry for your loss, my lord. Each of us here owes our lives to the Lady Adela and we will honour her memory."

"We will burn their bodies tomorrow. I hope that Father Peter will be here for I would know the words I need to say to send …" I found myself becoming filled with grief; it was almost too much to bear. I had to be strong. I was the lord of the manor. My feelings had to remain hidden. My father had taught me that. I coughed and it helped. "We have to stay within these walls for nine more days. Father Matthew said that if I survived ten days from the first contact then I did not have the disease." I saw the shock on their faces. That thought had not occurred to them. "If I become ill then you must give me the potion Father Matthew left. Erre knows where it is."

John the Steward said, "You should not have come, my lord. You have put yourself in danger."

I smiled, "It was meant to be. Had I not come then Father Matthews would have died without telling me what I needed to know. I do not feel ill and I believe that I will be spared but if not then Erre and John are in charge. I have left Wulfric to command the town." Smiling I said, "We all owe it to Lady Adela and Father Matthew to be better people after this. They have given us a new life and today you are all reborn. That, in itself, is a miracle."

When they smiled I knew I had said the right thing but in my heart, I felt like a hypocrite for I did not believe my own words. They had new lives but God had killed my wife, my unborn child and my daughter. I would find it hard to forgive.

We carried the bodies and laid them on the two pyres. Their ashes would be kept separate. My wife's servants and ladies used cochineal to give her some colour and arranged her clothes so that she looked as beautiful as ever. I slept through sheer exhaustion for there was still much to do.

When we rose, the next day, it was with a heavy heart. I went with Erre to the gate. There was a host awaiting us. Father Peter was there with Wulfric, Sir Edward and Sir Richard. All looked sombre. Baskets lay at the foot of the wall. "Throw the ropes to Erre and he will haul them up." While he did so I spoke with Father Peter. "We will have to burn my wife and Father Matthew today. We cannot bury them for…"

Father Peter nodded, "God will understand."

"I do not have the words, Father."

"When I see the smoke rise then I will know and I will say the words. Their souls will go to heaven."

I nodded. "Then we will begin."

When I reached the two pyres I saw that the women had found wild flowers which they had strewn over Adela's body. Erre handed me a torch. I saw that John held a third. It was the hardest thing I had ever done. I plunged the torch into the kindling beneath the logs we had used. The others did the same. My servants lit Father Matthew's pyre. The wood crackled and smoked and then the flames leapt up to consume first the wood and then the clothes. The women looked away but I watched in horror as my wife burned before my eyes. The image would ever live with me. It was not until that moment that I realised I would never see my wife again nor speak to her. She and my daughter were gone forever. I felt my eyes filling with tears.

The column of smoke rose and I heard chanting from beyond my walls. The smoke seemed to surround me and consume me. I felt strangely dizzy. Perhaps I was over tired. I had slept but an hour at most and I had not eaten. I continued to stare at the fire. I began to cough. It seemed that I was light as a feather for I felt as though I could float. I looked up and the sky began to spin and then all went black.

Chapter 14

I dreamed.

I rode Star but his hooves were not on the ground. He rode on clouds. My armour was now as black as night and matched the sheen of my mighty steed. Below me I saw a mighty host and they were fighting. I saw the Empress Matilda and she was assailed on all sides by knights wearing red surcoats. Rolf and his Swabians laid about them with their swords but no matter how many they slew more appeared as though sorcery was involved. I heard my wife's voice as she said, in my ear, "Go my husband. You are a Knight of the Empress. You serve her still!" I swung Star's head around and plunged towards the ground. His mighty hooves clattered and crashed into the red coated warriors. My sword rang against metal as I carved a path to the Empress. I hoisted her on to Star and we galloped up into the sky away from the death and away from the danger. We went higher and higher into the sky. The sky went from blue to black and then the stars disappeared and all was black. All was silent.

I opened my eyes and saw John and Erre staring at me with fear on their faces. I raised myself up. "Have I been ill?"

Erre said, "We thought you were dead my lord."

"How long was I out?"

"It is but two hours since we burned the bodies of your wife and Father Matthew. You fell to the ground and lay still. It was as though someone had struck you a blow. John said you breathed still and we brought you here to your chamber. We watched as you fought."

"I fought?"

"You waved your arm as though holding a sword and it seemed to me you were in a battle. Then you suddenly went still and lay there. We were afraid you had died and joined the Lady Adela."

John asked, fearfully, "Do you feel ill, my lord?"

"I felt… I know not how I felt but I dreamed." I swung my legs over the side of the bed. "And I know what we must do. We will not be idle. We will burn all of the bedding and the clothes of the dead. I will ask the villagers for clean clothes and we will burn the clothes you all wear."

They both nodded. I think they were grateful to have something to occupy them. "And the ashes of Father Matthew and Lady Adela?"

I pointed to the small pot containing Hilda's ashes. "My wife put my daughter in a pot. Find two good pots for Father Matthew and my wife. When the ashes are cold we will put them within. Father Matthew had niches in the church. They will lie within sanctified ground when we leave this place."

We busied ourselves.

I told no one of my dream. Even to this day that is my secret. I keep it buried deep within me. It did give me hope. God had deserted me but my wife had not and she had shown me what I needed to do. I was to protect the Empress. First, I had to survive the next days and then I had to make my men and my castle as strong as I could for I had to visit Anjou and Normandy. I would tell the others that I needed to visit with the King. They would understand that. The dream had been a premonition of danger. The Empress needed me. The spirit of my wife had told me that. As I look back, now, I can see that my soul was lost at this time. It all made perfect sense to me then as I led my people to scour the disease form my castle.

It took two days to clean and cleanse the castle. There was joy from my town that I lived and had not succumbed to the disease. It became a routine for me to parade my walls each morning where my men could see that I was alive and well. I took to running around the walls. I enjoyed the exercise and it gave me the chance to view my lands. Spring was well upon us and I saw green shoots spreading in the distance. Fields were filled with cattle and sheep. But for the disaster of the plague it would have been a happy time. Each time I appeared at the walls Father Peter would bless me. Those who were around would drop to their knees and pray for those within the walls.

When we ate, all together now, in my Great Hall, I saw all watching me carefully for signs of disease but there were none. I felt hale and hearty. There was a sickness but it was deep within me and I hid it from all.

When I woke on the tenth morning after the death of Father Matthew it was like being born again. I had not been stricken. In fact, if anything I felt stronger. I had worked during the ten days and eaten frugally. I would not waste my life. My wife's words which had come as she was ascending to heaven had made that clear to me. I strode to my gates and flung them open. There was a veritable host outside. I saw a mixture of anticipation and fear upon their faces. The disease had been contained within my walls; was it now outside? I walked towards Father Peter. In my arms I carried the pots containing the ashes of my family. We walked into the church. Behind me John carried the pot with Father Matthew's. We laid the two pots before the altar. I dropped to my knees before the priest and bowed my head. Silence reigned until Father Peter blessed me.

There was a long silence. Father Peter spoke a prayer in Latin and then led the congregation out. Everyone left but I stayed there. Father Peter returned to me. "You have suffered a great loss my son but it is God's will."

I turned and almost spat the words out. "There is no God! A benevolent God would have spared my wife and child who were innocent and blameless!"

"Those words would be blasphemous enough anywhere but here in this holy place they are a sin of such magnitude I can barely find the words to berate you."

He spoke quietly but it was as though my father was there chastising me in his own quiet way for an adolescent misdemeanour. I hung my head. I do not know why I had said what I had. Then I knew why. We were in the church. This was where we were closest to God. I had just lashed out in anger.

"God works in mysterious ways, my son. We cannot know his purpose. At the last judgement all will be made clear but until that time we are in his hands and we must trust to him. Do you see into the future? Do you know what is around the corner?" I shook my head. "Then do not abandon your faith because you are hurt. Think of all those who have lost loved ones before. Then you did not doubt the existence of God, why now?"

He was right. I was used to fighting enemies who had weapons. I had revenged myself on the killers of my father and Athelstan. I could not kill a disease. "I am sorry father, forgive me, I beg of you."

He shook his head. "The blasphemy is too great. I alone cannot forgive you. You need to show God that you are truly repentant. You must make a pilgrimage."

"York? Winchester?"

"No, it must be to the tomb of the Conqueror in Caen. I would say Rome but I fear the King would disapprove of such a perilous journey. You must go to Caen."

I nodded. I had already planned on visiting Anjou and Normandy. Perhaps this was meant to be. I was happy to be thus ordered.

Raising me to my feet he nodded, "We will put these urns safely within the church and then celebrate your recovery! Once that it is over you shall beg forgiveness at the Abbaye aux Hommes. There God can forgive you."

We did celebrate. Aiden and my archers had gone hunting and we held a huge feast in the open area before Ethelred's hall. I was assaulted by question after question. My son William asked the most. He had chafed at the bit whilst in Yarm and he refused to leave my side. Sir Richard told me that he had cried for two days when he heard of his mother's death. Since that time, he had put all of his energy into becoming a better warrior. I wondered at that. Would his grief rise to the surface at some later stage? Sir Edward said little but his constant stare made me wonder what was going on inside his head. He never said what had occupied his mind but he knew me as well now as any man and if any could divine my thoughts it was him.

John, my Steward, had told me there were many cases to be heard and so, at the end of the feast I stood. Unlike most of those before me I was almost sober, "I will hold sessions two days hence. Let all cases be brought hither. Then I intend to make a pilgrimage to the tomb of the Conqueror in Normandy. I intend to give thanks in the Abbaye Aux Hommes for our survival."

I received nods from all save Sir Edward. Like me he had drunk little.

As I bade farewell to our guests Sir Edward stayed close by. "It is a little far to go and give thanks. What of Durham, York or even Winchester?"

"Father Peter has ordered me to go there and besides it suits my purpose for I need to speak with the King." I lowered my voice. "I have suspicions of some of the lords. I think there may be plots."

"Barnard de Balliol?"

"He is one such. You know of what I speak." He nodded. "If our enemies think I am going to speak with the King then they might try to stop me. This way it is seen as an understandable journey which will arouse no suspicion."

He smiled, "I thought it was your heart which led you."

I smiled back. There are layers of deception. I had not lied to Sir Edward and, indeed, told him more than I would say to any other but it was not the whole truth. I pointed to the church. "That is where my heart lies."

"She was a good lady."

"She was more than I deserved and I now know that I should have been a better husband. I will now try to be a better lord. This ordeal will have one positive outcome, at least."

It took two weeks to put the affairs of the manor in order. I arranged for two ships to take us to Caen. Olaf arranged that. I took my squires, Wulfric and ten men at arms along with Dick and ten archers. The rest I left to serve Erre. He was determined to live up to the Lady Adela and her sacrifice. I knew that he would defend my home with his life. He and John promised to make my castle a home once more and to make the defences the best in the land. I knew that they would do as they promised and I had no worries about my valley and my town. We set sail for Normandy at the end of May. I did not know then that the next few months would change my life forever.

As we sailed south beneath a bright blue sky and a fresh north westerly blowing us south I could have foreseen the dangers that were ahead. I had been so consumed with the problems in the west and north as well as my own personal tragedies that I had forgotten the struggle in the west. Olaf was a well-travelled captain and one of our oldest friends. He brought us news and gossip from the mainland to which we now travelled. Wulfric, Dick and I would stand by him at the stern rail. William practised with John and Leofric.

Olaf was an easy man to talk with. He had sailed the seas these many years and knew us all well. He was not a knight, he was a friend. "Since the death of William Clito, Louis the Fat has been without allies. I have heard that he seeks an alliance with William of Aquitaine."

I looked at Olaf and the surprise must have shown on my face, "I know the Duke and his daughter Eleanor. Why would he make an alliance with Louis the Fat?"

"For the same reason that your King Henry married the Empress Matilda to Geoffrey of Anjou. He has no sons. Who will protect his lands, his people and his daughter when he dies?"

It made sense but it disappointed me. I had liked Eleanor and her father. I knew that she would not like to be used as a pawn in this game of thrones. Louis was a plotter. "Does this strengthen the French?"

"Aye, for there is much unrest in Maine and Normandy. King Henry is no longer a young man. His brother still rots in the Tower and there are some who would overthrow the King and put his brother on the throne as a figurehead."

"You seem to know about these things."

He laughed and tapped his nose. "I come from Norway and I am no Viking. I am trusted for my country has no ambitions. I fetch and carry for all sides. I hear things. Men do not think that a simple sailor can speak many languages. I listen." I wondered at his loyalty. He saw my look and added, "Ethelred and Alf are my kinsmen. Stockton is as close to a home as I have. I swear that I would never betray you, my lord."

I was relieved but Wulfric growled, "And if you ever did I would gut you like a fish."

Olaf nodded, "You need not threaten me Wulfric. I have Norse blood and I am never foresworn." He took the hammer of Thor from beneath his kyrtle. "I keep a foot in both camps."

"There will be war then?"

He lowered his voice. "I know not for certain but Eustace of Breteuil, the king's son in law and his illegitimate daughter, Juliana have been seen in Blois close to the border with the Île-de-France." Blois again; its threat never went away. "And there is more, the two families of brigands from Puset and Coucy, have now become barons. They too are close to the borders. They plague not only the French but the lands of Blois and Normandy. Their power has grown and every vagabond and renegade knight flocks to their banners for they promise great treasure and riches."

Wulfric nodded, "I have heard of them. Thomas Lord of Coucy is a cruel man. He enjoys gouging out eyes and hanging men by their testicles. Hugh, Lord of Puset is almost as bad."

"Hugh died in the Holy Land but his son, Roger, is cut from the same cloth as his father. And the Lord of Coucy has lost none of his appetite for cruelty; he seems to try to outdo himself with his bestiality and violence."

"Does the King know of this?"

"He has spies and I assume that he does," He shrugged. I know of gossip from those who work at the lower end; what the lords and kings do is beyond my reach." He smiled, "You are the noblest man that I know. If you do not know…"

"Thank you, Olaf." I stared ahead to the coast of Flanders, "And where is the King?"

"Rouen."

"The Empress and her husband?"

"They are at Angers."

Then it would be unlikely that I would see the Empress. It had been in my mind to visit with her but as her husband was reconciled with her it was hard to see how. My dream had suggested danger. Perhaps it was danger for the King but the Empress had been there and part of it. Now that I knew she was far away then I could do as I had told Edward. I would go to the tomb of the Conqueror and then visit with the King. I could hold my head high for I had not lied. I felt a sense of relief.

We did not sail all the way down the Orne to Caen. The water levels in the river were low due to poor rain in the spring. Instead we offloaded at Ouistreham which lay at its mouth. It was a short journey to Caen from there. We spent two days camped in the dunes by the sea to allow our horses to recover from the journey. We rode them in the sea for it strengthened their legs. I sent Dick to the castle at Caen to announce our arrival. Gone were the days when I could be ignored. I was now an Earl.

The citadel at Caen was magnificent. So long as it was garrisoned then Normandy was safe. I knew the castellan well and he was pleased to see me. "What brings you here so unexpectedly my lord?"

I told him of my loss and he was genuinely affected. I had spoken to him of my family on my earlier visits. "The tomb of the Conqueror is a good place to pray for the souls of your family."

"And I have heard of disquiet on the borders."

"Word has reached England then?"

199

"No, but it has reached me."

"The King is aware of the danger and he is gathering an army. He has summoned his allies from the south to head through Blois to deal with this while it is in its early stages. He will return here within a few days. It is timely that you have arrived for he often speaks of your skill. It is a pity that you did not bring your household knights."

"I came to pray and not to fight but we will give a good account of ourselves. It will make a change to fight knights and not the Welsh, the Norse and the Irish."

The castellan shuddered, "They are horse killers all!"

I went with my squires and William to the Cathedral. The tomb was plain and reflected what I knew of Henry's father. He had carved out a kingdom for himself against all the odds. I was doing the same. It was not a kingdom but it was my land. I prayed but the prayers were for my wife and daughter. I did not thank God for I had nothing to thank him for. I was still angry with him. At that moment I expected to spend eternity burning in hell but I cared not. Despite my angry heart, the peace and the darkness brought me some relief from my turmoil. The prayers of other penitents were like a heartbeat in the church. It felt alive.

The King arrived two days later. He was surprised to see me but I detected pleasure in the surprise. He put his arm around my shoulder as he led me to his private chambers, "I sense a story here, young Cleveland. Tell me all."

I began by telling him of my personal tragedy and then, after he had expressed his sympathy, I told him about the rumours I had heard. My words gave him cause for concern. I could see that in his face. "Balliol and Comyn eh? That is not a good alliance. I should have taken Gospatric's English lands from him before now." He smiled at me, "I am pleased you are here. Will you fight alongside me? We have a nest of vipers to remove."

"I am ever your servant, your majesty."

"Good. We just await Geoffrey of Anjou and then we can leave. It will be good to have two young cockerels fighting alongside an old warhorse like me."

I knew when to play the fawning courtier, "You are coming into the prime of your life, my lord. There is plenty of life left in you yet."

"Perhaps, but I now feel each stone in the road and every blow I take takes longer to recover. Still it is kind of you to say so."

Count Geoffrey and the Angevin knights arrived a day later. They made a colourful display. It must have been strange for the King's knights for until a few years ago they had fought against these very knights. When I saw the litters, I knew that Matilda had also accompanied her husband. That made sense for the Count would have had to leave many men to guard her in his castle in Angers otherwise. My heart raced and I felt guilty. My wife had just died and I was full of grief yet when Matilda came near I forgot her. I was a poor knight and a bad man.

Geoffrey of Anjou was introduced to me and I could not help thinking that my squires had more maturity than he did. He seemed to me an arrogant young man who was full of himself. He barely acknowledged any of us who met him despite the war scars of many of the King's household knights. Even the King himself seemed beneath him. I saw the embarrassed look on the Empress' face and I knew that the reconciliation had not gone well. I smiled and bowed. I was actually pleased that he did not even notice me. He strutted around as though he was the most important man in the room. The slight frown on the King's face told me that he did not like it. He was in a difficult position. This was not only his son in law this was the man whose lands protected Normandy's southern border.

201

The King regained control of the room by raising his hand. The last to finish speaking was Geoffrey. "Now that we are all here it is time you knew the purpose of this campaign. We ride to our eastern borders to punish the bandits who prey upon our people and to defeat Eustace of Breteuil once and for all."

Geoffrey laughed, "If they are the only problem then I will quash them with the knights of Anjou alone. I had thought we went to invade France."

The King waved a hand as though ridding the room of a fly. "Louis the Fat is getting old. His day will come. My first intent is to safeguard our Eastern border. We ride before dawn." Smiling he said, "Tonight we feast."

The squires were seated at a different table from us and I found myself amongst King Henry's household knights. Although I knew them, I had fought alongside them, we had little else in common and I sat and listened to their conversation. I watched the Empress who also appeared to be isolated. Rolf and the Swabians were the only ones who spoke with her. I smiled; they were not courtiers and would find small talk difficult. Her father spoke to her but her husband ignored her. She looked unhappy. Each time our eyes met we smiled. The night dragged on. I was glad that we would be going to war the next day.

When the Empress retired her husband stayed to carouse with his knights. Rolf and the other Swabians joined me at my now empty table. Rolf swallowed a whole tankard of ale and stared malevolently at Geoffrey of Anjou. He shook his head and held up his tankard for it to be refilled. I smiled at his obvious distaste. "I take it the young Count has not grown on you."

He shook his head. Gottfried snarled, "We have all thought of ending his young life but the Empress forbids it. He is her husband and she is loyal. She deserves a better man. He is a child and what is worse he acts like one."

202

Rolf nodded, "He does not spend time with the Empress; each evening he and his friends spend time with the ladies of the night. It is no wonder that the Empress is not with child."

"The King is keen for her to have a child. That way his lineage is assured."

"It is a shame that Robert of Gloucester is not legitimate. It would have saved all of this nonsense. The Empress could have married someone other than the youth."

"It was not meant to be, Alfraed. The world is not the one we wish it to be. It is the one we have to live with." He drank a good swallow of ale. "Enough of such depressing matters. Tell us about England. How are Edward and your lovely wife?"

I realised that they did not know of my misfortune. I told them and they were even more upset.

"You should have said something. Here we have been rambling on about the Count and you have had your family destroyed. The problems of the Empress and her husband are nothing compared with what you have lost."

Gottfried asked, nervously, "Were you not affected by the plague?"

I shook my head. "I had no ill effects."

Rolf nodded, "You know what they say; that which does not kill you makes you stronger. You have steel in you, my friend. This tragedy is like the heat of the forge. It will toughen and harden the metal within you." They all stared at me as though looking for a visible sign of the change within. "How is William taking it?"

"He appears to be coping well. I am grateful that Leofric and John spend time with him. They are both good squires and just a little older than William. They understand him. I do not know

203

how it will be when we return home. It is another reason I left Stockton."

"And the pilgrimage."

I shook my head, "I cannot lie to my oathsworn brothers. I came to the church but in my heart I now doubt that there is a God."

Devoutly religious themselves they all made the sign of the cross. "Do not say that, Alfraed. You will burn in hell."

"Unless I confess and recant on my deathbed. Perhaps I die unshriven and then I will burn in hell. The plague did not touch me but the deaths changed me. I wonder how I will fare in battle. Will this make me weaker or stronger?"

Karl nodded, "I have heard of warriors who, after such a loss, have the death wish upon them. Do not go down that road, my friend."

Rolf smiled, "He cannot do that Karl for there is William. He needs must care for his son."

As I made my way to my chamber I knew that they were right. No matter how much I was in the depths of despair I had my son to care for. The death of my wife and daughter, the treatment of the Empress by her husband, all were inconsequential next to the needs of William.

Chapter 15

I had the only mounted archers in the army. The other knights had crossbowmen who marched. With the foot who accompanied us it meant it was a slow pace we adopted as we headed east. When we crossed into Blois we were joined by Theobald, Stephen's brother. He was waiting at the crossroads. That day I was in the van. His face darkened when he recognised my standard.

"I did not expect to see you here."

"Nor I you, my lord. The King asked me to accompany him on this campaign," I smiled.

His knights watched and he was in a difficult position. "I thank you and your handful of men for coming to the aid of Blois."

I ignored the insult. I did not need to make excuses for the number of men I had brought. Each was worth five of his. "We come to make the King's borders safe. We are all one people are we not? We fight under the same banner."

"We do." He turned and pointed ahead. "There are forests ahead which are filled with danger. I have sent my scouts there already."

"Good. When we near I will send my archers to hunt out their sentries. It is time this Eustace learned of the skill of the English archer."

"Eustace is not there. He squats like a toad across the border in the Île-de-France. He sends money to Coucy and Puset. They do his fighting for him. He has lost enough of his lands already. He is like a louse which burrows his way under your skin but is hard to eradicate. I will join our cousin and tell him the enemy disposition." He paused, "I am grateful that you fight for Blois. It is unexpected."

Wulfric nudged his horse next to mine as the large conroi passed us. "I wonder where his brother is, my lord."

"My thoughts too, Wulfric." I waved Dick forward, "Be ready to take the archers into the forest when we near. If these are bandits then they will be dangerous in their lair."

Dick nodded, "It seems strange to me that the men of the forest should fight as an army."

"I think that they gained power during the wars between King Louis and the king. The two lords, Coucy and Puset took advantage of the chaos and anarchy to carve out their own fiefdoms. They attracted men as cruel and evil as they. I do not think these will be woodsmen such as the men of Sherwood. These are robbers pure and simple."

"Will they have a castle, my lord?"

"When I spoke last night to the King's household knights they told me that both men have well-fortified castles. The two barons use a river for defence but the castles are, I believe, made of wood. I suspect that they will try to whittle us down in their forests and bleed the King's army. That style of fighting is quite effective as you well know Dick. I think it will come down to a siege."

It was three miles later that we saw the huge forest ahead. We were still in the land of Blois but the last castle we had seen had been that of Theobald. Once again, I wondered at the lords of this land. Why had they not built a castle closer to the forest? The main road to the Île-de-France passed through the forest. It would have made a good barrier and a strong defence.

Dick and his men did not need orders and they went in two groups. There were only ten of them but they were deadly with the war bow. I saw that Aelric led half and he went to the north of the road. Dick took the others south. They dismounted and disappeared into the eaves of the forest.

We had not brought war horses and I rode Scout. His nose would be invaluable for he had the ability to sniff out danger. I patted his neck as I turned, "Ready your weapons." I smiled at William as he slid his blade in and out of his scabbard. My squires had taught him well. I had killed many enemies who had tried to draw weapons only to find them sticking. A good warrior checked that he could draw his weapon before danger struck.

Sir Richard of Redvers and ten of his men at arms rode up to join me. Sir Richard was a grizzled old warrior and one of King Henry's closest friends. He grinned, "The King sent me when the Count told him of this forest. He does to wish us to be surprised."

"Thank you." I pointed ahead, "My archers are entering even as we speak." I saw that the horses of my archers were being held just outside the forest. I could not see them but I knew that Dick and Aelric would be silently moving through the trees. It was their element. With war bows strung any brigand or bandit who crossed their path would be dead before they knew they were in danger.

I saw that Sir Redvers and his men had their lances ready. Ours were with the baggage train. I did not see the need for them. Until battle lines were drawn they would be an encumbrance. He turned in his saddle, "Column of twos."

I did not need to order my men to do the same for they were already riding in such a column. Behind me rode John with my banner. He was next to Wulfric. William and Leofric were behind Edgar and Brian at the rear of my column. Sir Richard rode next to me. As we neared the trees I saw that they were not as thick as they had looked from a distance. However, it was difficult to see more than forty or fifty paces inside them as there was no order to their growth. This had been an old Roman Road and was straight. However, the bushes and weeds had encroached as it was not maintained. The ditch which ran alongside could not be seen. It was a hidden danger. I only knew of its presence when I saw the body of one of Theobald's scouts lying face down with a savage wound across his back. I drew my sword and there was a soft hiss as my men did the same.

Sir Richard did as I did and we both scanned the trees to the side. He may have been even more wary that I was for he did not know my archers. I did not fear an ambush. We would have a warning from Dick. I turned to my right as I heard a cry. Sir Richard said, "Your men?"

"I would think so. Our flanks will be safe; for a while at least." I pulled my shield up a little tighter as we headed deeper through the forest. I knew, from the King's household knights, that de Coucy had a castle just on the other side of the forest. The ground was already climbing slightly for the castle was built on a natural hill. The forest seemed to go on forever.

There were one or two more shouts and then I heard a roar as though a dam had burst. Dick and his archers raced towards me. "My lord, you are under attack!"

"Get to your horses and tell the King." The van was half a mile ahead of the main battle. We would have to hold until then.

Sir Redvers said, "Back to back?"

"That would seem the best."

"Face the forest!"

The column split into two. We were now a long thin line two men deep. We prepared to face the attack. At first, we saw nothing but we could hear the enemy as they charged towards us through the trees. Then I caught the flash of flesh and saw them. I turned to my line of men. Half of them, Sir Richard's men, had spears. "On my command, we charge." I saw the nods along the line. It would not be much of a charge; just the twenty or thirty paces to the trees but it would enable us to use our horses. The horde which poured from the forest was a mixture of men at arms wearing helmets and leather byrnies and unarmoured brigands. There were an overwhelming number of them. If the King did not hurry then things would go ill with us.

Luckily for us they had few missiles save their javelins and spears. They would have to be held until the last minute. Normally I would be in the middle of the line but due to our formation I was on the end. I had the advantage that my shield was facing the empty road. I was happy that William was safely tucked in the centre of my men. I saw the enemy just fifty paces away and racing hard towards us. "Watch for the ditch! Charge!"

I spurred Scout who leapt forward. I leaned as far beyond his head as I could safely manage and the first brigand ran straight into my sword. It tore through his throat and came out of the side. He fell in a bloody heap. I turned Scout's head so that he faced the empty road and it gave me the opportunity to sweep my sword in a wide arc. The height of my horse, the length of my arm and longer sword meant that I was able to strike the two warriors who were armed with short axes and ran towards me. Even as they were falling to the ground I saw a man at arms run to me. He had a spear and a shield. I whipped Scout's head around and took the blow from the spear on my shield. I stood in the stirrups and brought down my sword. I aimed for his head but the helmet deflected the blade and it bit deeply into his shoulder. He fell screaming into the ditch.

"Back to the road!"

I backed up Scout and was relieved to see my men obey. One of Sir Redvers' men was surrounded by some of the brigands and they pulled him from the saddle and hacked him to death. I heard a trumpet and saw the line of knights galloping to our aid. The brigands fell back and disappeared into the forest. Their ambush had failed.

I turned Scout's head so that I could speak with Sir Richard. I saw that he had been hit in the cheek by a spear. Blood flowed. He shook his head. "A lucky blow!" Laughing he added, "Another scar, eh Earl? If I was younger it might attract some young wench!"

The knights were led by the King and he headed into the forest to catch those who were slow to run. I dismounted and handed my reins to John. "Did you suffer any hurt?"

I knew that holding the standard meant John had no shield to defend himself. He grinned and shook his head. "I have learned to use the standard like a second sword." He pointed to the two dead men who lay before him. "I hope they have coin about them!" He dismounted to claim whatever treasure lay on the men we had killed.

I walked down my line of men who had all dismounted and were doing as John was. I breathed a sigh of relief when I saw that William and Leofric were unhurt. William was animatedly telling Leofric something. I dare say it was how he had fought for there was blood on his sword. He saw me, "Father, I killed one! Him!" He pointed to a warrior who had been slashed in the neck and bled to death.

"Then you had better search him for treasure before the others do!" He leapt from his horse and began to search for a purse. "How did he do, Leofric?"

"He has courage, my lord, but I fear he needs more skills. The man he slew was slow. A faster man would have gutted him. I had two men to fight else I would have intervened."

"William will have to learn but I would appreciate it if you and John could spend as much time as you can to make him a better swordsman. I fear he has come to this too early. He is young and inexperienced yet. He needs more time to become skilful."

"We learned this way, my lord and we survived. Your son will too. He has your blood."

I had just returned to Scout when the King reappeared at the head of his men. "Well done Cleveland! And you too Sir Richard. I hope you did not lose too many men?"

Sir Richard said, "Just one. I will make the bastards pay next time."

The King nodded, "You have done well. When we leave the forest, we will camp. Are you both happy to be the van yet?"

I looked at Sir Richard and he nodded, "Aye my lord."

"Good. I hope we have made them think twice about ambush."

I shouted "Dick!" as the King returned to his place at the head of the main battle.

He rode up with Aelric and the rest of my archers. "My lord?"

"Ride ahead of us on the road and keep a good watch. We camp when we leave this forest."

It was an uneventful five miles we travelled. When we emerged from the gloom of the forest we saw, in the distance, a castle rising above the land. It was a mixture of stone and wood. It was well sited. The gate was stone and there were three courses of stone beneath the wooden palisade. The towers at the corners were all made of wood. I saw a large wooden keep within the castle. "Dick, ride to the castle and see how it is defended." We rode a little further away from the forest to allow the carts and horses room to spread out. A small stream to our left would give us water and this would be a good place to camp.

Dick and the archers returned when the first tents were being erected. The King was speaking with Sir Richard and me. Theobald of Blois was approaching from the forest road. Dick dropped to his knee and bowed, "Your majesty, I have ridden to the castle. They have a dry moat and a drawbridge. They are well fortified."

"Is the gate made of stone, archer?"

"It is my lord and they have two wooden towers filled with crossbowmen." He spat. "They have one less now for he tried to kill my horse."

The King laughed and threw a coin to Dick. "Well done." He turned, "Have men at arms cut down trees from the forest. We will make a ram. Count, take your men and stop them from escaping."

Theobald was not happy about that I could see but he had to obey. After all we were still in Blois. We would be relatively safe in this camp while he would have to watch for sudden assaults from the castle. "Yes, my liege."

Count Geoffrey of Anjou rode noisily into the camp long after we had finished erecting the tents. The King frowned and walked with Sir Redvers and me towards the stream, "My son in law decided to spend some time hunting. It is a sport he enjoys."

"Perhaps it will make him fresher for the fight."

"You are too kind. He is young. I try to give him advice but it does not work."

As we walked around the perimeter we heard the sound of axes in the forest as the men at arms cut down the trees. It would take the whole of the next day to make the siege engine and we would need to make it close to the castle. It would be both slow and ponderous to move.

As the sun began to set a rider galloped in from Theobald. "My liege the Count needs more men. There is a second gate and he is thinly stretched."

I saw a smile play around the edge of the King's mouth, "Count Geoffrey, Count Theobald is finding difficulty in surrounding the castle would you and your men be able to contain the southern gate? I know that your men are keen to show their mettle and I believe you are the man to take on such a responsibility."

"Of course! If these rebels dare to set forth then we will hunt them and slaughter them as we did the deer."

The young Count led his men towards the distant castle. The King shook his head, "Sir Richard, have the men at arms take down some tents and take them to the Count." Sir Richard laughed as he shouted to his sergeant at arms. "Perhaps this is a good thing. My daughter's husband can learn from experienced knights like Sir Redvers and yourself."

"We all have to learn your majesty."

"But as I remember from all those years ago when I was so nearly captured you were even younger than Count Geoffrey is and yet you behaved with great maturity."

"You had not seen me some months earlier when I was even more naïve than the Count. Had it not been for my father's oathsworn then I might have ended up a spoiled young knight."

"But you are not. Come let us sit by the fire for I would speak with you." As we seated ourselves around the fire he said, "I have watched you over the years. Outside of my son and my oldest friends you are the knight I trust the most. You are loyal, you are true and you are clever. When I die there will be some who will try to stop my daughter attaining the throne. You must swear to me that you will fight for her. I want you to ensure that my daughter becomes Queen of England."

"My liege we all swore an oath."

He nodded, "And you will keep that oath. Others will not. You have shown great affection and loyalty to my daughter but it will take more than that to hold the Kingdom for her. I made you an earl to give you more power than others hold. There is only my son who outranks you."

"And the Prince Bishop."

He smiled. I saw cunning in that smile. "There is no Prince Bishop yet. Twixt the Tees and the Tyne it is you who hold the power." I suddenly realised that I had underestimated the King. He had deliberately not appointed a Bishop. It strengthened my arm. "Your suspicions about Balliol match mine. When you return home, I would have you keep close watch on him. I have given you power; I expect you to use it."

Sir Redvers came back laughing, "They took no tents with them. I have no idea where the young Count thought he would sleep! Perhaps he thinks the ground is soft at this time of year."

"You and I have slept on the ground and in the open before now, Sir Richard."

"Aye, my liege, but we learned to take whatever shelter and comfort we could get!"

"Come and sit by me. We will work out our strategy for this castle."

Sir Richard said, "If the men within are of the same quality as those we met in the forest then it will not take long to bring them to their knees."

"Coucy is clever. His knights and men at arms will be within the castle. The ones we took were the ones he could afford to waste. He threw the dice and gambled but he did not wager much. The ram will breach the gate but it will be bloody work to fight our way in."

"My archers have the skill to use fire arrows my liege. Only half of the castle is stone. If we can set alight the wooden keep then their resolve may weaken."

"Good."

Sir Richard asked, "Who will lead the assault?"

"I would have liked either Theobald or Geoffrey to prove their mettle but I need a victory. If we assault and fail it will hearten our enemies and demoralise our men. It will be you two and your men at arms. I know that you will take the gate."

I did not mind. I wanted to kill. Inside I was still raging against God. The men in the castle would bear the brunt of my anger. Sir Richard said, "The first ones in get the lion's share of the treasure. I am happy."

We spent the rest of the evening working out the details. I then sought out my men to explain their role. As I went to my tent I saw my three squires talking. William looked unhappy. "What is the matter, my son?"

"We have had nothing to do while you spoke with the King."

"Well I shall now tell you what the King said to me and then you will know as much as I do." Surprisingly he seemed pleased by that. "Sir Richard and I will lead the assault on the castle when the ram breaches the ditch."

His face split with a huge grin. "I am to attack the castle!"

"No. The three of you will be with the archers and the horses. None of you have the skills I need. This will be hard and bloody work. You will watch, my son. It will be some time before you engage in such an attack but you can learn a great deal by watching."

The fact that he was not alone made him a little happier. He was all that I had left and I would not throw away his life lightly.

The ram was built just out of bow range from the castle. The King sent his own men to build it. The structure gradually took shape. Dick and his archers were sent to capture some cattle. When they brought them back they were slaughtered and their hides used to make a roof for the ram. The fresh hides would not burn easily and the meat was welcome fodder for hungry men. The fact that we deprived de Coucy's people of the food was also a consideration.

As the ram was being constructed Sir Richard and I went closer to the castle to see how good the defences were. We took our shields. The sentries tried a few desultory attempts to hit us with crossbows but they realised they were wasting their bolts when they thudded into our shields. We were both too experienced to be caught out like that.

The ground before the gate was a gentle slope and the ditch was but half the width of the ram. It meant that if the men who operated it could push hard enough then we would have our own drawbridge. The ram would break down the door and then it would be our turn to attack through the gate. I saw that they had an inner bailey and a second wall and gate which led to the keep.

"The King will need plenty of men to ensure the ram bridges the ditch."

"Blois and Anjou can provide the men for that." Sir Richard pointed to the gatehouse. "If they have any sense the men within the castle will have oil and water to hand."

"If my archers can set the keep alight then they may be too busy for that. I intend to wear a cloak soaked in water. It will give me some protection."

"Good idea. "As three more bolts smacked into our shields he added, "Let us return to camp. I fear we will be busy tomorrow."

When they were informed of the plan neither of the counts was much bothered by the fact that their men would have to push the ram up the hill. It was not as though they would have to do it and they chose their unarmoured men for the task. The hide roof and the wooden walls would afford protection for most of the men selected. There were those at the back who might be in danger but the King sent my archers and the crossbowmen to keep down the heads of the sentries over the gate.

My squires helped me to dress. I had my cloak soaking in a pail of water. John handed me my short sword which I would use until I had room to swing my arm. I knew from experience that the gap through which we charged might only be a small one. My long sword would not be of much use until we were in the open again. Forcing a gate was bloody, close-in work.

When I was dressed we went, with the pail and my weapons, towards the ram. It was being pushed slowly up the slope. The first part was the easiest section for no one was trying to kill them. I saw Dick lead the archers and crossbowmen closer to the walls. They had large wicker shields behind which they stood. Dick waited until the ram was close enough for the enemy to begin sending bolts towards it. He and the archers then began to pick off the crossbowmen on the walls. Our own crossbows sent their missiles at the men on the towers. The rain of bolts ceased. I donned my cloak which was heavy but would protect me from heat.

When the ram was within fifty paces of the gate it became harder for the slope was steeper. The King had anticipated this and another ten men rushed forward to help push it. Dick and our archers killed every crossbowman who appeared on the walls. Soon the crossbowmen were using the slits in the walls. They were not as effective for they could not hit the men at the back. Still they hit some of those pushing the ram and progress remained slow. Count Geoffrey had a good sergeant at arms and I heard him shouting at the men to increase their speed. The impetus pushed the ram over the gap and it struck the gate with a resounding crack. One of those inside the ram lost his balance and fell screaming on to the stakes which were in the ditch.

The men who had been at the rear ran back down the slope towards us. Sir Richard said, "Right, Earl, now it is our turn I think."

We marched, all twenty-two of us in two lines towards the rear of the ram. We had our shields ready in case of bolts but Dick and the others continued to keep down the heads of the defenders. As we passed them I saw Dick preparing the fire arrows. "Good luck, my lord. We will soon give them something to think on."

We could hear the thud of the ram as it struck the gate. It was like the sound of doom. I knew that, at first, it would appear to be ineffective but that was an illusion. Tiny, almost invisible cracks would appear and as the ram continued to strike they would widen as the gate became weaker. We stood at the rear of the ram and waited. The men at the front would tell us when it was breached. I turned to look at my men. They were all keen and ready for war. Behind them I saw the first of the fire arrows as they were launched at the enemy. I did not expect the first ones to work but Dick and his archers had made plenty. Eventually they would catch alight. Dick would aim for the roofs. It was harder to put out a fire there.

From within the ram I heard, "Almost ready, my lord. There is a large crack appearing."

Lifting the hide flap at the rear we entered the Stygian gloom of the ram. It was a tight squeeze to get past the men working the ram but I could see that there was a gap. The men had put down logs across the ditch and I walked over the narrow bridge. I held my shield before me for when the gate broke we would be exposed to the weapons those inside held. An arrow flew through the gap the ram had created and one of those working the ram fell to his death in the ditch. At that precise moment the bar holding the gate closed finally gave way and broke. The two sides of the gate moved inwards. I punched the shattered side with my shield and I leapt through the gap and into the castle.

I slashed with my short sword, blindly, as I stepped into the castle. My short sword found flesh. The man grabbed my blade with his hand. I saw two fingers fall to the floor. When he fell to the side he took my weapon with him. I saw an axe swing at me and I dropped to one knee and held up my shield. The axe blow was so hard it made my arm shiver. Weaponless I punched my mailed glove up between the legs of the man wielding the axe and was rewarded with a scream of pain. I stood and hit him with all the force I could muster. My shield knocked him to the ground; he clutched his groin. As he fell backwards I drew my sword and stabbed down on his helpless form.

Sir Richard had not yet come through the gap and the two men who had attacked me had slowed us down. I stepped away from the gate and began to move towards the horde of men who were racing to get at me. Although alone, I was more confident now. I had space to swing my sword. I released my heavy and wet cloak. I had not needed it and it would now encumber me.

Instead of waiting for them to attack me I charged them. The first two to reach me had spears. I blocked the blow of one and hit my sword against the haft of the second. The speed of their attack brought them close to me. I pulled back my head and head butted one. His open helmet afforded him no protection and he fell unconscious at my feet. He was replaced by a man at arms with a sword and the speed of his blade was like a snake's strike. I barely had time to block the blow. I swung my sword horizontally as I heard Wulfric behind me yell, "Die you bastard!" I knew not whom he had struck but I recognised the crunch of his axe hacking through flesh and bone. The man at arms I was fighting flicked his eyes to the giant that was Wulfric and that gave me the chance to angle my blade and hack across his neck.

Wulfric's shield appeared next to mine. "Where is Sir Richard?"

"He is coming, my lord, but it is just we two for the moment so let us just hold what we have and try not to take the whole castle singlehandedly?"

It made sense and my left arm was still a little numb from the blow of the axe man. The dead men around us had slowed the attack down but now I saw a knight approaching. He led six men at arms and a mass of brigands who looked intent on throwing out this tiny force of warriors. Sir Richard puffed his way next to me. "Sorry my lord, I got caught up on the gate."

I glanced down and saw that his surcoat was torn to ribbons. "You are here and we are now the tip of the attack. Wedge!"

I felt a shield touch my back and knew that we had some support. We had to clear a space before the gate so that the King could send in the reinforcements who were waiting outside the castle.

"Forward!" We marched towards the knight and his band of bandits. Behind him I saw that the keep was well ablaze. Dick's arrows had finally caught and the keep was lost. The drifting smoke aided us for it obscured the view of the men who were still on the walls.

Coucy's line was ragged and when they struck us it was like waves breaking on a harbour wall. We held. The knight who struck at me was a tall man and he used his height well. The sword came from a long way back. It did, however, expose his middle for he did not keep the shield as tight as he should. I stabbed with my sword and although his mail stopped a mortal strike I tore through his links and into his side. He grunted with pain. Once again, my arm ached from the blow of the sword.

"Push!"

My men behind us pushed so that when I stepped forward the knight I faced had to fall back. His men were too loose to support him. I took the initiative and brought my sword down again. He managed to get his shield in place but he was stepping back and he had little strength in the arm. I hit him between the neck and the arm. He screamed as something broke. The shield dropped and I pushed with my shield. As he toppled to the ground I stabbed him in the throat.

Wulfric's axe swept a space next to us as Sir Richard killed the man at arms. We suddenly had space and men at arms joined

221

Wulfric and Sir Richard. The line before us hesitated. I ran with my sword raised shouting, "King Henry!"

The men who faced me were taken by surprise for there were still many more of them. The first man I slew had no armour and my sword hacked through his ribs. He fell dead. I continued the swing and it went into the back of a second man. Wulfric's blow took the head from a man at arms and Sir Richard ran one through too. There was a gap before the three of us and we ran towards the inferno that was the keep. Within the walls was now pandemonium. The inner gate to the keep opened and the men fleeing the fire in the keep raced at us. I was not certain if they were trying to get at us or merely flee the inferno.

I heard a shout from behind as the King and the Count of Blois led his men to support us. We had them now. The Count of Anjou had the southern gate watched and they had nowhere to go. We were no longer a continuous line but our attack had cowed those we faced. We were not helpless travellers; we were well armed and skilled warriors. My sword sang as it carved a passage before me. The ones whom the three of us faced ran. It was now a series of individual combats. We held the advantage for more of us had armour than those that we fought. However, these were dangerous foes. They were like rats who were fleeing for their lives. They did not fight as knights and used a variety of weapons. I concentrated on keeping my shield tight and striking flesh.

"Let us find de Coucy and we can end this rebellion now!"

We ran through the inner gate and sought out the horses. I led the others beyond the keep towards the stables. Suddenly the door of the stables burst open and a huge knight with a great helm galloped out, followed by another eight riders all dressed in red surcoats. They all had a rampant black lion upon their shields and surcoats. It was de Coucy. The three of us braced ourselves for the attack but they swerved and headed for the south gate. "We have them. Anjou has the southern gate. Follow me!"

They galloped through the thick black smoke towards the gate. We could not see the gate for it was obscured by drifting smoke. We ran after the horsemen. I saw the gate ahead was open and I wondered why Geoffrey of Anjou had not joined in the attack. As we reached the gate I saw why. He had gone and the fleeing riders were heading east along with twenty or thirty men on foot. We had captured the castle but lost de Coucy!

Chapter 16

The three of us stood looking at the departing warriors. Sir Richard did not suffer fools gladly, "The arrogant young…. The King will not be happy about this." He shook his head. "And I have lost two good men at arms!"

I turned and looked to my men. All stood. I nodded to them. They raised their swords and shouted, "Earl Alfraed!" I saw that there was no more opposition. Men had thrown down their swords and were kneeling on the ground waiting to discover their fate.

The King strode up to us with his arms wide. "What heroes! You did all that I asked and more. De Coucy?"

Sir Richard pointed to the gaping gate, "They fled." He knew the King well enough to speak plainly and not disguise the truth. "The Count deserted his post."

The King frowned at Sir Richard's choice of words but he said nothing. Tight lipped he led us back past the keep which was now a raging inferno, towards the gate. As we neared the gate he saw the Count of Anjou. He strode around the bodies of those that we had killed as though he had been there with us.

The King's face was as black as thunder as he approached his son in law. "Why did you leave your post?"

The young man said sulkily, "There was no fighting. We came here to fight and not be guards on a gate!"

"Had you stayed at your post then you would have captured De Coucy. Then you could have fought!" Silence filled the castle. He turned to the assembled warriors who were looking eagerly at the armour and weapons of the dead. These had been bandits and stolen from the rich who passed through their lands.

"All of the plunder from this castle shall be shared by Sir Richard and the Earl of Cleveland. They have shown us all how real knights fight."

We both bowed and said, simultaneously, "Thank you, my liege."

Theobald of Blois said, "And what of the prisoners? Do we execute them?"

The King smiled, "No, the Count of Anjou can escort them to your castle. We will put them to work building better defences."

"I am to be a guard again?"

"Perhaps the journey to Blois and back will help you to reflect on your actions." I thought he would refuse but the King lowered his voice and, closing with his son in law said, "When I die you and my daughter will rule England and Normandy. I would see that you are ready for such responsibilities." He said it so quietly that only four of us heard it. The young man nodded. "We will wait here for your return."

It took a whole day for the fire to die down. The King told Theobald to build a stone castle on the hill. "This will protect your lands from the east and it is rich hunting around here."

The Count of Blois nodded, "Do we pursue Coucy?"

"We do. Thanks to Anjou we still have the leaders of this rebellion at large. He will flee to Roger of Puset and Eustace. The next time we will not have such slight losses." He turned to me. "Had you had all of your knights, Cleveland then, I believe, we could have ended the war today. I wish that you had brought them."

"I came not to fight a war my liege but to make a pilgrimage. I did not expect that I would have to fight and besides

225

they are needed on the Tees." I looked at the Count of Blois, "No offence, Count Blois, but this is not my home for which we fight."

Theobald nodded. The King said, "But it is my home and you fight for me."

"Always, your majesty." I was suitably admonished.

The plunder was extensive. Coucy and his men had escaped but they had had to leave their ill-gotten gains. While we waited for the Count of Anjou to return I had my men make a wagon for our share of the gold, armour, weapons and treasure. They would all be rich men. The men of de Coucy did not trust their fellows and all carried purses with gold and silver and their necks were adorned with gold and silver jewellery. The ones who wore armour had finely made pieces. Their swords were also well made.

Geoffrey of Anjou returned four days later. Theobald of Blois had sent out his scouts to discover the enemy while we waited. He had found them. They were at Thymerais. It had been a border castle captured by William the Conqueror before he had invaded England but the French had recaptured it. Since then Louis of France had lost his citadel. Now it was the last refuge of the rebels. Close to the border with the Kingdom of King Louis the Fat, the rebels would have to risk the wrath of that king if they fled. Puset and Coucy had been a thorn in the side of the King of France just as much as the Dukes of Normandy.

I sent my treasure back to Caen with two of my men at arms who had suffered slight wounds. I would not risk them. Sir Richard did the same. It meant he only had four men at arms to serve him. It was decided he would join the household knights of the King.

This time Geoffrey of Anjou demanded the van. I think he was keen to prove himself. I did not mind. If I could I would have returned to Caen with my treasure. I had hoped to see the Empress and that had not been meant to be. I had William ride next to me on the journey to the last stronghold of the King's enemies. "Having been on campaign, my son, do you still wish to be a knight? You have seen men die."

He nodded, seriously, "But I have seen glory too father. All the men spoke of how you, Wulfric and Sir Richard faced the enemy and made them flee. I was so proud. Even the men who follow other knights would serve you if they could. I would be like you when I grow up and become a knight."

I smiled, sadly, "You see the outside, William. You do not see the turmoil within. Enjoy these days when you are free and life has not turned sour."

We rode in silence as he ruminated on my words. "You mean mother and Hilda."

"I do."

"It was God's will that they died. Father Peter told me that it was an honour for mother and Hilda to be taken for they were with God."

I was on the horns of a dilemma. The priest had given my son comfort but I did not agree with the words. I looked at the innocent face of William and I nodded; it was a lie but I knew not what else to do. As we approached the castle at Thymerais I saw that our task would be a harder one this time. The Count of Anjou had placed his men before the gate but I could see that there was no way that a ram could break down the gate this time. The road which led to it had a twist right at the end. There was a bridge over a deep ditch and a barbican defending both ends. Unless there was a ditch at the rear then we would need a catapult. I was not certain if we had men with the skill to build such a machine let alone operate it.

Sir Richard, who had arrived with the King, was organising the camp. The King held a council of war as darkness fell. I was invited as was Sir Richard. Geoffrey of Anjou spoke. For the first time since I had met him he seemed deflated and flat. "There is but one gate. The town is also within the walls. They have six stone towers." He pointed in the darkness. "The barbican has four small towers."

The King said, "They will be well supplied then." We all nodded for Puset and Coucy would not worry about the townspeople. They would let them starve. The warriors within would be well fed. "I had thought to besiege them but we would suffer more than they would."

I could not help being positive, "There can, however, be no relief force coming this way."

The Count of Blois said, "Unless King Louis decides to throw in his lot with them."

That was as depressing a thought as I had heard. It made perfect sense. Sir Richard said, "Then we must make a catapult or a bolt thrower."

"Have you experience of them, old friend?"

"I have seen them and I know how they work but..."

I remembered that Wulfric had spoken of some men at arms who had served abroad. "There must be men at arms who serve with us who have seen them."

"You are right, Earl. That is our plan. We besiege them and try to make a machine of war and batter down their walls."

"Can we not assault the gate?"

"We can, Count Geoffrey, but it would be costly in terms of men."

228

"I saw what Cleveland and Redvers did. They lost but a couple of men. My men are not afraid."

"I know and it may come to that but let us try the machine first."

There were some of Theobald of Blois' men who had served in the Holy Land and seen such devices. They set to building the machine. Reinforcements from Normandy reached us and the mood of the camp improved. They brought archers, arrows, bolts for the crossbows and more men at arms. If we could force the gate or the walls then we had a good chance of defeating those within.

It seemed to take an age to build the machines. The King insisted upon two in case one failed. Men at arms were sent to find large rocks which were brought to the site where we were building the two machines. They would be used to break down the walls. We did not have the luxury of round stones. It meant that the irregular stones would make it difficult to hit the same spot each time. It could not be helped. One advantage of a single gate meant that there was no way that they could easily escape as they had at de Coucy's castle. Individuals could slip over the wall but they would be on foot. The King had mounted patrols riding around the walls and we caught four such escapees. They gave us an accurate number of the men within the castle before they were killed.

The King wisely had the two machines tested out of sight of the enemy walls. One broke immediately. The two men who had made it were embarrassed and fearful of punishment. The King, however, was remarkably patient. "Better to break now than when we attack."

They set to repairing it with a will and soon made them both stronger. Two days later and they were tested once more. This time they both worked well. The army was arrayed before the gate. Normally terms would be offered but these rebels were cruel bandits and the time for words was passed. Geoffrey of Anjou was chosen to lead the attack on the bridge once the barbican and walls were destroyed. As we now had more archers and crossbows than hitherto, the King intended to batter those who tried to stay on the walls. He was a clever man. Inside the castle they would have to endure the noise of our assault and yet have no decent report of what was going on outside.

The archers and crossbows sheltered behind their wicker shields. Before we hauled up the mighty machines they cleared the walls so that the war machines could work without fear of attack. Sir Richard supervised the barrage of stones. The rate of release was not great. It took ten men to wind back the basket and then another four to load the stones. After our practice we had an estimate of the range but it was loose. It was why we had decided to attack the barbican. We had a greater margin of error. If we missed the barbican we might still hit the walls.

The first machine whooshed as it sent the first rock at the walls. There was a huge clatter and a cheer. Dust flew from the stone and the wall. There was an audible groan from our men who had thought that we would have had an instant effect. The gate and the walls looked barely touched. The second one missed the barbican but hit the wall. A large piece of masonry fell. That evoked a cheer. It seemed to take forever to reload the basket but soon they had a rhythm. It was hard to see that we were achieving anything.

Sir Richard said, "Be patient. One of my sharp-eyed men has seen a crack appearing in the tower. The gate is nothing if the towers are destroyed. More stones flew towards the walls and the towers. Sometimes they hit the same place but that was rare. The right-hand tower suddenly collapsed as the weight of stones took its toll. It was spectacular. I saw men who were sheltering in the barbican fall to their deaths in the stake filled ditch. One side of the gate still hung from its hinge but, as a barrier, it was now useless.

Our whole army cheered but Sir Richard said to me, "We only have ten more stones left. We will have to find more."

By the end of the attack of the catapults one and half towers on the barbican had been destroyed and a small section of the wall had collapsed into the ditch. I felt quite hopeful. The first set of gates no longer functioned and the wall around the inner gate looked to have been damaged. I could see us being able to demolish the barbican by the next day and then Geoffrey could attempt an assault.

The last assault on the walls saw the barbican become indefensible. Those who survived the stones and the missiles withdrew to the town walls. We heard banging as they shored up the damaged gate. If we had had enough stones we could have breached the last gate before dark but we had to find more.

Dick, the archers and the crossbowmen moved within range of the gate. They sheltered behind huge shields while the catapults were moved closer to begin to rain their stones on the interior of the town. King Henry hoped to demoralise the defenders. The catapults only managed until late afternoon before they ran out of ammunition and one of them broke. The two siege engines were drawn back out of danger. The men who had built them would need to repair them. They were fragile things. They had served their purpose and Count Geoffrey formed his men up for the attack. They would have to march along the length of the wall before they could cross the bridge and attack the gate. The King insisted that he take the best six axe men from the army with him to batter down the gate. I do not think that the Count had thought of that.

The bows and the crossbows kept the heads of the defenders down but once they reached the gate then the arrow slits in the walls would be used and I had no doubt that they would use either oil or boiling water. The Count discounted my advice and he did not take dampened cloaks. We had the whole army ready to take advantage of any breach in the gate. Even though Dick and the others were hurting the defenders I saw two of the Angevin warriors fall into the ditch as they marched towards the last gate. They had to move slowly in order to keep a solid line of shields facing the enemy. They turned and formed up. The ruins of the barbican caused a problem none of us could have foreseen. The Count's men could not keep a solid line as they clambered over the stones of the ruined defences. They could not keep a tight formation. I saw men at arms falling as arrows struck home. The young Count did the right thing once he reached the bridge; he ran towards the damaged gate. It minimised the time they had to endure the rain of spears, stones and bolts.

"Well that is the first part completed and we had fewer casualties than I could have expected. Count Blois, move your men to the foot of the ramp. You will assault next."

The men of Blois formed up and marched towards the bottom of the slope which led to the walls. I heard a cry and looked to the gate. They were pouring boiling water down on the attackers. I could see why they did not use oil or pig fat. They could not risk it igniting. If the gate and the bridge caught fire then the siege would be over. Two men spun away from the gate and were felled by arrows. More boiling water was used and the Count ran. His men followed and, even before Theobald of Blois had reached the foot of the road the Angevin were fleeing back towards us. They had lost heavily. I saw the disappointment on the King's face. I saw the scars in the wood which showed that the men with the axes had almost succeeded in breaking through the wooden gate but it had all been in vain. They would now spend the night repairing the gate and all of the Count's men's sacrifices would have been in vain.

"Call back Blois. There is little point wasting his men in an attack. We will try again in the morning. Sir Richard, see if you can get the catapults repaired. We will try to attack the gate with the stones the men can collect. It may have been weakened."

The Count of Blois was relieved that he and his men did not have to assault the walls. The men who had suffered the boiling water bore terrible burns. Geoffrey of Anjou was angry. I could not tell if the anger was at his own failure or the humiliation of having to retreat. He went directly to his tent.

That evening there was an air of depression in the camp. Although we had not lost many men the effect of the failure made the numbers seem greater. "Theobald, you will lead the attack on the morrow."

"What of the boiling water?"

We still had the hides we had used on the ram. "Make shelters from the cattle hides. They keep water out. They will not stop all wounds but they will save your men from the more serious effects of the water."

"Thank you, my lord. I will heed your advice."

The King added, "The gate has been weakened. If we can hit it with the stones then your work may be so much easier."

That evening it was just the three of us who sat and talked; the King, Sir Richard and I. "This is a thorn which must be removed. I have more important things to do than to bring these brigands to heel."

I felt hopeful, "The castle will fall tomorrow. We have seen how effective the stone throwers are. If they do the same tomorrow as they did today then we can breach the gates and enter the castle and the town. This time the rats have nowhere to run."

"You are right." I could see that he was still distracted. I began to wonder at his motivation in this foray east. It was Blois land for which he fought. Why had he come to lead this army personally? He could have let one of his knights lead his men.

Then it came to me; he had wanted to see his son in law in action. He was disappointed. I knew I was right when Sir Richard spoke.

"It is your daughter and her husband who are the real problem."

"You are right, old friend. They say you choose your friends but can do nothing about your family. My father knew that. Had my brother Robert not rebelled then things might have turned out differently."

"You cannot change the past, my liege."

"I know Richard." The King looked at me. "Look after your son, Alfraed. He is your future. I curse the day my son sailed on the White Ship. I would not be in this situation if he had stayed in England."

I stretched, "You cannot say that, your majesty. Suppose he had been suborned as your daughter was?"

He cast a briefly, angry look and then smiled, "You are an honest fellow and you are right. At least I have no reason to doubt the loyalty of my daughter."

Sir Richard mumbled, "Just the competence of her husband." He paused, "If he could have given the Empress a child then it might be better."

"You are right. I need a male heir. Perhaps he needs to eat more oysters or lampreys!"

Sir Richard said, with a straight face, "I believe the effects of oysters are over rated your majesty. Last month I ate twelve in one sitting and only ten of them worked!"

He was a dry old knight and I liked him. The King and I laughed until the tears coursed down our cheeks. The joke was not that funny but it relieved the sombre mood.

I was awake before dawn. Even so I was not up before my squires. Although I had not used them for some days the three of them were putting an edge on my sword and oiling my mail. I was grateful to Leofric and John for they were teaching my son good habits. Count Geoffrey was an example of someone who had not been taught good habits. As the catapults were hauled into place and the men of Blois prepared to attack I ate last night's cold ham and stale bread. Soon we would have to go on short rations for the King had expected a swift victory. We had eaten the supplies we had captured. We would need to take the town and use what lay within its walls. I suspect he was disappointed that the Count of Blois had not provided more. These might be the enemies of the King that we fought but we were in Blois land.

I had just mounted Scout when there was a trumpet sound from the castle. I reached the King and Sir Richard who were also mounted. "What is this? Some trick?"

The gates opened and a knight made his way down the road towards us. He did not ride and he carried neither shield nor sword. It looked to me like an overture to peace. I looked over to Dick who had an arrow knocked. "My captain of archers can end his journey whenever you wish, your majesty."

The King smiled, "It is one man we will let him approach. The two counts had joined us. "Do you recognise him?"

Theobald of Blois said, "I believe him to be one of the knights of de Coucy I saw him at a tourney."

"Let him approach."

The King cleverly made him walk all the way towards us. He had to march between the waiting men at arms. To give him credit he did not seem to worry overmuch about it. I saw him glance to the side as he passed the two catapults. He reached us and gave a slight bow. "I am Guiscard de Dreux, my master,

Thomas Lord of Coucy asks for a truce so that he may put a proposal to you."

"Where?"

The knight waved a hand towards the wall. "Half way between the road and your camp; your leaders only." He cast a look of derision towards the Count of Anjou.

Geoffrey coloured, "I will not take an insult from this man."

"Hold your peace. I will meet with the rebel leaders but I choose whom I bring. If you do not like it then we attack again!"

Sir Guiscard nodded, "I will give my master your demands. "

As he rode off Count Theobald said, "It must be a trap."

I pointed to the gate. "That could be taken easily with a determined attack and the catapults are both repaired. Did you not see him examine them surreptitiously as he passed them?"

It was obvious they had not. The King nodded, "Sharp eyes! We will meet with them. Cleveland here is right. We can attack again and overwhelm them. I would prefer not to for it would result in many losses. If we can negotiate their surrender then there will be many ransoms and we can end this rebellion quickly." He turned to Sir Richard, "The five of us will ride to meet them."

"Doesn't that give them an easy chance to kill us all?"

"Earl Cleveland, have your archers watch them for treachery."

"Dick." When Dick came over I said, "We are to meet with our enemies. Have the archers watch out for treachery."

"Yes, my lord."

There were many things to worry about but my archers' accuracy and loyalty were not amongst them.

The three enemy leaders were the first ones to approach the meeting place. I saw that they did not use horses. The wrecked barbican had given them few options. As we headed to meet them I could see why they had asked for this truce. Our siege engines, crude though they were had been more effective than we had thought. The two counts flanked the King while Sir Richard and I rode slightly behind. I kept my sword and shield ready. One of the three we were to meet was the King's son in law. With a stroke his wife would have a claim to the throne.

The King waited for them to approach. He must have enjoyed their discomfort for they had to look up at him. I recognised Thomas de Coucy. He had no helm but he still wore the same armour with the rampant lion. It reminded me of the Scottish lion. The King ignored him and addressed himself to Eustace of Breteuil. "This is not the first time you and my daughter have dared to rebel against me. The last time I took from you the lands I gave to my daughter. It seems I must now take your lives."

Eustace spoke and he seemed almost petulant. "We have not rebelled. We live here in the castle of Hugh de Puset. We are victims. We have to rely on the hospitality of others for you have made us paupers."

The King laughed, "The castle de Puset stole from Blois." He stared at them. "Will you surrender or shall we break down your gate and put your people to the sword?" Roger de Puset had the temerity to shrug. The King shouted, "I know you care not for your people or any people for that matter. I grow tired. You asked for this truce. What are your proposals? Do you surrender?"

Hugh of Puset smiled, "If you attack us you may well win but how many men will you lose? The Count of Anjou suffered

237

badly in his attack yesterday. I know that he was the least experienced and valuable of your leaders but..."

Count Geoffrey's hand went to his sword, "I will kill you for that insult!"

The King shouted, "This is a truce! Stay your hand!" The voice carried across the field and there was silence. "And you Puset; watch your tongue."

De Coucy spoke for the first time. He had a silky voice which I did not trust for an instant. "We have a proposal. Let me fight one of your knights. If you win then we surrender and throw ourselves upon your mercy. If I win then you let the three of us and our household knights leave and then you can sack the town."

The King shook his head in disbelief. "Is there not an ounce of honour between any of you? You would throw your people on my mercy while you escape with your lives?" He turned his horse's head around. "I have heard enough..."

"You are afraid then, Norman? I thought better of you."

"I fear nothing, least of all a robber baron like you."

"In that case you cannot lose. Unless you fear that I will defeat your champion."

He had been clever. If we rode back and continued the fight then the belief would be that King Henry did not value his own men. It would demoralise the army. The King turned his horse back and de Coucy knew that he had won. "Whom would you fight? Me?"

"And kill a king? That would be regicide. No, I will fight the knight whose name is known throughout these lands as the best knight in England, Alfraed, Earl of Cleveland."

I was almost amused by the look given to me by Count Geoffrey. It was almost as though he was seeing me for the first time. I kept my face impassive even though every eye was upon me. I knew that the King had taken the bait when he said, "And you will surrender unreservedly when the Earl of Cleveland defeats you?"

"If he defeats me then you have our word, all of us."

"You so swear?"

They nodded and said, together, "We so swear."

The King turned and looked at me. Although he said not a word I could see his eyes pleading. He could win the war and not lose a man if I accepted the challenge and fought as his champion. I nodded.

"Very well then we meet here at noon."

He nodded and said, "Between these war machines? And we can bring our household knights?" The King gave Eustace a quizzical look. "So that we may leave if Sir Roger wins."

"Agreed."

We turned and went back to our lines. "You can beat him, Alfraed."

"I hope so, your majesty, but if not then I pray you take my son as a ward."

"I swear I will honour him as though he were my own, but you shall win."

I was not certain. Adela was gone and my life was empty. Perhaps it was my fate to die here so close to the place where I had first met the King and my fortunes had changed for the better. I would know in a very short time. I could fight this de Coucy knowing that I had done all that I could for my son. If I fell then it would be an honourable end.

Chapter 17

The King and the other four took themselves off to discuss the events. I walked towards my men. They had no idea what was going on. Wulfric approached. "Do they surrender, my lord? Are we to return home?"

I gave him a wry smile, "In a manner of speaking, yes. I am to fight de Coucy. If I kill him then they surrender. If he kills me then they leave the castle and we can go home." I turned to Leofric, "I need my helmet."

Wulfric shook his head, "It is not right sir. You are taking all the risks and you will not reap the reward."

"Perhaps. Fetch Dick. I have need of him."

John and William stood close by. "Should we do anything, my lord?"

"The sword is sharp?" John nodded. "Then I shall need a long dagger." He went off.

"Will we be allowed to watch you kill him, father?"

"You are so confident?" He nodded. "I expect so. When Dick and Wulfric return I want you to listen to what I say to them. It is important."

My squires and my men returned at the same time. The rest of the camp was filled with men at arms and knights preparing themselves to witness the combat. I strapped the dagger to my waist. "Wulfric, you and the men at arms will guard my squires. I suspect treachery. Dick, you and the archers need to position yourselves to the north of the combat but remain hidden. If there is treachery then you know what to do."

"Can we not be closer to you, my lord? If there is treachery…"

"If there is treachery then I trust you and your bows. You would not be allowed to be closer, for it is household knights only. That is why I suspect treachery. The fight will be between the catapults. The King did not appear to notice the significance of that but I do. You will need to be outlaws once more and approach like wraiths."

"We have not forgotten that skill."

I looked at Wulfric, "If I am to die the King has promised to make my son his ward. I do not doubt him but I charge you with protecting Stockton until he becomes old enough to command."

William's mouth opened and I saw him take in the words. "You cannot die! Not after mother and…"

"William, you are young in years but you must grow quickly. We have no time for tears or doubts. If I am to die this day then so be it but you will be the next lord of Stockton. Until you are old enough then Wulfric will rule."

He nodded. I saw him fight to control what he felt within, "When will I be old enough?"

"When Wulfric tells you."

Sir Richard reached me, "It is time, Earl." I nodded, "I suspect treachery my friend."

"As do I." I pointed to Dick who was organising the archers. "My archers will be close by if there is."

"Can you defeat him?"

"We will be fighting on foot and he has the advantage. He is a bigger man and he has a great helm. My stroke is normally

242

twixt the helmet and hauberk. I cannot do that with a great helm. I will have to use my feet and my speed." I rubbed my left arm. My worry is this arm which has still to recover from the blow I received at de Coucy's castle."

Wulfric growled, "He fled from us that time, my lord, if you recall. I would expect such a trick again."

Until his body lies at my feet I will expect all tricks. John, fetch my banner. It will fly above me." I smiled at William. "Your mother's hands sewed the stars and the wolf upon it. Perhaps she will watch over me too."

Sir Richard led us to the two siege machines. The King and our household knights stood on one side. He was flanked by the two counts. Ahead of me I saw de Coucy and Hugh of Puset leading their knights. Of Eustace and the King's daughter there was no sign. I frowned as I looked to the gate. The rubble had been cleared in the night. What did that portend? Had they deliberately come on foot to lull our suspicions?

I stood next to the King. I was his champion. Sir Richard took Wulfric and my squires to stand in the middle of the knights. He was protecting my son as best he could. I said quietly to the King, "There will be treachery. We do not fight honourable men, my liege."

"You think I should not have accepted his terms?"

"I think you did the right thing, your majesty, but let us just say that I am suspicious."

"As am I. Fear not we will watch out for tricks."

As the enemy approached I said, "He has played his first trick already. We are evenly matched in terms of numbers. Look at the men he brings. They are hardened warriors all." Lowering my voice to a whisper I added, "We have two thirds of our army who are inexperienced. Most of them stand behind us."

He had not thought of that and now it was too late. De Coucy and Puset were no fools. They knew that Geoffrey of Anjou was little more than a boy and Theobald of Blois had allowed the bandits to take his land. He was obviously no threat. No matter what happened if they chose to they could begin a battle which we would lose.

De Coucy left his confederates and stood confidently in the middle of the open space. His armour was good armour. I saw that he had his shoulders protected by metal plates. Each bore a rampant lion upon them. Another of my blows would be useless. His knees were similarly protected. He had put his ill-gotten gains to good use. I saw the sword in his hand. At least our swords were the same length. There would be no advantage there.

I walked towards him with my sword drawn. I was looking for danger the whole way. I saw that he stood on a flat piece of dry ground. That suited me. His voice seemed disembodied as it came from deep within the helmet. We were far enough away from the others so that no one else could hear our words. "You will die today. I think you know that. I looked in your eyes before and I saw a man dead within. This day marks the end of King Henry's expansion. Soon Blois will be ours and then Normandy. And when the King dies then England will be ours too. I promise you this, Earl of Cleveland, I will make your end swift. I saw you fight and you are a brave man but your life ends here on this field."

I did not respond. Instead I pondered his words. I had suspected the brothers Blois as being behind the plots in England and the borders. Perhaps I was wrong. If Blois was to be captured then the brothers would lose out too. It looked like it was Juliana who was plotting against her father. He was a clever man and he had distracted me with his words.

The blow when it came towards me was quicker than I had expected. Athelstan's training took over and my body reacted before my mind. I spun away from the blow which struck air only. There would be no more words now. Words wasted breath and distracted the mind. This was now a deadly game between the two of us. The difference would be that one mistake would result in death.

I feinted towards his shoulder. He did not react but swung his sword sideways at my middle. It was a swift strike. I barely had time to deflect his blade and the two swords rang off each other. He was not afraid of a blow to the shoulder. He knew that his metal plate would stop it. I looked for a weakness. I could see none. I would have to create a weakness. I stabbed forward as quickly as I could and found a gap between his sword and his shield. It tore through his surcoat and along the mail links. He brought his shield across to try to trap my sword but I pulled it away swiftly before it was lost. I danced away from the counter strike which, again, hit air. Those blows tired a man.

I could not see behind the helmet but I knew that he, too, was trying to work out a way to fight a man with hands as quick as mine. He suddenly launched himself at me. He was quick but my feet were even quicker. Athelstan had taught me to spin on one foot. It was a dangerous move as it exposed your back to an enemy but I spun so that it was his shield close to my back rather than his sword. As he lurched past me I swung my sword hard across his back. I used the edge of the blade and the momentum of my spin to add power to the blow. The grunt from the helmet told me I had hurt him. More importantly I saw, through his ripped surcoat, that I had damaged the links of his hauberk.

He too tried to spin but it is a move which needs to be practised and he had not. He stumbled and I took the opportunity to dart my blade along his side again. This time I heard my sword tear the links of his hauberk. To those watching it would look as though we were evenly matched. They were too far away to see the rips and tears in his mail but the two of us knew of them. I was making his mail weaker. It was a slow process and we would both be tired by the time I had succeeded.

He faced me once more. He held his sword a little higher than he had done before. He was changing his strategy. As a taller, bigger knight he could bring the sword down from on high. He was going to batter me to death. I braced myself to endure blows which I knew would come quick and hard. I pulled my shield a little tighter to my side and I shifted the weight, subtly to my left leg. When he swung his sword I just raised my shield a little higher and took the hit using my braced left leg for support. The sound of the sword hitting the shield echoed across the field and I heard a cheer from his supporters. My shoulder ached and I felt numbness in my left arm again. My fingers tingled. It was my old weakness returning.

I turned slightly so that my right leg was behind me. He swung again and this time the blow was a backhand one across my shield. This strike did not have as much force as the first. He was tiring slightly. Had my arm not been weakened then I would have punched him with my shield. I just had to take the hits. His strike however, had exposed his side again. I jabbed my sword towards the tear in his surcoat. This time he grunted and there was a tendril of blood on my blade. The cheers from his supporters still sounded for they only saw the massive blows he was making. I was forced to recoil with each one.

As he pulled his sword up again for another strike I prepared to move. My right foot was behind me and my left planted firmly before me. I did the unexpected. As he swung his sword towards my head I stepped into him with my right foot. The pommel of his sword caught the side of my helmet as he struck at me and the blow made me briefly see stars but I was able to push my sword across his mail. This strike was higher than the ones which had wounded him and I heard the mail links as my sword grated along them. I continued my move and, as I stepped behind

246

him I pushed hard with my shoulder. His blow had already overbalanced him and he had to take two or three steps to regain his balance. I was on him in an instant. Whilst he was struggling to stand upright I brought my sword in a wide sideways arc to sweep into his weakened mail and wounded side. This time I did strike flesh. Blood spurted and it was the turn of our men to cheer. The blood was clearly visible on my sword although his red surcoat hid the damage from his men.

Perhaps the cheer distracted me for he brought his own sword around in a mighty blow to smash into my shield and weakened arm. I lost all feeling from my shoulder to my hand. Now I was in trouble. I forced myself to concentrate on his sword and to recall Athelstan's words. '*A fight is never over until you lie dead at the feet of an opponent*'. I could still move my feet and I could see that he was bleeding in two places. I just had to stay away from his sword and keep my left side as protected as possible.

I saw that his sword and his shield were held slightly lower than they had been. He was tiring. There was nothing wrong with my right arm and my hand darted forward to strike beneath his helmet. He was taller than I was and the tip of my sword beat his defence and forced his head up. I had no feeling in my arm but I used my body to push my shield into him. Overbalancing he fell backwards. He was a large man and I felt the ground shake as he hit. I was also losing my balance. I had one chance. As I stepped over him I stabbed downwards. Perhaps fortune guided my hand or Athelstan's training took over; whatever the reason the blade went beneath the metal plate which protected his left shoulder. As I tumbled over his body I kept hold of my sword and felt it grate along bone and then tear free. He screamed in pain.

I was on my feet in an instant and I spun around. He lumbered to his feet. His shield hung from his now useless arm. We were both even now and similarly weakened. Blood flowed freely. It was a mortal wound but he was not yet dead and he was dangerous. I would not underestimate him. I had seen men last for hours with such a wound. I could hear his heavy laboured breathing as he circled me. Suddenly he raised his sword high in the air. I thought it was the precursor to a strike but it was a signal. The rebel knights lurched forward towards our line. I was almost distracted by the movement and de Coucy lunged at my head. He was like a wounded bull and I stepped out of his way but left my sword pointed at him. The force of his charge knocked me to the ground but drove the sword deep within him. He fell dead on my right arm.

I saw a bandit above me with an axe. I tried to move my left arm to bring up my shield but there was no power. My left side was numb. As the edge of the axe bit into my arm an arrow appeared through the side of his head and he fell at my feet. I struggled up. I felt the blood flowing from the wound. It could have been worse. Had the arrow not slain him I would have lost my arm. I saw the siege engines were being destroyed but also that the focus of their attack was me. Another two men fell to the arrows of my archers as they defended me from afar. I wearily swung my sword at the wild warrior who ran at me. It was a weak blow but it bit into his unprotected neck. I saw four mailed warriors run at me and knew that my time was done and then I heard a roar as Wulfric led my three squires into a frenzied attack on the men at arms. I believe Wulfric was so angry that he could have slain them all on his own but my three squires fought like terriers. With the men at arms dead they stood before me in a protective wall.

Then the King and the other knights arrived and the battle began to go our way. I tried to raise my sword but I had no strength. I saw the blood puddling at my feet and I sank to my knees. I heard Wulfric roar, "Edgar!"

As I lay panting on the ground William took my sword and held it. "You have won father!"

Then Edgar appeared, "Lie down my lord, you are losing too much blood."

Leofric took off my helmet as John laid me on the ground. I stared up at the blue skies filled with scudding clouds and heard the sounds of battle around me. It felt strange and I remembered my dream. Then I seemed to be floating and now it felt the same. Was I dying?

I must have blacked out for the sky disappeared. I knew I was not dying when I heard William's voice close to my head, "Do not die father!"

I forced my eyes open and sat up. Edgar said, irritably, "I pray you stop moving, my lord. I am trying to staunch the bleeding!"

I saw that he had pulled away the damaged mail and ripped my sleeve. I saw that it was a deep wound but he had tied a piece of cloth around my upper arm. Having seen the wound, I knew I would not die, at least not yet. "Leofric, fetch a torch. You must cauterize it, Edgar."

He laughed, "You have seen my needlework then, my lord." He turned to William, "Fetch your father two goblets of ale from the camp."

He looked at me and I said, "Obey Edgar, he is a healer."

As he ran off I surveyed the battle as I could see it from my prone position. Wulfric's rapid arrival and my archers' skill had stopped this becoming a disaster. I now saw that the fight had been planned so that they could destroy our siege engines and catch us unawares. It had been the arrogance of de Coucy which had saved us. He should have given the signal earlier but he wanted the glory of defeating me first. John could see further. "How goes the battle?"

"There are horses coming from the castle, my lord."

That would be a disaster if they attacked our men. It was a mêlée and there was no order. A line of mounted men could sweep through our lines and the King would be in danger. Leofric arrived with the torch. Edgar took it and said, "You two lads hold tightly. He will thrash around. I am sorry, my lord."

I felt John and Leofric grip my shoulders. My right hand was still on the ground. I closed my eyes and nodded. I felt warmth become heat and then smelled burning hair and flesh before an excruciating pain raced up my arm and through my body. I gritted my teeth and waited for the agony to subside. I kept my eyes closed and then felt a sudden shock of cold. I opened my eyes and saw that Edgar had poured one of the goblets of ale on to the wound. He handed me the other. I drank it down. I needed wine to numb the pain but the ale helped.

As John stood he said, "My lord, the horsemen! They are fleeing south! The enemy are running."

It seemed that Puset and Breteuil were fleeing to fight another day. I lay back down. We could go home. I must have dozed off for the next thing I knew I was in a tent in the camp. Wulfric stood over me. He smiled when I opened my eyes. "I have sent the men and the squires to collect the treasure from de Coucy and the men we slew. The men of Blois and Anjou hung back a little too much for my liking. That was a good fight, my lord. He was a tough warrior. I knew you would defeat him but…" He nodded towards my arm. "I am sorry I was too slow to stop that bastard with the axe. It was a good job that Dick had his wits about him."

"Did we lose any men?"

He shook his head, "Their best men rode off while the bandits were slaughtered. The King is in the town now. He is an angry man."

"And what of the counts?"

"The Count of Blois is with the King." He sniffed, "He is like a dog picking up scraps. Sorry my lord, I spoke out of turn." I waved a hand to show it did not bother me. "The Count of Anjou is gathering his men. He intends to follow Hugh lord of Puset. He seems to think he was insulted."

"What says the King about that?"

"He does not know. He is still in the town."

"We shall return to Caen when the King has finished with the burghers of Thymerais. I do not think he will be in a conciliatory mood. I have had enough of this land. I would return to Stockton."

"Aye my lord and perhaps the pestilential air will have been cleansed from our home by then."

We did well from the battle. I would need a new hauberk and surcoat but the armour of de Coucy was well made and Alf would be able to use many parts of it. We had gained no horses but there were many coins and weapons from the dead. Some of them had been taken in battles with the French. My three squires did particularly well out of the battle.

It was night by the time the King returned and I was rested and dressed. I had left the tent. I wanted an open sky above me. I saw the smoke from the burning corpses drifting towards the town. I saw that the King's standard and that of Blois flew from its towers.

King Henry strode over to me. He had a worried look upon his face. "Once again, I am in your debt, Cleveland. You were right about treachery and I thank God for your archers. I intend to make a decree that every manor in England must train archers such as yours. Things would have gone badly else."

"That is a wise move, my liege. Archers will save England. The town is ours?"

"It is. I shall stay here for a few days to make it defensible. I would not wish Louis to take advantage of the blood of Anjou." He suddenly looked up. "Where is my son in law? I saw him not."

Wulfric said, hesitantly for he was in awe of the King, "His is pursuing Hugh of Puset, your majesty. He said his honour had been impugned."

"The fool! Then I shall have to follow him. I cannot have my daughter widowed a second time."

"You will return to Caen?" I nodded, "Do not leave before I return. I will not be long."

"I had hoped to begin to rebuild my life in the north, my liege."

"I know but I needs must speak with you about…" he was suddenly aware that others were around, "well you know of what I speak." He turned to William, "Your father is someone whom you can admire and emulate. He is a true knight. He is probably the finest English knight in the land. Chivalry and honour course through his noble veins."

After he had gone I issued my orders, "Wulfric have the men ready to leave in the morning. I care not how you get them but find as many spare sumpters as you can. I think that, for a while at least, we can use the good offices of my name."

Wulfric laughed, "Do not worry, my lord, we will have enough horses for all that we have taken." He looked at my arm which was heavily bandaged. "Shall I have a litter made for you?"

"If you do then you can find another master to ride upon it! I will ride Scout!"

We rode at a leisurely pace for our animals had worked hard and we had no spares. Even so it only took us a day longer to reach Caen than the outward journey had taken. The first treasure we had captured was there with Sir Richard's men. The news of our new victory had not reached Caen. It did not take long for the news to spread. The castellan insisted that we stay in the keep. It suited me. My men would be in the warrior hall but it would be more peaceful in the half empty keep. I intended to sleep and rest as much as I could. Despite my words to Wulfric the combination of the blows to my arm and the wound from the axe made me worry about my left arm. This was where I missed the surgeons from Constantinople who knew how to deal with such injuries. The healers in the castle were often relying on guesswork.

I had just reached my chambers and my squires were about to help me take off my mail when there was a knock at the door. It was Judith, the Empress' lady in waiting. "Sorry to disturb you my lord but the Empress would like to invite you to dine with her in the Great Hall this evening. She has been lonely since her father left. Rolf and the Swabians will be there. She asks if your sergeant at arms might join her too."

"We would be honoured."

After she had left and my squires took off my mail and helped me to bathe I pondered her words, *since her father left*. Not her husband but her father. What was the significance of that? Leofric promised to pass the invitation on to Wulfric. He would come but he would be less than happy. He hated having to watch his manners. He was always happiest in the company of men. He would never marry for that reason. Still I knew that there were many Wulfrics spread across England, Scotland, Wales and Normandy. He might shun their polite company but Wulfric liked women and they liked him in return!

Chapter 18

I still had some fine clothes which I had brought with me from my last visit to Constantinople. Leofric trimmed my beard and hair. He anointed my face with the sweet-smelling lotion we had brought from the east and when he was satisfied he left. Edgar had told Leofric to make sure I wore a sling for my arm. Leofric insisted that I obeyed orders. Later that night I was pleased that he had for it ached the whole time. Had I not had the sling then the pain would have been unbearable.

I was the first one to reach the Great Hall. The Steward had obviously had his orders from the Empress. He waved a servant over to me with a goblet of the heavy red wine she knew I liked. I sat by the fire and stared into the flames. I had learned the habit from my father who swore that he could see battles and great deeds in the flickering firelight. I found my mind drifting. I had told the King I wanted to return home as soon as possible but was that really true? Perhaps I had been deluding myself. I wanted to be here in Caen. Stockton was now a place of haunted memories for me. Every room and corridor would remind me of my wife and my child. My empty bed would make me feel lonely. The meals with just my son for company would reinforce the fact that I lived in a home without women. I had grown up in such a house and I knew how it had eaten away at my father. It was another reason he had left the villa to come to England.

My melancholic reverie was ended by a clap on the back and a roar from my Swabian brothers. "If it is not the hero of Thymerais. We would have been here sooner but we spent some time with Wulfric, Dick and your squires. Do you have to win every battle single handedly?"

"I just follow orders."

"Do not lie to your blood brothers Alfraed. You went into battle with this giant thinking you would die. That is why you asked the King to take your son as a ward."

"I was thinking of my son it is true but I did not want to die. That would be a sin."

"You are not speaking the truth again; you know that your men would have raised your son as Athelstan raised you. Speak the truth and shame the devil!"

He was right of course. I had thought that I would die and now be with Adela. It seemed that I was incapable of fighting badly. I changed the subject. "The Count has taken himself off after Hugh of Puset. He thought he had been insulted by him. The King is not best pleased about that. He is a brave enough youth but he lacks both manners and judgement."

"And there you are being kind for we have not seen any behaviour like that in Anjou."

I did not like to be seen to be belittling the Count, "We have, at least, recovered the lands which Blois lost."

"I am surprised that Stephen is not here. I hear he is in England still."

Rolf was a clever man and he kept a close eye on the Blois brothers. Like me he knew of their attempt to abduct the Empress. The four of us, along with Edward were the only ones who really knew of the perfidy of the King's nephew. The sixth member of the Knights of the Empress, Sir Guy de la Cheppe lived in France. We had not seen him for some time but I knew that he too would have his suspicions about the Blois brothers.

Wulfric joined us. I hid my smile for it was obvious that he had made a valiant attempt to tame his mane and his beard. He had failed. This was not his natural environment. He could never make the change from man at arms to knight as Edward had done but I would not exchange him for any ten knights. Gottfried was also fond of him. They enjoyed the same activities and they greeted each other like two he bears. Wulfric's entrance stopped us talking politics and, instead, he embarrassed me by telling the Swabians, in even more detail the battles I had had in Wales and in Scotland.

Rolf took me to one side. "I envy you my friend. We are bodyguards only. We do not go to war. If we did not practise each day then I fear we would forget what a sword is for."

"You could ask to be relieved of your duty. The Empress must be safe now for she has a husband."

Rolf shook his head, "There have been two attempts on her life already. One was a poison. We caught the woman but she managed to take her own life with a draught of the same poison. The other was an attack in the forest. Karl's quick reactions saved her that day. We would have caught and tortured the assassin but he tripped and broke his neck whilst fleeing from us. Someone wants her dead. There are many who wish the throne of England for themselves."

"I did not know but having seen Juliana and her husband I am not surprised. The only child of the King who supports the Empress is Robert Earl of Gloucester and he is in England."

"And I hope he stays there for he must secure the throne for the Empress when the King dies. I do not think her husband can win it for her."

Our conversation was interrupted by the arrival of the Empress. She swept in and looked every inch an Empress and the daughter of a king. She was stunning. The three of them, the Empress and her ladies had obviously gone to great lengths to impress us with their appearance. Matilda, however, stood out. I could not take my eyes from her. Perhaps the heavy red wine had gone to my head but I felt intoxicated just looking at her. When she coyly smiled at me I felt my heart race. I am ashamed to say that all my thoughts of Adela left my head. I was a shallow creature who could be swayed by a smile and the hint of perfume.

"Come, Alfraed, the wounded hero shall sit next to me. I would hear from your own lips of your great deeds. My ladies shall sit between the other warriors for you are all dear to me." She came over to Wulfric and gave him a medallion made of gold. In the centre it had her image cast into it. It was a smaller version of the ones she had given the Knights of the Empress. "And you Wulfric of Stockton, this is for you. I have heard how you saved the life of my champion. You may not have the title of a knight but you have the heart of one and I would be honoured if you would champion me as the others do."

Wulfric blushed and clumsily dropped to one knee, "Empress it would be an honour!"

She took his hand and lifting him to his feet kissed him on both cheeks. I was at the side and I saw his face. He was enchanted, quite literally, by her presence. From that moment on he was as fervent a follower as we were. The ladies sat down and we followed suit. All thoughts of treachery and plots disappeared. We only had eyes for the three visions of loveliness. The five of us were warriors who were used to war and wounds, battles and blood but that night we were just men entranced by the beauty and conversation of three ladies.

Despite my enjoyment with the company, the food and the conversation, my arm began to ache. It had been hard enough eating one handed as it was but when my whole left side began to throb I became distracted. The Empress was not only an astute woman she seemed to know what troubled me. "What ails you, Earl? I see pain upon your face."

"It is just the wound." I laughed, "I have been fortunate thus far and avoided wounds. Perhaps it is a sign that I am getting old."

She leaned over my body to my left arm and sniffed the wound. I was intoxicated by her perfume and briefly forgot the pain. "There is no smell of putrefaction."

"It will pass."

Wulfric, who was normally silent, voiced his own concerns. "My lady, he has not been right since he took many blows on his shield at the attack on Coucy's castle. When he fought the single combat, he dropped his shield. There is something wrong with the arm. He thought to hide it from us but we knew that there was something amiss."

She frowned, "Then I will have my physician look at it in the morning and Margaret will bring a potion this night to aid your sleep."

I laughed, "I think the wine alone will make me sleep."

I resolved to smile for the rest of the evening and avoid scrutiny of my arm. Wulfric was correct. I had not been able to use my left arm as I should have been able to since that first attack. I feared I had some wound which was deep within and would never heal.

As the evening went on Wulfric showed a side I had never seen before. He began to relax and to drink more. He could hold his ale and his wine and he did not become unpleasant. However, he did begin to sing, at Judith's request, some songs and he had a fine voice. The songs became more and more ribald. I feared he had offended the Empress and tried to quieten him.

Matilda put her hand on my right hand and said, "I am not offended. It is good that we laugh so. I have not laughed so much

258

in years. Your sergeant at arms has a gift from God; he has a fine voice. Let him use it."

And it did make all of us smile. I think I was not the only one who was sad when the ladies retired for the night. Before she left the Empress came to me and, putting her hands on mine said, "Thank you for the evening Alfraed and I will send Margaret with the potion and the salve. The Empress needs her knights. Who knows when danger may strike?"

After they had gone Wulfric engaged in good humoured banter with Gottfried. Karl fell asleep and Rolf joined me by the fire. He pointed to my left arm. "Did the feeling go from your arm from here to here?" He moved his hand from my shoulder to my fingers.

"Aye."

"And you found it hard to grip and to move."

"Aye."

"I have seen this before. Despite the Empress' words I am not certain that her physician will be able to cure it. I knew of an older knight, when I was a young squire, who suffered in the same way. In his case it was the result of a hammer on his shield. He lived to a ripe old age but sometimes, in the middle of battle and for no reason, his left arm would not function. After a while feeling would return."

"How was he able to fight?"

"He had well trained horses and his shield was tightly strapped to his left arm so that when the feeling left him he was still protected." I nodded, "You could do worse than copy de Coucy and have a plate over your left shoulder. That is where you are vulnerable, even with a tight shield."

"Thank you, my friend. We never know when we will suddenly become old do we?"

He laughed, "You are not old. You are younger than I and I do not feel old. This is caused by the death of your wife. It may seem harsh but you must forget her or put her deep within the back of your mind. She would want you to become stronger following her death and not weaker. Would she want you cloistered in a monastery?"

I laughed, "No, not Adela. She loved life." I nodded, "You are right and I have William to look to. Until he becomes a man I must be mother, father, lord and mentor to my son. He does not need an old man yet."

Wulfric and Gottfried picked up Karl and carried him to bed.

Rolf stood and clasped my arm. "This has been the most enjoyable night I have had for some time. Thank you for your company."

"And thank you for your company and your advice. I know it comes from the heart."

Once in my room I took off my sling. I regretted that my squires were in the warrior hall. How would I undress? Almost before the thought had disappeared into my head the door opened and Margaret came in with her jar of salve and the leather bottle. She took one look at me and shook her head. She put the jar and bottle on the table and said, "Come, my lord, I will help to undress you."

I was embarrassed, "No, Margaret, it is not seemly."

She laughed, "You think you will be the first man I had seen naked. You have nothing I have not seen before. Come, my lady commands me to tend to you."

I surrendered. She was very gentle as she took my clothes from me. She was careful not to cause me any more pain. I do not think I had ever seen such a gentle woman.

As she laid my clothes on the table she said, "Lie on the bed so that I may tend to your arm."

She brought over the salve and removed my bandage. In the candlelight the wound looked red and angry. I saw bruising running all the way up the arm. She sniffed the bandage. "You will need this no longer. The wound is healed or it is healing enough to need God's air upon it." She gently began to dab the salve around the wound. It smelled very pleasant with a hint of rosemary and there was something in it which had heat. Seemingly satisfied she rubbed more of the aromatic salve on the rest of the arm. She had a touch like the professional masseurs in the baths of Constantinople. "There, now I will give you a draught of this potion. There are herbs within this too. It will help you sleep and it has powers to heal from within." She looked deep into my eyes, "In the body, the head and the heart."

"Are you a witch, Margaret?" I asked the question for she seemed to read my mind.

She laughed, "My mother healed in my village and some said she was a witch." She shrugged, "I know how to heal and I know how people think. If that makes me a witch then I am a witch." She poured me a small goblet of wine and added a few drops of the potion.

"What is this?"

"Nothing to fear. Now drink it." I did as she commanded. "If you shout out in the night then I will come to you. Our rooms are just across the corridor." She leaned over and kissed me on the forehead like a mother with a sick child. "Now sleep, my lord, and you will be a new man when you wake in the morning. I promise you that."

She covered me with a quilt and after blowing out the candle left. I smiled as I rolled over to sleep. I felt like a child again. I fell asleep quickly and dreamed. The dreams were little flashes and pictures which made no sense. I saw Adela nursing Hilda then an axe came through a door and I saw a grinning and bleeding de Coucy above me. I saw the King leading a charge of warriors and I saw my castle burning. I woke and found myself sweating. I suddenly realised that I was not alone. I could smell Margaret.

"Who is there?"

A low female voice whispered, "You cried out. I came to see why."

A shadow came towards me and slipped beneath the quilt. I felt gentle fingers on my chest and then I was being kissed. I did not resist and I kissed back. I had not felt this way for years not since …

"Matilda!"

Her husky voice was close to my ear as she said, "Not tonight. We are just two people who should have been together for all time. That can never be but for tonight we are as one. Fear not, Margaret stands guard outside the door. Do not fight this, my love. It was meant to be."

I do not know if it was the drink I had consumed or the potion but I did not fight it. To my shame I wanted this and the two of us lay together all night and made love. We dozed and woke. We spoke and we embraced but mainly we made love. As the first hint of light began to come through the slit in the wall the door opened and Margaret's voice hissed across the chamber, "My lady. You must be hence. The servants rise."

Matilda leaned over to me and kissed me one last time. "This was not wrong, Alfraed. God sent my child husband to fight and returned you to me for one night. My prayers have been answered and for the only time in my life I have been held by a real man whom I love. We can never do this again but I shall cherish the memory of this one night to my grave. Thank you," she hesitated, "my love. And I pray that God will reward this tryst with a child. It is my fervent hope."

I held her hand, "You cannot leave me now. Flee with me and we will find a new life together."

"Flee? To Constantinople perhaps?" She too had read my mind. "That was my idea once my love and you persuaded me that it would not end well. You were right. We both have responsibilities. If we fled then England and Normandy would be in turmoil. Your home and people in Stockton would be razed. Would you want that? The price we pay for the peace is our unhappiness. Know that I will think of you always and I know that you will think of me. In the next life we shall be together."

She left the room and I closed my eyes. Suddenly the wound in my arm seemed as nothing. It was the wound in my heart which would never heal.

When I rose and met the Empress and the Swabians for our first meal of the day it was as though the previous night had never happened. There was no sign from either Margaret or the Empress of the events of the night. I felt confused. We had just finished when a small man, I recognised him as a Greek, appeared at the door. The Empress smiled at him, "Ah Basil." She looked at me, "This is my physician. He will examine you. If there is a cure for what ails you then he will find it." Her eyes met mine and that day began a conversation without words. I knew the meaning of the look.

When Basil spoke, in my chambers, he spoke in Greek. "The Empress said you came from the Great City. It is good to speak my language rather than the jabber they use here. That way there will be no confusion." He sniffed my arm and smiled, "I see the witch has been at work. Fear not she has skills but not I think the skills you require. Tell me how you came to be wounded."

I told him all and, mindful of Wulfric's words, included the first blows.

He nodded and began to feel around my elbow. "I will just try something." He opened his leather bag of instruments and took out a scalpel. It was thin and sharp. He smiled. "Look away and then tell me if you feel anything."

He held my hand and I felt pain as he stuck it in my palm, "Ow!"

"Good, and now?"

"Nothing."

"And now?"

"Nothing."

"Good."

I felt a pain in my shoulder, "I felt that."

"It is what I expected. You may look at me now." He held my elbow. "The problem lies here and there is, I am afraid, no cure. You felt no pain when I stuck my scalpel into your elbow. The effect will occasionally spread. I fear that in your world you will have to endure many blows to the arm and they may well spread the numbness down your arm. One day, perhaps, the numbness will remain and you will not be able to use your left hand and arm. There is nothing I can do. The only solution would be to stop being a knight."

"I cannot do that."

"I know. Then you should continue to use the salve but just on your elbow. I will have the witch prepare a large batch of it." He shook his head, "She will enjoy that! And if you can protect your left side then so much the better." He stood and said, "Perhaps padding on the inside of your shield?"

"That may be a solution but it would have to be hidden. If my enemies know of my weakness then…"

"Quite so."

After he had gone there was a knock at my door and my squires were there, "Good. You may help me to dress and then I have a task for you but it is one which must be carried out in secret." As they dressed me I thought about the previous day. It had changed my life. I knew that. The Empress was quite right. We could never be together, not unless her husband was dead. If she had a child then things might be different but Henry would never rest until he had a legitimate male heir. And I was now a wounded warrior and would be so for the rest of my life. My reputation was such that I would always be sought out in a battle. As Earl of Cleveland, champion to an Empress and a King, I had nowhere to hide.

Once I was dressed I confided in my squires. "You are my oathsworn and within these walls our words remain. Is that clear?"

They all nodded, "Aye my lord."

"My arm will be weak now. I need the three of you to pad my shield on the inside but make it so that no one knows. I also need shorter leather straps so that the shield will be tight to my arm."

Leofric was the thinker, "That will make it harder for you to fight on horseback, my lord."

"I know. I will have to learn to fight differently. When we return to Stockton that will be our task to give me skills I do not have now so that I can be stronger than I am now."

They left to find my shield and I knew that they would do a good job. They were loyal.

The King and the Count of Anjou returned just six days after we did. Sir Richard sought me out. He shook his head, "It was fortunate that the King followed his son in law. He nearly walked into an ambush which would have slaughtered them all. Even so he lost heavily. The King is not happy." He lowered his voice, "He told him to father a son quickly or he would have the marriage annulled."

I suddenly felt guilty. What if the Empress was now with child? That child would be mine and not her husband's. A shiver ran down my spine. That wild night was just a memory; would it be a memory which would return to haunt me?

Perhaps the King's words had had an effect for Count Geoffrey sought out the Empress and we did not see them until the evening feast. The Count strutted as though he owned the whole farmyard. I was seated next to the King and the Count sat amongst his knights at the opposite side of the room. I saw the disappointed look on the faces of Rolf and the Swabians. They would have preferred our company. The Empress, however, kept up the mask. However, when she glanced over at her father our eyes met and we spoke.

King Henry was quite concerned about my wound. "My daughter's physician has told me of your injuries. I am sorry. If I had known what would happen then I would never have agreed to the combat. I was tricked."

"We cannot change the past. Who knows, if we had assaulted then the outcome might have been the same save that de

Coucy might have escaped. At least one of your enemies has died."

"Aye and the serpent of a daughter and her husband are now in Paris where they conspire with Louis. I have heard that he is making moves to marry his idiot son to Eleanor of Aquitaine. That is a dangerous prospect for Normandy; we would then be encircled. The sooner my daughter has an heir the better."

"Amen to that." Sir Richard was as aware as I was of the danger of a civil war after the King's death.

We ate well that night. The King's favourite food, lampreys, was served. I did not particularly enjoy them and I played with them just to satisfy my host.

"When you return to England I want you to keep a close watch on Balliol and try to send spies to discover the whereabouts of Gospatric. I had intended to return home and help my son to watch over my realm. Events here have conspired against me. You have my permission to fortify the castles of your knights."

That was a great honour. Kings did not like castles, other than their own, to be crenulated and heavily fortified. It showed the trust he had in me. "Thank you, my lord, but I should warn you that the strongest castle other than my own is Barnard Castle; it is Balliol's castle. It has a naturally defensive site and sits atop a rocky crag."

"Watch Balliol and use your authority to curb his ambitions. My clerk is drafting a decree increasing your powers."

"And Durham?"

He smiled, "Let us just say that so long as you control the Tees there is little point in appointing a Bishop whose loyalty is in doubt. The Pope keeps suggesting names and each one arouses suspicion in me. No, it is best we leave it as it is. Besides I have appointed Henry of Blois as Bishop of Winchester. The Archbishop allowed that. It increases my influence in the south of the land."

"As you wish." I spoke to hide my feelings. I liked not the fact the brother of Stephen and Theobald held such a prominent position. The King trusted the brothers. I did not.

"And Cleveland, do not grieve overlong for your wife. Find another woman. One son is never enough. I learned that. A man should have as many sons as he can. Your wife would wish it."

"I will try but there is a dearth of suitable ladies in the north."

He nodded distractedly. His advice given he moved on.

We left a week later. Margaret came to me just before I was leaving and handed me a jar of salve. She spoke quietly. "Your lady sent me with this." Her words lifted my heart. "She said she will always think of you and prays for you each night."

"As I do her."

She gave me an intriguing smile. "Next year will be a better year for us all; I promise you that."

As I left the castle I could not help looking back. Would I see her again and, if I did we would be as strangers? I could never lie with her again.

I had sent word to Olaf that I needed his ship again and it was waiting for us at Ouistreham. We sailed north back to Stockton. I had lost so much during the year and I had come close to death more times than enough yet somehow, I felt stronger. I was ready for the challenge of the north and ready to fight for what was mine.

Epilogue

The salve seemed to help as we sailed north with a ship laden with the fruits of our labours. I smiled as I listened to my three squires speak of what they intended to buy with their share. I spent much time with Wulfric and Dick. They were now as close to me as Edward and the Swabians. I would not be sailing home but for their efforts and skills.

"We will need to make up the numbers of men at arms and archers again."

Wulfric gave a scowl. "This time we take none who have come from the east eh my lord?"

"You are right. I would use much of this gold to buy more horses. Dick, when we return I wish you to take your archers and go to the horse country to the south of us and buy horses."

"Aye my lord and I will send men to Sherwood to find more archers."

And so we planned. It helped me to forget the pain of losing Adela and the pain of being apart from Matilda. My one night of joy would never be repeated. I had seen the Holy Grail and had it taken from me. I would never know happiness again. When we had finished planning we spoke of the battles we had fought and how we would fight in the future. I had much to live for now. Sadly, my enemies continued to grow. I did not doubt that Hugh of Puset wished me dead too.

I felt a sense of dread as we sailed into the Tees. My banner still fluttered from my tower but I wondered if I could settle within its walls once more. William came to stand next to me. He had grown, both physically and mentally. He looked little different these days to Leofric. John still towered over him but soon there would only be Wulfric who was bigger. William had seen great slaughter and fought his first battle. Those things changed a person. "It will be hard father but mother and Hilda are with God now. They are happy." I looked at him and I saw not just my child and my squire but someone to whom I could talk. He had endured what I had endured. "The Empress' ladies, Judith and Margaret, were kind and they spent time talking with me. Margaret said she believed that mother's spirit was happy. I think she is right."

I was curious, "How do you know?"

He came a little closer, "I have dreamed and I have seen her face. She looks as she always did, happy."

Perhaps I needed that innocence of youth too.

We stepped ashore and there was a party waiting to greet us: John, my steward, Erre, Aiden and Alf. John spoke for them all, "Welcome home, my lord. We have cleansed the castle and the town."

"Aye sir, we burned all those buildings which showed signs of disease. Our town is healthy once more."

"Thank you, Alf." I looked at Erre. "And how are the men?"

"We are all determined to serve you better than ever. We owe it to the memory of those who did not die with a sword in their hand. That is no way for a warrior to die."

"You are right." I waved a hand at Olaf's ship which was being unloaded, "And we have more treasure, mail and weapons. I am home to stay."

I saw a priest walking from the town gate towards the jetty. John said, "This is Father Henry the new priest appointed by the bishop."

The young man gave a slight bow. "I am Father Henry. I hope I can serve you and this parish as well as Father Matthew. I have much to live up to."

"None of us can hope to be a man as great as Father Matthew. Alf, I would like to commission a bell for the church. I would like to name it Matthew."

That seemed to please everyone and it gave me something to worry about other than the affairs of my heart. Alf too enjoyed the task and five weeks later it was finished. My father and his oathsworn believed in something they called, '*wyrd*' or fate. It was truly '*wyrd*' when the bell was rung for the first time. It was a few weeks after its erection and we had not even used it to summon the congregation to church. It was such a shock that we all ran to the church.

Father Henry came out with a huge smile on his face. He clutched in his hand a document. "This is great news. The King has sent it to the Archbishop of York and he has sent it to me. The Empress Matilda is with child! The King will have a grandchild. It is cause for great celebration."

Hardly daring to hear the answer I asked, "When will the child be born?"

The priest re read the document, "March of next year! What wonderful news."

As I turned to walk back up to my castle I began to count back the months. Nine months from March was the time when I had slept with the Empress. Her husband had arrived back a week later. Who was the father? Was it the Count of Anjou or had I fathered a bastard? The only way I would know would be to speak with the Empress. I now yearned to be back in Normandy but I was not. I was on the Tees. I was Earl of Cleveland and I would spend the next months with the thought that I might be the father of a future ruler of England. That one night of passion might come back to haunt not only me but the whole of England and Normandy. I climbed to my south-east tower and stared out across the German Sea. The land for which I fought was now even more precious to me.

The End

Glossary

Allaghia- a subdivision of a Bandon-about 400 hundred men (Byzantium)

Akolouthos - The commander of the Varangian Guard (Byzantium)

Al-Andalus- Spain

Angevin- the people of Anjou, mainly the ruling family

Bandon- Byzantine regiment of cavalry -normally 1500 men (Byzantium)

Battle- a formation in war (a modern battalion)

Booth Castle – Bewcastle north of Hadrian's Wall

Cadge- the frame upon which hunting birds are carried (by a codger- hence the phrase old codger being the old man who carries the frame)

Cadwaladr ap Gruffudd- Son of Gruffudd ap Cynan

Conroi- A group of knights fighting together

Demesne- estate

Destrier- war horse

Fess- a horizontal line in heraldry

Gambeson- a padded tunic worn underneath mail. When worn by an archer they came to the waist. It was more of a quilted jacket but I have used the term freely

Gonfanon- A standard used in Medieval times (Also known as a Gonfalon in Italy)

Gruffudd ap Cynan- King of Gwynedd until 1137

Hartness- the manor which became Hartlepool

Hautwesel- Haltwhistle

Kataphractos (pl. oi)- Armoured Byzantine horseman (Byzantium)

Kometes/Komes- General (Count) (Byzantium)

Kentarchos- Second in command of an Allaghia (Byzantium)

Kontos (pl. oi) - Lance (Byzantium)

Lusitania- Portugal

Mansio- staging houses along Roman Roads

Maredudd ap Bleddyn- King of Powys

Mêlée- a medieval fight between knights

Musselmen- Muslims

Nithing- A man without honour (Saxon)

Nomismata- a gold coin equivalent to an aureus

Outremer- the kingdoms of the Holy Land

Owain ap Gruffudd- Son of Gruffudd ap Cynan and King of Gwynedd from 1137

Palfrey- a riding horse

Poitevin- the language of Aquitaine

Pyx- a box containing a holy relic (Shakespeare's Pax from Henry V)

Serdica- Sofia (Byzantium)

Surcoat- a tunic worn over mail or armour

Sumpter- pack horse

Tagmata- Byzantine cavalry (Byzantium)

Turmachai -Commander of a Bandon of cavalry (Byzantium)

Ventail – a piece of mail which covered the neck and the lower face.

Wulfestun- Wolviston (Durham)

Maps and Illustrations

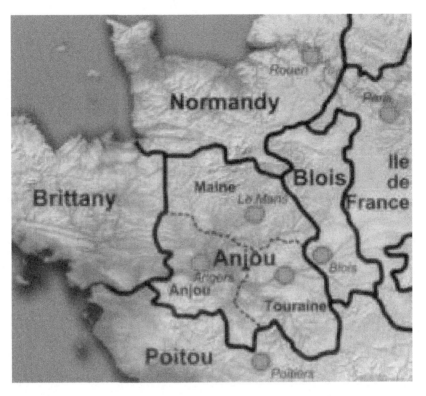

Map courtesy of Wikipedia

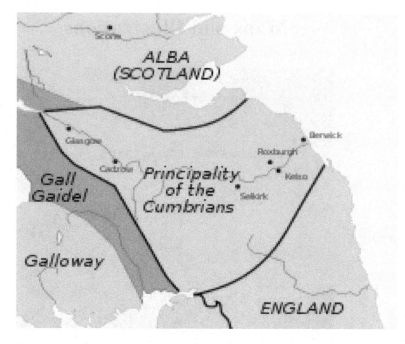

Courtesy of Wikipedia –Public Domain

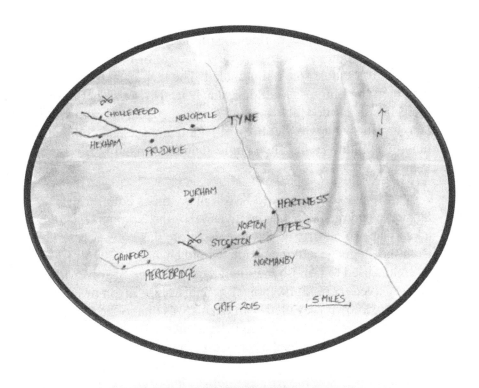

279

Historical note

The book is set during one of the most turbulent and complicated times in British history. Henry I of England and Normandy's eldest son William died. The king named his daughter, the Empress Matilda as his heir. However, her husband, the Emperor of the Holy Roman Empire died and she remarried. Her new husband was Geoffrey of Anjou and she had children by him. (The future Henry II of England and Normandy- The Lion in Winter!)

I have used the word Saxon many times both for the language and the people. The invasion of the Normans had only taken place some fifty or sixty years before this book was set. Both the language and the people would change and evolve. The Normans tried to impose their language upon the Saxons who already lived there. It did not work and Anglo-Saxon or English as it became known prevailed. Part of this was due to the fact that the Norman ladies used Saxon/English nannies to look after their babies and children. As they spoke to them in their native tongue the young Normans grew up speaking English. Of course, many Norman words became part of English- honour, chivalry, ham, lake but it took another century, until after the time of Richard 1st, for one language to be used throughout the land. In my next book I will change the word Saxon for English. By the time of Henry 1st's death the ordinary folk thought of themselves as English.

A cog was a small trading ship which developed from the Viking knarr. It had high sides and a flat bottom. There was one sail and steering oar on the starboard (steer board) side. By this time some had had small wooden castles built at the bow and stern and these were used to house archers. These ships would be built bigger as the centuries wore on. They had no deck save at the stern where the ship was conned. The holds were covered with canvas when they had goods to transport.

I have introduced Eleanor of Aquitaine here. She was about 8 in 1129 and her father was Duke William. As she eventually marries Matilda's son I thought I would introduce her. The Empress Matilda did leave her husband in 1130. It was not a happy marriage.

The Emperor John Komnenos fought against the Hungarians under King later Saint Stephen. He lost and had to sue for peace. The incident with our hero is purely fictional.

There was never an Earl of Cleveland although the area known as Cleveland did exist and was south of the river. At this time the only northern earls were those of Northumberland. The incumbent was Gospatric who rebelled against England when King Henry died.

The Scots were taking advantage of a power vacuum on their borders. They did, according to chroniclers of the time behave particularly badly.

"an execrable army, more atrocious than the pagans, neither fearing God nor regarding man, spread desolation over the whole province and slaughtered everywhere people of either sex, of every age and rank, destroying, pillaging and burning towns, churches and houses"

"Then (horrible to relate) they carried off, like so much booty, the noble matrons and chaste virgins, together with other women. These naked, fettered, herded together; by whips and thongs they drove before them, goading them with their spears and other weapons. This took place in other wars, but in this to a far greater extent."

"For the sick on their couches, women pregnant and in childbed, infants in the womb, innocents at the breast, or on the mother's knee, with the mothers themselves, decrepit old men and worn-out old women, and persons debilitated from whatever cause, wherever they met with them, they put to the edge of the sword, and

transfixed with their spears; and by how much more horrible a death they could dispatch them, so much the more did they rejoice. "

Robert of Hexham

Meanwhile Matilda's half-brother, Robert of Gloucester (one of William's bastards) declared for Matilda and a civil war ensued. The war went on until Stephen died and was called the anarchy because everyone was looking out for themselves. There were no sides as such. Allies could become enemies overnight. Murder, ambush and assassination became the order of the day. The only warriors who could be relied upon were the household knights of a lord- his oathsworn. The feudal system, which had been an ordered pyramid, was thrown into confusion by the civil war. Lords created their own conroi, or groups of knights and men at arms. Successful lords would ensure that they had a mixture of knights, archers and foot soldiers. The idea of knights at this time always fighting on horseback is not necessarily true. There were many examples of knights dismounting to fight on foot and, frequently, this proved to be successful.

The word Fitz shows that the owner of the name is an illegitimate son of a knight. As such they would not necessarily inherit when their father died. There were many such knights. William himself was illegitimate. Robert of Gloucester was also known as Robert of Caen and Robert Fitzroy.

Ridley, the father of my hero, was in three earlier books. There were two regiments of Varangians: one was English in character and one Scandinavian. As the bodyguards of the Emperor they were able to reap rich rewards for their service.

The Normans were formidable fighters. The conquest of England happened after a single battle. They conquered southern Italy and Sicily with a handful of knights. Strongbow, a Norman mercenary took a small mercenary force and dominated Ireland so much that as soon as a force of Normans, led by the king land, all defence on the island crumbled. In one of Strongbow's battles a force of 100 knights defeated 4000 Irish warriors!

Ranulf Flambard was the controversial Bishop of Durham who was imprisoned in the tower by Henry for supporting his brother. Although reinstated the Bishop was viewed with suspicion by the king and did not enjoy as much power as either his predecessors or his successors. He had been something of a womaniser in his younger days and he tried to make up for that by giving to the poor when he was older. He was responsible for much of the defensive works of Durham Castle and was truly a Bishop Prince. He died around 1128. The incident with the Bishop being held captive is pure fiction. However, he died in 1128 and there was a great deal of unrest while King Henry was away in Normandy. The Gospatric family did show their true colours when the Scottish king tried to take advantage of the internal strife between Stephen and Matilda and invade England. A leopard does not change his spots. The land between the Tees and the Scottish Lowlands was always fiercely contested by Scotland, England and those who lived there.

Hartness (Hartlepool) was given to the De Brus family by Henry and the family played a power game siding with Henry and David depending upon what they had to gain. They were also given land around Guisborough in North Yorkshire.

Squires were not always the sons of nobles. Often, they were lowly born and would never aspire to knighthood. It was not only the king who could make knights. Lords had that power too. Normally a man would become a knight at the age of 21. Young landless knights would often leave home to find a master to serve in the hope of treasure or loot. The idea of chivalry was some way away. The Norman knight wanted land, riches and power. Knights would have a palfrey or ordinary riding horse and a destrier or war horse. Squires would ride either a palfrey, if they had a thoughtful knight or a rouncy (pack horse). The squires carried all of the knight's war gear on the pack horses. Sometimes a knight would have a number of squires serving him. One of the squire's tasks was to have a spare horse in case the knight's destrier fell in battle. Another way for a knight to make money was to capture an enemy and ransom him. This even happened to Richard 1st of England who was captured in Austria and held to ransom.

At this time a penny was a valuable coin and often payment would be taken by 'nicking' pieces off it. Totally round copper and silver coins were not the norm in 12th Century Europe. Each local ruler would make his own small coins. The whole country was run like a pyramid with the king at the top. He took from those below him in the form of taxes and service and it cascaded down. There was a great deal of corruption as well as anarchy. The idea of a central army did not exist. King Henry had his household knights and would call upon his nobles to supply knights and men at arms when he needed to go to war. The expense for that army would be borne by the noble.

The border between England and Scotland has always been a prickly one from the time of the Romans onward. Before that time the border was along the line of Glasgow to Edinburgh. The creation of an artificial frontier, Hadrian's Wall, created an area of dispute for the people living on either side of it. William the Conqueror had the novel idea of slaughtering everyone who lived between the Tees and the Tyne/Tweed in an attempt to resolve the problem. It did not work and lords on both sides of the borders, as well as the monarchs used the dispute to switch sides as it suited them.

The manors I write about were around at the time the book is set. For a brief time, a De Brus was lord of Normanby. It changed hands a number of times until it came under the control of the Percy family. This is a work of fiction but I have based events on the ones which occurred in the twelfth century.

I can find no evidence for a castle in Norton although it was second in importance only to Durham and I assume that there must have been a defensive structure of some kind there. I suspect it was a wooden structure built to the north of the present church. The church in Norton is Norman but it is not my church. Stockton Castle was pulled down in the Civil War of the 17th Century. It was put up in the early fourteenth century. My castle is obviously earlier. As Stockton became a manor in the 12th century and the river crossing was important I am guessing that there would have been a castle there. There may have been an earlier castle on the site of Stockton Castle but until they pull down the hotel and shopping centre built on the site it is difficult to know for sure. The simple tower with a curtain wall was typical of late Norman castles. The river crossing was so important that I have to believe that there would have been some defensive structure there before the 1300s. The manor of Stockton was created in 1138. To avoid confusion in the later civil war I have moved it forward by a few years.

Vikings continued to raid the rivers and isolated villages of England for centuries. There are recorded raids as late as the sixteenth century along the coast south of the Fylde. These were not the huge raids of the ninth and tenth centuries but were pirates keen for slaves and treasure. The Barbary Pirates also raided the southern coast. Alfred's navy had been a temporary measure to deal with the Danish threat. A Royal Navy would have to wait until Henry VIII.

The Welsh did take advantage of the death of the master of Chester and rampaged through Cheshire. King Henry and his knights defeated them although King Henry was wounded by an arrow. The king's punishment was the surrender of 10,000 cattle. The Welsh did not attack England again until King Henry was dead!

Matilda was married to the Emperor of the Holy Roman Empire, Henry, in 1116 when she was 14. They had no children and the marriage was not a happy one. When William Adelin died in the White Ship disaster then Henry had no choice but to name his daughter as his heir however, by that time she had been married to Geoffrey Count of Anjou, Fulk's son and King Henry was suspicious of his former enemy's heir. His vacillation caused the civil war which was known as the Anarchy. However, those events are several books away. Stephen and Matilda are just cousins: soon they will become enemies.

In the high middle ages there was a hierarchy of hawks. At this time there was not. A baron was supposed to have a bustard which is not even a hawk. Some think it was a corruption of buzzard or was a generic name for a hawk of indeterminate type. Aiden finds hawks' eggs and raises them. The *cadge* was the square frame on which the hawks were carried and it was normally carried by a man called a codger. Hence the English slang for old codger; a retainer who was too old for anything else. It might also be the derivation of cadge (ask for) a lift- more English slang.

Gospatric was a real character. His father had been Earl of Northumberland but was replaced by William the Conqueror. He was granted lands in Scotland, around Dunbar. Once the Conqueror was dead he managed to gain lands in England around the borders. He was killed at the Battle of the Standard fighting for the Scots. I have used this as the basis for his treachery. He was succeeded by his son, Gospatric, but the family confirmed their Scottish loyalties. His other sons are, as far as I know my own invention although I daresay if he was anything like the other lords and knights he would have been spreading his largess around to all and sundry!

Hartburn is a small village just outside Stockton. My American readers may be interested to know that the Washington family of your first President lived there and were lords of the manor from the thirteenth century onwards. It was called Herrteburne in those days. In the sixteenth century the family had it taken from them and it was replaced by the manor of Wessington, which became Washington. Had they not moved then your president might live in Hartburn DC!

The King of Gwynedd, Gruffudd ap Cynan, recaptured Anglesey from the Normans and his son, Owain who later became known as Owain the Great began to encroach upon the Norman lands around Cheshire. Robert of Gloucester might have subdued South Wales but North Wales was a different matter. Eventually the men of Gwynedd would defeat the Normans and it was not until the time of Henry II that they began to suffer heavy defeats. The Welsh were aided by Vikings from Dublin as well as Irish mercenaries. Owain had been brought up in Ireland and his mother had family there. It gave the Welsh an advantage for the Vikings brought heavy armoured infantry to aid them. The Vikings continued to raid England until the fifteenth century but at this time they were no longer the fearsome warriors who conquered so much of the world in what we now term, the dark ages.

Ranulf de Gernan was Earl of Chester and was married to another Matilda/Maud- the daughter of the Earl of Gloucester. They seemed to have used a limited number of names at this time! I have tried to use real names where ever possible. I apologise for any confusion.

The plague and pestilence were two terms used for contagious diseases which usually killed. The Black Death was a specific plague which could be attributed to one cause. Influenza, smallpox, chicken pox even measles could wipe out vast numbers. The survivors normally had antibodies within their blood stream. Medicine was of little use.

The Lords of Coucy were robber barons who plagued Louis the Fat and the lands of Blois. They were as cruel as I suggest and I have made nothing up. Henry's daughter and her husband, Eustace, did rebel and Henry took away their Norman lands. King Henry had to spend a great deal of his time in Normandy and the lands in England were left to Robert of Gloucester and his small coterie of friends like Sir Richard Redvers, Roger of Mandeville, Richard d'Avranches and Robert Fitzharmon. My fictional hero also fits into this category.

The ram and the stone thrower were siege engines used at this time. Later weapons such as the trebuchet would render the stone thrower redundant. This was the time before skilled engineers such as those used by the Romans but the Crusades and warriors who had fought in the east brought back knowledge and skills in this area.

Alfraed could not have slept with the Empress Matilda- he is fictional. The Empress did become pregnant in1132 and gave birth to Henry II in March 1133. I use real events whenever I can but I write about the grey areas. Geoffrey was much younger than his wife and they did not get on. It seemed to me possible that she would take a lover. Ironically her son Henry II also married a much older woman- Eleanor of Aquitaine who, like Matilda, had formerly been married to a ruler. In her case it was the King of France. My fiction is no stranger than the truth.

Books used in the research:

The Varangian Guard- 988-1453 Raffael D'Amato

Saxon Viking and Norman- Terence Wise

The Walls of Constantinople AD 324-1453-Stephen Turnbull

Byzantine Armies- 886-1118- Ian Heath

The Age of Charlemagne-David Nicolle

The Normans- David Nicolle

Norman Knight AD 950-1204- Christopher Gravett

The Norman Conquest of the North- William A Kappelle

The Knight in History- Francis Gies

The Norman Achievement- Richard F Cassady

Knights- Constance Brittain Bouchard

Griff Hosker September 2015

Other books

by

Griff Hosker

If you enjoyed reading this book, then why not read another one by the author?

Ancient History

The Sword of Cartimandua Series (Germania and Britannia 50A.D. – 130 A.D.)

Ulpius Felix- Roman Warrior (prequel)

Book 1 The Sword of Cartimandua

Book 2 The Horse Warriors

Book 3 Invasion Caledonia

Book 4 Roman Retreat

Book 5 Revolt of the Red Witch

Book 6 Druid's Gold

Book 7 Trajan's Hunters

Book 8 The Last Frontier

Book 9 Hero of Rome

Book 10 Roman Hawk

Book 11 Roman Treachery

Book 12 Roman Wall

Book 13 Roman Courage

The Aelfraed Series (Britain and Byzantium 1050 A.D. - 1085 A.D.

Book 1 Housecarl

Book 2 Outlaw

Book 3 Varangian

The Wolf Warrior series (Britain in the late 6th Century)

Book 1 Saxon Dawn

Book 2 Saxon Revenge

Book 3 Saxon England

Book 4 Saxon Blood

Book 5 Saxon Slayer

Book 6 Saxon Slaughter

Book 7 Saxon Bane

Book 8 Saxon Fall: Rise of the Warlord

Book 9 Saxon Throne

The Dragon Heart Series

Book 1 Viking Slave

Book 2 Viking Warrior

Book 3 Viking Jarl

Book 4 Viking Kingdom

Book 5 Viking Wolf

Book 6 Viking War

Book 7 Viking Sword

Book 8 Viking Wrath

Book 9 Viking Raid

Book 10 Viking Legend

Book 11 Viking Vengeance

Book 12 Viking Dragon

Book 13 Viking Treasure

Book 14 Viking Enemy

Book 15 Viking Witch

Bool 16 Viking Blood

Book 17 Viking Weregeld

Book 18 Viking Storm

Book 19 Viking Warband

The Norman Genesis Series

Rolf

Horseman

The Battle for a Home

Revenge of the Franks

The Land of the Northmen

Ragnvald Hrolfsson

Brothers in Blood

The Anarchy Series England 1120-1180

English Knight

Knight of the Empress

Northern Knight

Baron of the North

Earl

King Henry's Champion

The King is Dead

Warlord of the North

Enemy at the Gate

Warlord's War

Kingmaker

Henry II

Crusader

The Welsh Marches

Irish War

Poisonous Plots

Border Knight 1190-1300

Sword for Hire

Return of the Knight

Modern History

The Napoleonic Horseman Series

Book 1 Chasseur a Cheval

Book 2 Napoleon's Guard

Book 3 British Light Dragoon

Book 4 Soldier Spy

Book 5 1808: The Road to Corunna

Waterloo

The Lucky Jack American Civil War series

Rebel Raiders

Confederate Rangers

The Road to Gettysburg

The British Ace Series

1914

1915 Fokker Scourge

1916 Angels over the Somme

1917 Eagles Fall

1918 We will remember them

From Arctic Snow to Desert Sand

Wings over Persia

Combined Operations series 1940-1945

Commando

Raider

Behind Enemy Lines

Dieppe

Toehold in Europe

Sword Beach

Breakout

The Battle for Antwerp

King Tiger

Beyond the Rhine

Other Books

Carnage at Cannes (a thriller)

Great Granny's Ghost (Aimed at 9-14-year-old young people)

Adventure at 63-Backpacking to Istanbul

For more information on all of the books then please visit the author's web site at http://www.griffhosker.com where there is a link to contact him.

Made in the USA
Columbia, SC
29 April 2019